TAKEOUT DOUBLE

A BRIDGE MYSTERY

JIM PRIEBE

MASTER POINT PRESS | TORONTO, CANADA

This is a work of fiction. All the characters and events portrayed in this book are fictitious, and any resemblance to real people or events is purely coincidental.

Master Point Press
331 Douglas Ave.
Toronto, Ontario, Canada
M5M 1H2
(416) 781-0351
Website: http://www.masterpointpress.com
Email: info@masterpointpress.com

We acknowledge the financial support of the Government of Canada through the Book Publishing Industry Development Program (BPIDP) for our publishing activities.

National Library of Canada Cataloguing in Publication

Priebe, Jim
Takeout double: a bridge mystery / Jim Priebe

ISBN 1-894154-89-4

I. Title.

PS8631.R53T34 2004 C813'.6 C2004-902171-0

Editor Ray Lee
Cover and interior design Olena S. Sullivan/New Mediatrix

1 2 3 4 5 6 7 09 08 07 06 05 04
Printed in Canada.

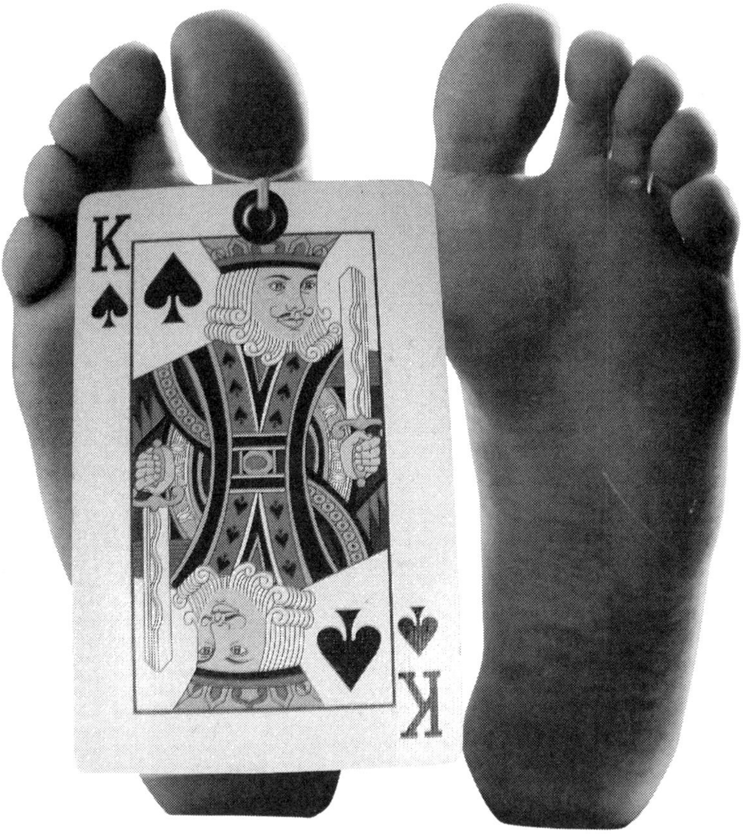
K

I wish to acknowledge the boundless energy and
encouragement of my wife Joan
during the writing and editing of this book

CHAPTER 1

THE SMALL SALTBOX-STYLE HOUSE THAT BELONGED to Jack Duffy and his wife, Helen, was in a quiet residential area of suburban Buffalo, New York. Like most of its neighbors, the house and driveway enjoyed the cover of the tall, mature trees that lined the street. The trees added beauty during the day, but by night, they shrouded the street lamps, cutting the intensity of the light and leaving the neighborhood in dark, heavy shadows.

The would-be intruder who arrived at nine one evening in early November noted the eerie appearance with satisfaction. Carrying out his task in near-darkness meant that chances of being spotted by a curious neighbor were virtually zero. The frozen state of the ground and the lack of snow also pleased him because it meant he would be leaving no footprints. His all-black clothing and blackened face would help to conceal his presence. A ski mask, covering his face completely, might have aroused suspicion, but the camouflage coloring would look natural to anyone except a close acquaintance. He was not expecting to encounter close acquaintances on this junket. Thin, black, leather gloves allowed a good sense of feel in his hands and would make sure he left no fingerprints. He had visited Jack and Helen several times and was familiar with the layout; he knew exactly how he was going to enter the house.

As he drove around the block twice, he noticed a light on in an upstairs window. What was that about? Jack, he knew, would be at the bridge club for another hour and a half. Had Helen decided not to take the kids out after all? He looked carefully, but there were no other signs of life; no flickering from a television, no other lights on downstairs. He decided that they probably left a light on whenever the family was out. The street was still empty and silent.

He selected the darkest spot he could find to park, well down the block from Jack's house but within a few seconds dash if he needed to reach his car quickly. On visits to Jack's parties, he had noticed that an outdoor light attached to a motion sensor would pick up movement coming from the street. He had to approach the house through the western neighbor's lot so as to slip in under the sensor and get to the backyard. He managed that without incident, and pried open the window of the small washroom where he planned to enter. He opened the window as quietly as he could, but the noise from the wood splitting crackled in the cold air like a broken loudspeaker. His heart was beating well above its normal rate, and the exertion of forcing the window caused him to break out in a sweat in spite of the sub-zero temperature.

He paused. The task at hand, which had seemed so clear and simple during the planning phase, now seemed ill-judged and impossible to complete without detection. A sudden stab of panic tempted him to close the window and flee. Then he calmed himself. No one could possibly be aware of his presence. He reassured himself that his plan was a good one and that no one was going to catch him. He took a breath and continued. The opening was barely large enough for him to squeeze through, but he managed it, landing in an untidy heap on the floor below.

With his heart pounding, the intruder paused to look around, recalling the details of the house plan. He closed the window behind him and quietly made his way to the den. The den, which he knew Jack used as a home office, was almost certainly the room where Helen would store the box he was after. It was directly beside the downstairs washroom. He fiddled with his penlight for a few moments and managed to produce a small beam of light. That helped, and his eyes slowly adjusted to his surroundings. A few guarded steps gave him confidence, and he was soon able to move with caution around the house.

He followed his plan to set up a fast exit route. Emergency or otherwise, he thought. The patio doors along the back wall of the den were easy to locate, and he pulled the locking pin that secured them from outside entry. Then he unlocked the door, and carefully pulled it open a few inches. An icy blast of air forced him to close it almost all the way.

He began to look around and search for the carton he wanted. Where was the most logical place to put a box of books? Would Helen go to a lot of trouble to hide the package? He looked into a corner, and his heart jumped at the sight of a cardboard box. To his disappointment, he found that it contained office supplies. Taking a step backwards, he almost tripped over a chair. Damn, he thought, looking around at the clutter. Got to be careful. How could anyone work in such a shambles? How does Jack find anything in here?

He noticed a pile of hunting equipment on a cabinet — a shotgun, a box of shells, warm clothing and waders. A heavy canvas belt had a water bottle and a good-looking knife attached. The intruder took the knife from its pouch and examined it under his light. Beautiful, he thought. Without thinking, he slipped it back and slid both the pouch and knife into his jacket pocket. Continuing his search for the carton he wanted, he looked through all the shelves that were clearly visible. His frustration mounted. Surely, Helen had brought it home with her. He had counted on Helen having it in her home and storing it in the den. Had she hidden it somewhere? Was there a safe in the house? That might make his quest impossible.

He looked around and noticed bookcases full of books, and filing cabinets tightly closed, but nothing that he was really interested in. Then he noticed some boxes on an upper shelf that resembled the type of sealed box he was looking for, and decided to investigate. He moved a chair carefully over to the point below them, clambered on to it, and cursed softly when he found that he could not reach far enough. Retreating to the floor again, he piled a pair of dictionaries on top of the chair. That worked fine, and now he was able to look around the shelves, but still had no luck finding what he wanted.

From his new vantage point, he looked round the room once more, and his eyes returned to the pile of hunting equipment that he had first looked at. The equipment was stacked on top of a filing cabinet, and he realized that he had not looked under the clothing when he first started his search. Maybe, he thought. As the thought struck him, he noticed his watch, and realized that it was much later than he had thought. He had used up almost all the time he had allowed for his adventure. He had not pictured a long search for his goal. A quick in and out was all that his plan allowed.

Hurriedly, he began to descend, intending to look under the pile of clothing, but in doing so he lost his balance and crashed to the floor. His mouth hit something hard (the waste paper basket?), and he immediately sensed the taste of blood. Had he broken a tooth? He heard his penlight clatter away. The light went out. What a careless move, he thought. He started to pick himself up, and then, as though his fall had triggered some kind of alarm, all hell seemed to break loose.

He heard a door opening and saw light come on in the front hall. Bleeding now, and stung by the blow he had received when he fell, he felt consumed by absolute panic. His heart pounded so hard he was afraid someone would hear it. What to do? Get out, he thought. Now. Forget the booklets. He remembered that he had left the patio door open slightly to prepare for a quick escape. Thank God. He almost tripped over his lost penlight, and bent over to pick it up. Better not leave anything behind, he thought. He hurled himself through the patio door.

Just as he stepped out, a loud scream added to his panic and he started to run in the wrong direction. In a second, he oriented himself. Remembering the direction in which he had parked his car, he turned quickly. Thankful that Jack had no fence enclosing his yard, he took a deep breath, and moved rapidly and quietly through the dark. Remembering to duck under the sensor light again, he hurried to his car. No one seemed to notice him on the street. He jumped in and started away, squealing his tires loudly on the street as he floored the gas pedal. Speeding down the street, he thought he saw headlights appear behind him, starting from the vicinity of Jack's driveway.

After a few sharp turns, he was at the freeway entrance, and he relaxed as he saw nothing but darkness in his rear-view mirror. Even if he had been followed, they had lost him now. No further problems. Not tonight. He was sure no one had seen his license plate, although they might have seen the car. And tomorrow I get the new car, he thought. What a stroke of luck. He was picking up his new, red, Hyundai Sonata. That's about as far as I can get from a black Chevy Cavalier, he thought. The timing couldn't be better. Still, he was mad at himself for failing to accomplish his mission.

☠ ♥ ☠

Jack Duffy left the bridge game at Stewart Appleton's club not focusing on the cool temperature or the clouds of breath condensing on the windows of his Chrysler. Jack's build was chubby, the result of years of office work and little physical exertion. His normal complexion was pinkish, but shades of red approaching that of a radish or a beet surfaced readily when something provoked him. Tonight, his face had displayed its full spectrum of reds.

When he started the car and drove homeward, he was angry, but not out of control enough to do anything stupid with his vehicle. He still loved the leather, the sound system, and the complete lack of rust. Good for a ten-year-old car.

His mind was sifting through the events of the evening's game. The evening's rot set in during the very first hand. They had actually achieved a fine score on the hand although Jack's partner, Henry James, had bungled along aimlessly, and in the end, had had to rely on an opponent's error. But Jack had made the mistake of lecturing Henry on the way he had played the contract. Henry had resented it, and from that moment on, they were adversaries instead of partners.

As the evening wore on, Jack himself had misjudged the play of two hands and thereby given the partnership very poor results. Henry had lit into him both times, extracting full revenge for Jack's earlier lecture. Now it was Jack's game that was a mess. His mind dwelt on the two hands he had misplayed, wondering how he could have missed such obvious points. His concentration lapsed and finally disappeared completely. He ended by making an opening lead out of turn on the last hand, which had led to another bad result, and the pair had left quickly when the game was over, not waiting to see the scores and not even saying goodnight to each other. Jack wondered at himself. Angry! Always angry. Why did he play bridge if it had this effect on him? He thought of Henry's outburst tonight, and how it had destroyed his concentration and his game. Perhaps that's what I do to Helen when we play together, he thought. Maybe I'm the reason she can't focus.

When he turned in to his street, he was not expecting to see a police cruiser with its lights flashing parked in his driveway. It seemed as though all the lights in the house were on. A few neighbors, bundled in winter parkas, were standing in a group on his frozen front lawn. Suddenly frightened, Jack pulled the car to a stop behind the police car and jumped out. "What's going on?" he shouted.

The nearest uniformed officer asked, "Who are you, sir?"

"I'm Jack Duffy. This is my house. Where are my wife and my kids?"

"They're inside. They're all fine, sir. Come with me please."

Jack shrugged off the guiding arm of the officer, and then realized the man was trying to help. They entered the house together. "What in hell's happening?"

"You had a break-in tonight, sir. Everyone's fine. There's your wife, I believe."

Jack saw Helen looking remarkably composed, an arm around each of their children. He was relieved to see that they seemed fine and went over quickly to give them each a hug. "You're late," said Helen. "You missed the excitement."

"What happened?" asked Jack.

"We're fine," said Helen. "But this scared the dickens out of me, Jack. Sandra and Rick and I just got back from the movie. We came in the front door and were taking off our coats and boots when I noticed a big draft. The curtains were billowing in the living room. I went into the den and the place seemed awfully cold. Then I noticed the patio door was open and the wind was blowing in. The window in the washroom had been pried open and someone came in there. I hollered and phoned emergency."

The uniformed officer said, "Look over here. Whoever it was broke in by your downstairs bathroom window. Then he left through your patio doors. The door was still open when I got here. They usually set up an escape route in these break-ins."

"I see. Thanks, officer. You guys okay?" he asked, looking at Rick and Sandra.

"Yeah, Dad," answered Rick. "We never saw the guy. He was gone when we got here."

Sandra piped up, "You should have heard Mom yelling."

"What time did all this happen?" asked Jack.

"I guess we got here about ten-thirty or so," said Helen. "Whoever it was must have left just as we got here. Maybe we disturbed him. I started to scream and turn lights on."

"I suppose your scream put some fear into him," said Jack.

"The old camp scream. I do a pretty good coyote."

The officer told Jack, "Your wife did all the right things. Most of these prowlers are looking for an easy place to rob. If someone disturbs them, they take off in a hurry."

"Hey, officer, I saw the car – got a good look as he drove off." They looked round at the short, balding man who was hurrying across the road to them.

"Who are you, sir?" asked the policeman.

"Harry Easton – he lives across the way, in that red bungalow," said Jack. "Hi, Harry. You say you got a good look? What did you see?"

"Evening, Jack. I was just pulling into my driveway and I hear the squeal of tires. This little car about fifty yards down the street shoots off, no lights on, at a heck of a clip. It was too dark to see the number and I was too slow thinking about following him."

"Did you get enough of a look to ID the model?" asked the officer.

"Yes, I did," said Harry. "It was a black Cavalier. Chevy Cavalier. A 2001 model."

"How can you be so sure of the model and year?" asked the policeman.

"That's my business," smiled Harry, "I look at them every working day." He offered a business card. "I'm the sales manager at Woodhearn Motors in Tonawanda – the GM dealership."

"Interesting. We'll need you to give us a statement."

"Sure. Glad to help out. I'll bet it was some neighborhood teenagers."

"Could be. There's not much chance of finding out who without a plate number. But you never know."

Jack thanked his neighbor, returned to Helen's side and asked, "Anything stolen?"

"Not as far as I can see," she answered. "My jewelry, the stereo, the TV, everything's still here. The guy was in your den, but I can't think what anyone would want from there. An old computer? Your Playboy magazine collection?"

"My hunting stuff is in there. My shotgun, some shells, gun-cleaning equipment. I'd better have a look."

But he and Helen could find nothing missing, and the break-in remained a puzzle.

Charles Werkman, that night's intruder in the Duffy home, was an addicted practitioner of duplicate bridge. He was interested neither in social bridge, which he classed as a form of idle chatter without serious thinking, nor in playing for a monetary stake. Dedicated money players were few in number and included no one whose game Charles respected. Besides, money bridge offered no opportunities of the type that Charles enjoyed most: serious partnerships, with detailed, complex agreements on what each bid meant. He loved to read about the exploits of the great champions. Most of all he loved to win. Win at all costs? Absolutely. He loved to see his name in print among the list of winners. The game had become his main source of self-respect, the battlefield where he wanted to make his mark.

Charles worked in the industrial division of a major paint company translating orders from customers into specific quantities, with prices, billing and delivery dates. The large customers liked to deal with him. He had an encyclopedic memory for details. They might request a yellow color for a line of earth-moving equipment, and Charles would gently remind them that they had ordered twice as much last year and had run out in the middle of a production run. He might let on that they usually ordered equivalent amounts of primer, and ask if they had forgotten to put that on the order. His ability to cover occasional mistakes delighted the agents in his customers' purchasing groups. But work was a source of income, never a means of gaining real satisfaction. It challenged only a minor part of his abilities.

As he neared forty, Charles was feeling more and more frustration at his lack of real recognition. Not athletic in his youth, and never a great student, he knew no way of winning the admiration of schoolmates. When he matured and needed respect, bridge seemed to be a way he could gain it – perhaps the only way.

That is not to say that Charles was a great bridge player, although he was reasonably good. In fact, Charles was a cheat. But even that had not, so far, got him what he wanted. Local victories got him local publicity — fine as far as it went, but the real prize would be a win in a national event or an international competition. For instance, there were a few games each year in which players from all over North America and in some cases, from a hundred or so countries around the world, competed against one another. Everyone played the same hands on the same night and the game was scored on a continent-wide or a worldwide basis. The winners were announced in headlines in major bridge magazines. He knew the schedule of these games and coveted the publicity that a win might earn him.

One such game was scheduled in mid-November and one of the sessions would be at Stewart Appleton's Cheektavia club. Part of the fun in taking part was that each player received a booklet after the game, with an expert commentary on how the bidding and play ought to go on each hand, so they could compare their own results. Charles knew that if he could somehow get a copy before the game, just one single copy of the booklet, he would be almost sure of winning the local game; he could probably score well enough to have a chance at taking national honors, and maybe even top the worldwide competition. He had puzzled for months about a way to accomplish this without making any progress when suddenly a possible answer had fallen into his lap.

His favorite partner for the past five years had been Jack Duffy, but that was because Jack happened to be the best available partner just now. Jack was not someone that he expected to play with forever, as Charles did not see him improving at a fast rate. The two had only once taken the opportunity to play in really tough competition, in a North American Championship. There, a win or even a high placing brought long-term recognition. But in such events, even minor mistakes cost heavily in final standings. Charles cultivated top-level players as best he could, but his overtures were always rebuffed. The experts he approached were friendly enough, and answered questions he asked, but made it only too obvious that unless he was offering money to cover their professional fees, they had no interest in games with him. "Catch 22," he thought. "I can't establish a partnership with a top professional until I have a partnership with a top professional."

He resented the fact that none of the top players would ever schedule a game with him, yet he himself would have dumped Jack in a minute had an opportunity surfaced to play with a better partner. He knew, too, that he could never expect Jack's full commitment as a partner because Helen was always in the background. Whenever Jack arranged teams to play in a tournament, he always included Helen as his partner or a teammate. Helen was a fine player, but not good enough for the kind of success Charles had in mind.

The previous week he had been standing with Jack after a game at Appleton's club, checking over their scores, when Stewart Appleton himself came over. Stewart drew Jack aside but Charles could hear every word of their conversation. "The worldwide game's coming up next Wednesday."

"So I hear," responded Jack.

"Is Helen planning to run one at the golf club?"

"Oh yes," said Jack, "she always does. Her clientele always turn out for it. She generally gets ten tables or so. Is that a problem for you?"

"No," said Appleton. "The folks that play in her game don't like to come here anyway."

"They love the hand records and the analysis. I'm not sure just why. Most of them forget a hand five seconds after they play it anyway. They're just social players."

Anyone monitoring Charles' heart rate at that instant would have noticed that it rose several points and stayed up. This might be just what I'm looking for, thought Charles. If Helen takes the booklets home at night, maybe I can find a way to get hold of them. All I need is one book. I could do it so that no one could tell what happened. That ought to be easy. Charles made a mental note of the date of the event, a Wednesday, and the fact that he would somehow have to break into Jack's home and get at the package.

He knew that Jack often played bridge at the club on Tuesdays, and that when he did, Helen usually took the kids to a movie. That fit his plan very well. Could he make sure, somehow, that Jack would indeed play next Tuesday? That would help. Would Helen and the children be home? That would certainly complicate matters. He would have to postpone the whole idea if Jack's place was not deserted.

He scheduled a game with Jack for that Tuesday night, and then a further game with Henry James, another local expert with whom Jack played occasionally. His plan was to cancel with both at the last minute, and suggest that they played with each other. He could plead most any excuse — illness, some business problem. Better still, he could just be open, call it a mistake, and leave them an opening to play together. He was sure that neither would be the slightest bit concerned by his actions. If events did not fall into place, he would wait for the next opportunity. He became excited as he thought about his plan and mentally ran over the details.

When Tuesday rolled around, Charles had his plans well fixed in his mind. He phoned Henry James first and then called Jack at his office. "Jack, I double-booked a game tonight. I just looked over my calendar and I have you and Henry James both lined up for tonight. Sorry. But listen. I just talked to Henry and he's okay to play with you if you want. I can find something else to do tonight."

"Henry wants to play? That'll work fine. Do I need to call him?"

"You can if you want. I just talked to him and he says he's confirmed unless he hears from you."

"Okay. That'll work. Helen is taking Sandra and Rick to a movie, and I don't want to spend the night alone."

"We're still on for the worldwide game tomorrow?"

"Yes. That's all set."

"Well, have a good game with Henry tonight. See you tomorrow."

Yes, things were working out just fine.

CHAPTER 2

THE ADAM'S MARK HOTEL IN BUFFALO WAS MUCH like thirty or so other Marks across the country, and not unlike ten thousand other hotels that bridge bureaucrats patronized, frequented, took occasional freebies from, and arranged tournaments in. These hotels all had in common huge rooms where bridge organizers could assemble tables to play, tables to set out supplies, and tables from which directing staff could control operations. Not all were as well appointed as the Adam's Mark in Buffalo. Players universally liked the Marks' facilities, whether they were in Buffalo or St. Louis, San Antonio or Philadelphia, because of the thick carpets, high ceilings, and massive chandeliers casting bright, even lighting over the playing area. Of course, some players considered the hotels in New York City, Washington and San Francisco to be superior, but they were also almost twice the price.

The directors of the December regional tournament at Buffalo's Adam's Mark were expecting a continued run of quiet days to cap off an orderly tournament. However, the events that took place on the final Sunday balanced off several months of quiet times.

A ruckus started even before the game began when a lumbering giant by the name of Jim Lemone accosted another man, Bob Smithers, and warned him in no uncertain terms to stay away from Lemone's wife. He threatened severe violence to Smithers if he learned of any further contact between the two. Smithers was a small man, about half the size of Lemone, but no coward, and he challenged Lemone to try something. Two of the directors happened on the scene at the right time and quelled the conflict before either individual was harmed. They warned Lemone and Smithers that they would both be barred from the tournament immediately if anything further erupted between them. Lemone's very pretty, very tiny wife, Muriel, steered Jim away from the scene with abrupt orders to stop making a fuss.

In the middle of the game, Jack Duffy and Charles Werkman sat down at the same table as Smithers. For a while, the play was uneventful, then in the course of bidding a hand, Charles paused for several seconds before making his bid. Smithers noted the hesitation instantly. He knew that when a player pauses in a manner obviously out of his usual tempo, the fact that he has a problem often gives his partner information about his hand. The ethics of the game, however, require the partner to ignore the hesitation and any information it might convey, and the vast majority of players are very careful to do so. Immediately after Jack's next bid, however, almost everyone in the room could hear Smithers bellow "Director!"

Jack's temper immediately rose to its boiling point. "More of Smithers' nonsense," he snarled at Charles. "What an asshole."

The director arrived quickly and listened to both sides, taking time to examine the cards each of them held. Charles claimed that he had not made a significant pause. Jack admitted that there might have been a small hesitation but felt he had made an obviously correct bid with his own hand.

The director looked uncomfortable, but said to Jack, "I'm going to rule that there is unauthorized information, and I am sorry but I have to roll the contract back to three hearts."

Smithers added, "Not only that, but this man insulted me. Why don't you tell the director what you said? I won't repeat it."

Jack fumed, "Oh, for heaven's sake. How low are you going to go?"

The floor director said, "Not again, Jack? Let's see what Paul has to say." He summoned the head director and explained the situation.

The head director said, "Jack, you know you are under probation for behavior problems and I should suspend you for this. This kind of conduct is just unacceptable. We can't put up with it."

Jack flushed. In retrospect, he realized that he had overstepped the bounds and said, "I'm sorry. I shouldn't have said what I said."

"You'd better make an apology to Mr. Smithers right now."

Jack turned to his opponent. "I apologize for my statement," he mumbled, in a tone that could have conveyed any feeling except a sincere apology.

The directors headed off with a parting shot at Jack. "Take this seriously. You won't get away with it again."

After the eighth and final round of the Swiss team event, the directing staff were expecting to announce the winning team in the usual routine manner. However, Bob Smithers, not having had enough excitement for one day, called a director to his table during the last match and registered another complaint about his opponents' actions. This time the director had little sympathy with Smithers' point, whereupon Smithers announced that he was lodging a protest and asking for an appeals committee to review the ruling.

As soon as the round was finished, the directors convened a committee of three experienced players to hear the case. Smithers and the opposing captain, Lew Orono, represented their respective teams and presented their points of view. Orono simply stated that he had wanted to know the meaning of an artificial bid, and had asked a question about it during the auction at his turn, as he was entitled to.

Smithers added color to the bare facts of his case. "We all know that when a player asks questions about an artifical bid, he often has values in that suit. Everybody at the table knew that my opponent wanted a club lead. I call that cheating."

This inflammatory statement was not well-received by the committee, but in the end they did overturn the original ruling, which resulted in the Smithers team taking first place instead of their opponents. As the committee members terminated the hearing and everyone rose from their chairs, Orono, captain of the displaced victors, turned to Smithers. He was a mean-looking, powerful man, and made his displeasure known by shoving Smithers in the chest and propelling him backwards a few feet. "I am not a cheater, you son of a bitch," he said. He followed this with an advance on the smaller man and made an effort to seize his shirtfront and deliver a lecture, at least. The directors on the spot, luckily, again saved Smithers from physical violence. Smithers brushed imaginary dirt from the spot where Orono's hand had been and looked pleased with himself. Orono sent a menacing look in Smithers' direction as he walked away toward his teammates.

Sometime in between these two separate incidents, Charles Werkman was involved in a third situation which, had the directors been aware of it, would have tested their skills to the breaking point. When Charles had first decided to cheat at bridge, he had prepared patiently by teaching himself to become adept at handling decks of cards. He used his dishonest skill in team games, like the one today. He wore trousers with multiple pockets — ideal for carrying a few decks of cards, which no one else would be likely to notice. Charles arranged the cards in these decks so that he could deal them without cutting or shuffling and wrapped each of them with an elastic band so that the cards retained their position while bouncing around in his pocket. These pre-dealt hands were always difficult, high-scoring freak hands, almost sure to determine the outcome of a short match, and unusual enough that regular players would seldom get an optimum result.

The hands for pairs games were always preset by a computer program, but in most team matches the players themselves simply shuffled and dealt all the hands before play started. Most tournaments ended with a Swiss teams event involving seven or eight short matches over the course of the day, a scenario that was ideal for Charles' purposes. At the start of each new round, Charles hurried to the table where his next match would take place. When he managed to arrive ahead of the opponents and his partner, he would remove the cards from one of the duplicate boards, slide them into a convenient, empty trouser pocket, pull one of his decks out of another pocket and place it on the table. To anyone arriving now, it appeared that he had just shuffled the deck and was ready to deal the cards. If anyone else was nearby when he first got to the table, his partner or an opponent, he abandoned his act for that match; if he were ever to be caught, it would mean being barred from tournaments for life, and he wasn't going to take any serious risk of that.

When he was successful in inserting one of his own decks, he knew the exact layout of the cards and had a major advantage in the match. Occasionally he managed to work two of his hands into the same match and then his team had enormous odds in their favor. The scheme was ideal for matches near the end of an event. These were the most important matches of the day because the format dictated that contending teams would lock horns during the late stages. The pairings had to be chosen carefully at this point and the time between matches expanded from the usual five minutes to ten minutes or longer. Players milled around the scoring table, checking their standings and waiting for their seating assignments. When Charles was in luck, his assignment went up early enough for him to hustle around and do his dirty work. He did it only when his team was in contention to win or to place well; otherwise, it was not worth the risk. No opponent had ever noticed Charles dealing one or two hands without shuffling or cutting. No one had ever raised an objection. The method was fool-proof, far too clever a scheme for anyone to figure it out.

The procedure had paid off handsomely during a tournament in Toronto that past Easter, when his team had been in contention for first place. He had managed to get a hand into play during the very last round which involved a difficult slam in which declarer had very few high cards but succeeded by executing a double squeeze. His team included Jack and Helen, and they had won the event. Of course, the couple was completely ignorant of Charles' cheating practices.

On the infamous Sunday at the Adam's Mark in Buffalo, Charles and Jack were teamed with Jack's wife Helen and an older player named Hermann Volcker, an excellent card player with an old-fashioned approach to bidding. At the midpoint of the event, they were cruising along in the top group in the field, right where Charles wanted them. In the first match after a break, Charles had inserted a hand where he could succeed in making a vulnerable game by dropping a singleton king offside, usually an anti-percentage play. He hesitated for several seconds before making the crucial play, giving opponents the impression that he was deep in thought about the correct action. They won the match comfortably, and were now leading the field by the smallest possible margin.

The schedule had them playing the second-place team next. Charles' pulse quickened as he mentally reviewed his plans. He spotted their assignment before anyone else and surveyed the table where he and Jack would be playing. It looked deserted and he hurried over. He sat down, removed the cards belonging to the board in front of him, stuffed them in a pocket and pulled out one of his pre-dealt gems. This operation was not as smooth as usual and Charles had to fumble momentarily to get the deck out of one of his lower trouser pockets. Bob Smithers was walking by as he went through his machinations. The whole affair could have turned into a non-event had Charles simply stopped and waited for Smithers to move on, but Charles did not see him and was confident that no one was near. Smithers was puzzled by the sight of a player pulling cards out of his trousers, but it all happened so quickly that he did not know what to make of it at first.

After the round was finished, Charles needed a break, and he found his way to the washroom. Smithers was also there. After the briefest of intervals, Smithers said, "What in blazes were you doing pulling cards out of your pocket?"

Charles said nothing.

"You son of a gun," continued Smithers. "I'll bet you were swapping the decks. Cheating."

"Like hell I was. You're a bloody troublemaker. You always have to start something. No wonder everybody hates your guts."

"We'll see," said Smithers.

They left the washroom without noticing Hermann Volcker slouched over a wash basin. Hermann had excused himself to Helen, slipped his convention card carelessly into his hip pocket, and made his way with some urgency to the men's washroom. After he finished the task at hand, he pulled his trousers up, fastened a couple of buttons, went to wash his hands, then disgusted himself by knocking his convention card onto a wet part of the countertop. He retrieved it quickly, saw that it had minimal damage, but needed a good drying before he was ready to return to the game. As he stood by the drying machines trying to transform his convention card from a state of soaking wet to merely damp, he overheard fragments of the conversation between Werkman and Smithers. The voices sounded familiar, although he could not see the speakers to identify them positively. The noise of the hand dryer drowned many of the words and Hermann had trouble following the conversation. The older voice said, "— cards in your trousers, — swapping decks, — cheating — ."

The younger one replied, "— hates your guts —."

The voices tailed off. Hermann finished drying off his card as best he could, and then hurried back to his table, embarrassed and a little angry with himself. He could not understand the significance of the conversation he had just heard, but it bothered him for the rest of the day. Hermann's inattention, coupled with Charles' distraction, made the last two rounds wretched for the whole team, and they closed with a dismal placing in the event.

CHAPTER 3

THE WORLD HAS COLDER PLACES, BUT UPPER NEW York state, at five-forty a.m. on a December morning, will satisfy most people's need for a cooling off. The man delivering the morning edition of the New York Times to the downtown Buffalo Adam's Mark hotel was driving slowly along Bingham Street abreast of the cut-rate parking lot under Interstate 190. With the heater in his Caravan turned up full, he comfortably mulled over ways to postpone the moment when he would have to get out of his vehicle to battle the wind, ten-below-zero air, and driving snow.

A lone car in a remote corner of the parking lot made him curious. No lot attendant had arrived yet, and he decided that circling for a look was a good way to gain a few extra seconds of warmth. As soon as he pulled up beside it, he began to wish he had minded his own business. A pair of shoes stuck out from under the back of the car. When he lowered his window for a better view, he could see that the shoes were connected to a pair of legs, and presumably a whole body. He called the emergency number from his cell phone and received instructions to wait at the site. He had no intention of leaving the comfort of his van, so sat quietly with the motor running, listening absently to the perky banter of a morning radio talk show. Upset because his other deliveries were going to be thrown off schedule, he hoped that the police would hurry so he could finish his work without a whole lot of delay. He began framing excuses for his boss, thinking that he had used plenty in the past year, although this one would actually be true. The hotel coffee shop opened at six-thirty, so at least he would be able to get something warm inside him before long.

At six-fifteen, a white Ford Crown Victoria with no markings slid to a halt beside his van. Two plain-clothes men stepped out and motioned him to join them. "Lieutenant Nelson," said the shorter, "and this is Detective Wilson," motioning to his colleague. "What can you tell us?"

"Got to get goin' with the papers," said the man. "Late already."

"Faster you tell us everything, faster you get going," said Nelson.

"All I seen was them shoes. I drive over and see there's a body layin' under the car. So I called you. That's it."

"Okay. You didn't touch anything, I hope?"

"You kiddin'? Never got out of my van. Wish I'd never come over to this side of the lot."

Nelson and Wilson stumbled through the snow as they walked around the car to look at the body. "God, whoever did this guy could have picked a better day to kill somebody." Nelson shivered involuntarily as he looked at the body. "Russ, get the paper guy's name and address, will you? We'll need him later."

Notwithstanding Nelson's complaint, the pair looked well prepared for the snow and cold with parkas, leggings, wool hats and heavy gloves. The paper distributor could not see that they were wearing pajamas under their outer clothing. The constable on duty at the station had phoned Nelson at home, Nelson had called Wilson, and the pair had answered the call with their usual promptness.

"How's 'bout a coffee, anyway?" said the paper man. "Small price for what I done."

"Here's the man who was in a big hurry. Sure. Go ahead in and order us three coffees and some donuts."

"I'll order if you're payin'," said the wary paper man.

Nelson nodded assent. "Russ, why don't you go in with him? We've got to contact the coroner anyway. You might as well do that inside. I'll stay here and get started."

By seven-thirty, the air had warmed to minus nine degrees, although wind gusting to thirty miles per hour kept it feeling much colder. Nelson moved slowly, glad of his heavy coat and gloves. Although the body was not heavy, it was stiff as an icicle and difficult to deal with. Wilson arrived with two cups of coffee and several donuts. They sought the warmth of their car and lingered over their feast.

When the coroner arrived, they returned to the frozen air of the lot once again and greeted him. "Hi, Wilbur. I dragged the body out from under the car and got his wallet. Name's Robert Smithers, and he's fifty-six. Local address; wonder what he was doing here?"

"Great timing, Bryan," complained the coroner. The trio worked together to examine the remains. The victim was small with a slight build, in his mid-fifties.

Wilbur Cornwell, a veteran of hundreds of such scenes, muttered aloud as he made observations. "An easy mark for somebody with maybe average strength and decent physical condition. The knife in his chest is presumably the cause of death. No blood on the body. Eyes wide open."

Nelson added, "His face shows what you might call surprise, disbelief. Like he didn't think the guy was going to attack."

Wilbur continued, "Yes. And the angle the knife went in shows that the killer was facing the victim when he did it. I reckon the killer knew him. It all happened quickly. See, there are no wounds on the victim's hands. If there was any move to self-defense, you'd get some cuts on the hands. The knife went straight into the heart. One slash got through the overcoat, the sweater, and into his chest."

"Wonder why he left the knife in the body?"

"Hard to tell till we get him back to the lab and thawed out, but my guess is it lodged on a bone, and got stuck. That happens sometimes. He wouldn't want to stick around the body too long in case someone saw him."

The trio moved Buffalo's sixty-first murder victim of the year, a frozen, solid, flat monolith, into the back of the coroner's purple Chevrolet Astrovan for its journey to the morgue.

Detective Wilson had made a note of the name engraved on the handle of the knife used as a murder weapon: BUCK NIGHTHAWK. It looked expensive; the name meant nothing in particular to him, but maybe it would to someone. You never knew what could turn out to be important.

Glad of an excuse to get indoors, the two officers next searched out the manager on duty at the hotel and informed him of the murder right next to hotel property.

"Smithers was not a guest of the hotel last night," said the manager, defensively. "We have no record of anyone by that name."

"Can you tell us anything else that was going on in the hotel yesterday? Weddings? Meetings? Conventions? Anything that happened over the past twelve hours that might have a connection?"

"Sunday was relatively quiet. We had a few check-ins for a seminar starting today. And our regular business travelers. The only event taking place on Sunday was a bridge tournament; that was quite big – a few hundred people, maybe. It ended yesterday evening, but I can look up the names of the organizers if you like."

When the officers nodded agreement, he continued, "We'd prefer it if you could keep your enquiries here as discreet as possible. I can give you a conference room for the day for your interviews. It has a phone, too, if you need one. "

The officers took advantage of all the help they were offered. A search of Smithers' pockets and his car soon established a definite connection to the bridge tournament: a couple of magazines, a tournament schedule and some old scorecards made it clear Smithers was a bridge player, and the event seemed the obvious explanation for his visit to the hotel. Clearly, they needed to talk to the people running the event if they were going to figure out whether the murder was connected to it in some way.

Once Nelson felt he had collected enough basic information on the Smithers murder, he needed to update his boss, Captain Jim Kesten, as soon as possible. After calling and relaying some essential facts of the case, he asked for an urgent meeting with Kesten. They settled on an appointment immediately after lunch.

The architecture of the police station provided occupants with constant reminders of exactly where they stood in the hierarchy. Russ Wilson, as a lowly detective, shared a small cubicle with three other detectives, who, mercifully, were seldom present at the same time. Lieutenants had larger rooms with the benefit of single occupancy. Bryan Nelson liked the old-fashioned oak furniture that had been the standard for the past twenty years and was capable of going for another forty. Other lieutenants had availed themselves of an upgrading program a year earlier in which the police commission, in an unexpected burst of generosity, had offered officers the option of replacing their old furniture. Most of them liked their new, leather-upholstered, padded chairs, but would cheerfully have traded the flimsy metal desks for the old oaken species.

Nelson was right at home with faded walls and old-fashioned furniture. The chips and scratches in his oak desk were familiar and welcome works of art. The chairs were designed for longevity rather than for comfort. Nelson had installed a now-tattered foam cushion on his, but the three visitors' chairs were plain hard oak. A message board with a few expired messages adorned one wall, and a well-used telephone with a built-in speaker was the only item on the desk. There were no family pictures, and no artwork of any kind hung on the walls to indicate Nelson's interests.

To Nelson, the Spartan surroundings were familiar and comfortable. He blended into the room perfectly. A small man, he was all muscle with no fat on his body. A few assailants over the years had found, to their subsequent sorrow and regret, that they had taken on a wildcat. His dress was always tidy and always predictable. When he became a detective he traded the official blue uniform for one of his own choosing: two gray suits, one plain and one striped, both well-cut, both now shiny, both matching the color of his hair and small, neat mustache. He owned police-issue black shoes, several white shirts, and, as his only concession to fashion, a variety of bright silk ties.

Jim Kesten, as befitted a captain, had the benefit of a large corner office, but although he had a view of the outdoors, he preferred looking at closed blinds instead of the ill-watered lawns and poorly tended flowerbeds. His room was large by police standards. The furniture was comfortable and included his massive desk and a small conversational grouping with a sofa, coffee table and chairs. Jim used this grouping for meetings when he wanted to descend from the throne behind his desk and project a common touch among his visitors.

The call from Nelson relating the news of Smithers' murder had set him thinking, and he decided now was the time to implement a plan of his own that had been brewing for a few weeks. He called Gordon Bryder, the police commissioner, to enlist support for his scheme.

"Good morning, Gordon," he said. The pair usually got right to business, and this call was no exception. "You know how we discussed Art Fraser's application for a move into homicide?"

"Refresh my memory on Fraser."

"He's been with us for eleven years now. He spent the last seven as a lieutenant in the vehicle section. He did some excellent work tracking down a stolen car ring operating out of Mexico. He's thorough, and shows plenty of initiative in starting and completing investigations. He's an ambitious guy, too; spends a lot of hours on the job."

"Yes, I remember now. He almost flunked out of law at Cornell, as I recall."

"True, but he was near the top of his class in every subject at the police academy. Everything he touches is well done. He's a natural for police work."

Bryder asked, "And you say he's looking for a homicide assignment?"

"Yes, he is. We have an ideal opportunity here to move ahead with that."

"Tell me."

"We had a murder this morning. The victim apparently was a bridge player. The whole affair may tie in with a big tournament that just finished at the Adams' Mark hotel."

"And?"

"Fraser is a keen bridge player. He knows everybody in the bridge crowd and everybody knows him. He's an ideal man to head up this investigation."

"Who's got the case?"

"Nelson and Wilson were the first men on the spot. Nelson phoned me this morning."

"Nelson's a pretty solid man. His nose will be out of joint if you go ahead with your plan."

"I expect you're right. Nelson is going nowhere, though; he'll still be a lieutenant when he retires. We've all agreed that Fraser has potential for bigger things. I have no doubt that the investigation will go more quickly if we put Fraser in charge."

"It's your call, Jim. I don't see any flaw in your logic. Just advise Fraser to use some sense dealing with Nelson. He's been a good cop, and we don't need a younger man with a streak of arrogance moving in and turning him off."

"I will certainly do that."

When Nelson arrived, Kesten motioned him to a seat on the sofa, took a leather chair for himself, and asked what was up. When Nelson finished his quick review, Kesten seemed to go into deep thought.

After a moment he said, "You and Wilson could use some help on this thing. You've got a lot of angles to cover."

"Russ is pretty good," responded Nelson warily. "We've handled a lot of cases together."

"It will look better for both of you if we get this one sewed up quickly."

"What's on your mind?"

"I see your case likely has some connection with the bridge tournament. Someone familiar with that group might help a lot."

"Know anyone who might fit?"

"Art Fraser…" Kesten let the name dangle in the air for a few seconds. "Maybe you don't know, but he plays a lot of competitive bridge."

Nelson had to hold himself severely in check to avoid spluttering at the mention of Fraser's name. Lieutenants were competing for very few promotion opportunities in their district in the New York State police. Nelson didn't need anyone on his investigation team who held the same rank as he did, and the fact that Fraser was also a lieutenant meant that matters could be very awkward. Just how awkward would become evident in a matter of minutes.

The two men had first met eleven years ago when Fraser was a cadet and Nelson was director of the pistol range. Fraser had turned into an excellent shot under Nelson's coaching and the two had been friendly enough ever since. Fraser had gone on to become senior man in the vehicle theft section of the criminal investigation branch and proved to be a good officer. His composed and educated manner allowed him to work well with insurance companies and individual owners. He developed the knack of assembling most of the relevant information on a case quickly. He had made a name for himself by uncovering a ring of car thieves headquartered in Buffalo, who picked up late-model Japanese cars and shipped them to Mexico for parts. Nelson could see that Fraser was making impressive progress and had been promoted early to lieutenant — a level that had taken Nelson fifteen years to achieve.

"Yeah, well, if that's so, we could run some of the stuff by him if you like. Can't do any harm," conceded Nelson.

"Well, actually, my thought was that Fraser would take charge of this one," Kesten corrected.

"You mean I work for him on this case?" asked Nelson, a touch of hoarseness slipping into his voice. "He's never worked a homicide, has he?"

Kesten smiled thinly, understanding Nelson's real problem. "Bryan," he said, "I don't make all these decisions. Not at all. You're a senior, well-respected man in this department. But the commissioner intends to move Fraser into the homicide group and promote him. I know it's going to be tricky having two lieutenants on the same case. But you guys can surely get along. From where I sit, if we cut the investigation time in half, everybody looks good. You, me, the commissioner, Wilson. Oh yes, Fraser too. But nobody loses. What do you say?"

There was a pause. Then, "Whatever it takes," sighed Nelson.

"That's great," said Kesten. "If we assign him officially, he'll do a lot of work on the case."

"Fine," said Nelson, wishing he had never shown up in Kesten's office this Monday morning. How did this all happen? He suspected that Fraser had called the chief earlier and suggested the whole idea. Damn! Help comes in many forms. Wanted. Unwanted. Right now Nelson wanted help, but not from Kesten. And especially not from Fraser.

"Jim," said Nelson. "Can I ask you a question?"

"Anything," replied Kesten.

"Who handles traffic issues while Fraser works on the murder?"

"Fraser can handle both ends for a short while, anyway. This murder investigation has priority."

Nelson left feeling sorry he had asked his last question. He returned to his office, sighed and sat for a few minutes meditating before calling Wilson in. He felt a sense of humiliation that Kesten was bringing someone in to take over and head up an investigation that he had started. He briefly considered resigning and looking for a position as chief of a small town force. That would solve nothing, he knew. He debated how he should cover the Kesten visit with Wilson, knowing that it would set Wilson thinking about why he was still a detective after twenty years on the force. Maybe Wilson could use a little extra juice right now, anyway. Wilson could be lethargic, although he was not shirking on any aspect of the Smithers case so far.

"I talked to Kesten this morning. He asked if we needed more help. The guy never made a decision in his life; now he's asking, 'Do you and Russ need more help?' Damn. He wants us to get together with a bridge insider. Someone who knows the ins and outs of the game, knows all the people and has contacts. A friendly person we can trust and level with. He's suggesting Art Fraser ought to join us – even head up the case."

"It won't hurt to stay on the good side of Fraser. The word is he's gonna make captain, and sooner rather than later."

"Yeah?" said Nelson.

"I'm just repeating what the guys say," Wilson replied. "He's a bright guy. A lot of the fellows think that way."

Nelson's ears burned at this remark. "Is that so? The guys aren't the ones doing the promoting though. There's lots of good people to choose from who can do the job," he said. He caught himself before adding more acid comments. "I told Jim we could use help. We might shorten the time of the investigation, if we're lucky. Fraser is well connected in the bridge group. He may even know Smithers."

Wilson said, "I know you don't like it that he's gonna be the next captain." Nelson reddened at this and had a half-formed response starting when Wilson continued. "Okay, but listen. Fraser is good. But he's also a politician. You can't knock him for that. I'm no politician. Maybe you're not cut out for police politics either. So what? A guy can be a damned good cop without being good at the politics."

"My ex-student, for God's sake. I taught him how to use a pistol at the academy," said Nelson. "Now I gotta work for him."

Wilson raised his eyebrows at this remark. "I don't think there's a better cop in New York State than you, Bryan. You see what I'm saying? We gotta tie this one up; who cares where we get help?"

Nelson sat looking at his desk for several moments. "Sometimes, Wilson," he said, looking up, "sometimes you make perfect sense. We need help. From the inside. You in a hurry?"

Wilson laughed. "I got all day," he said.

CHAPTER 4

LIEUTENANT ART FRASER WAS SENIOR MAN IN THE traffic department of the New York State Police District seven, which included the county of Genessee and the city of Cheektavia. At six feet, two inches, and just under one hundred and eighty pounds, Art had a gaunt look when clothed in the single-breasted suits he wore on his police assignments. Underneath the clothing, there moved the lithe body of a man who enjoyed keeping himself fit.

The head of criminal investigation, which included homicide, was scheduled to retire within three months, and Art saw himself as a candidate to assume that position. He had long felt that an assignment to homicide investigations would help his career enormously, and he had lobbied vigorously among senior officers and people he knew in the police commission for such an assignment. The call he got that Monday morning seemed to fit the bill exactly.

"Hi, Art," said a gruff voice over the phone. "Jim Kesten calling."

"How you doing, Jim?" Fraser asked. "What's new?"

"Something important has come up. Come on over and I'll tell you all about it."

"I'll be right there."

Art put away the papers he was working on, locked his desk, donned his parka, pulled up the hood, and braced himself against the wind and drifting snow as he walked the few yards over to the administration building where Kesten had his office. The men exchanged greetings and Kesten started the conversation.

"I just finished talking to Nelson. We had a murder Sunday night. A Robert Smithers, a bridge player apparently. You might know him."

"Bob Smithers! My God, I saw him at the tournament yesterday. He was a man who collected lots of enemies."

"He won't collect any more. His body was found early this morning outside the Adam's Mark. Somebody knifed him last night and left the body in the parking lot."

"No kidding. What a way for guy to end up."

"I thought your background might be useful in the case. I'd like you to join our investigation team. Head it up, matter of fact. I already cleared it with the commissioner. How would you feel about it?"

Fraser did not know quite what to say. He did know that a contribution to solving the murder of Bob Smithers would be a giant step forward in his career. Therefore, saying no was not an option. "I can do that. Who's working the case?"

"Nelson and Wilson. They were on the scene early this morning and got the details. I've already told Nelson I'm putting you in charge, and I'm sure he's told Wilson by now. You've got two pretty good cops to work with. But be aware that Nelson's nose is a little out of joint here. You need to make peace with him and treat him with respect." Kesten's words ended on a note of anxiety. He really believed that Fraser could do the job if he handled himself with diplomacy and avoided internal feuding that might even provoke sabotage by Nelson or Wilson.

"That sounds good. I'd love to tackle the case," said Fraser, with an air of confidence that did not reflect his real feelings.

"Just be careful not to get too close to it – you realize that it's possible someone you know well, even are friends with, could have done it."

"Well, I don't think that's very likely, but of course, I'll keep it in mind."

Fraser started to rise from his chair, but Kesten waved him back to his seat.

"One more thing, Art; let me give you some advice on a delicate issue," continued Kesten. "A number of the higher ups in this organization want to see you promoted."

Fraser looked up, pleased at this remark.

"Not everyone feels that way. There is some talk that you are a little full of yourself. Is there any reason they should feel that way?"

"I step on people's toes at times," said Fraser. "That's bound to hurt feelings. But I only do it as a last resort. If a case is bogging down, sometimes you need to give it a kick to get it moving."

"Okay, but that's not really what I mean. I agree with you about keeping your work moving. God knows, enough things crop up to slow us down. But here is my point, and I'm going to be blunt about it. You won't be a success as a captain unless you get people on your side. If you build up animosity in your subordinates, you will be a loser. Am I making sense?"

Art thought of all the reasons why Kesten's assessment was wrong. He was tempted to blurt out a defense of his own behavior, but his political instincts took over. The correct political action would be to agree with his boss and think it through later, at his leisure, when he could work out what it all meant.

"Leave it with me," said Fraser. "I'll see what I can do."

Back in his office, Fraser thought about Smithers' murder, in a mild state of shock. All of the regular players were well aware of Smithers' habits. Capable bridge player. Charming and considerate to all females. Womanizer. Continual liaisons. On the other hand, his attitude toward men varied from general curtness to downright insolence. Except for a select few, the male crowd responded with indifference or out-and-out hostility.

He called Nelson's number and was pleased to find him in. "Morning, Bryan. This is Art Fraser. I hear you made an early call this morning."

"It was cold as hell on that parking lot. Killers could be a little more considerate."

"Jim told you he wants me involved?"

"Yeah. I got the word. Jimmy wants you on the case." Nelson never called Kesten by that name to his face. "He says you know a lot of the bridge crowd."

"Actually, I knew the victim, too. It's not that big a group, and all the good players know one another. Can we get together soon and make some plans?"

"Wanta come over and meet with us right now? Me and Russ, Wilson that is, we're going over a few things. If you're too busy we can always meet later."

"How long do you think we'll need?" asked Fraser.

"We're figuring on a couple of hours," said Nelson.

"Okay. I can be there in ten minutes. Do you guys serve good coffee?"

"We could," laughed Nelson. "And we'll open a couple of bottles of wine too."

Fraser arrived shortly and winced as he took the hard chair offered to him. "Comfortable quarters here," he noted.

"The best, " replied Nelson. "It helps to keep meetings short. How do you see things?"

"I know very little about the case except what Jim told me. We've certainly got to look for a bridge connection. I'm sure you know Smithers was a player and we had a tournament on over the weekend at the Mark."

"Right," said Nelson. "The hotel manager offered us a conference room for today if we want to do interviews down there. More relaxed for any witnesses, we figure."

"Sounds good," said Fraser. "Plenty of people out there hated Smithers. And almost anybody at the game last night might have had the opportunity to kill him. We've got to look at the whole crew and then narrow it down."

"If you know where to start, fill us in," said Nelson.

"We might talk to Judy Regal first. She was the tournament chairperson. We ought to get the head director in too. Paul Walters. He might have some information that will help. Then we can make up a list of suspects."

Russ Wilson set up an early afternoon appointment at the hotel with Judy Regal and a later appointment with Paul Walters. Fraser decided that all three officers ought to be present during these first interviews so that they could start their work on the case from a common knowledge base. The Adam's Mark hotel provided admirable quarters for their interviews. The room was brightly lit and furnished with a modern, good-sized conference table surrounded by comfortable chairs. An attendant wheeled an urn of coffee and several cups into the room.

"Maybe we could move our offices down here," said Wilson.

"Could you afford the rent?" Nelson asked.

Judy was a well-turned-out, talkative lady in her mid-sixties. Fraser introduced her to Nelson and Wilson, and prefaced the interview by telling her that the pair did not play bridge, and would appreciate detailed explanations of any of the points Judy covered. She expressed shock and surprise at the news of Smithers' murder and agreed to help the investigation in any way she could.

"Maybe you could start by telling us who might have had a grudge against Smithers," said Fraser.

Judy leaned forward and said, "How long do you have? Bob must have upset most people at one time or another."

"What about this weekend in particular?" Fraser probed.

Judy grinned maliciously. "Well, there is one incident you will surely want to hear about. Bob Smithers was in the middle of it. I was sitting right beside them, at the next table, so I heard the whole thing." The detectives were not quite sure what she was talking about, and encouraged her to go on.

"It happened during the last round. That's when all the winners are decided, " she added, glancing at Nelson. "The first seven rounds are just preliminaries." She looked knowingly at the officers and saw they were interested in what she was saying. "On the last round, two teams are playing each other. Orono and Smithers. Lew Orono and Bob Smithers."

Please get on with it, lady, thought Wilson.

"These teams are fighting for first. One of them is going to win and the other..."

Is going to come second, thought Wilson. For goodness sake, say it.

"The other can end up fourth or fifth. Nowhere, you might say. So it's an important match. At the end, they compare scores, and a big cheer goes up at Orono's table. High fives all around. They think they have won. Then the head director comes over to their table and tells them that Bob is protesting the result on one hand and is calling for a committee. And the committee agreed with Bob and overturned the table result. So the Smithers team ended up winning, and Orono was in fourth place. That's quite a comedown, don't you think?"

Nelson and Wilson barely followed the jargon. Looking blank, they dumbly nodded assent. Fraser understood Judy perfectly.

She continued, "Okay. Now, here's the interesting part. Lew Orono was boiling mad, and he's not a character you want to fool with. He has a really ugly side. I distinctly heard him mutter to Smithers, 'You'll pay for this.' "

"Wait a minute. A guy could get mad enough to kill someone over a bridge game?" asked Wilson.

"Believe it," responded Judy. "Your normal rules of behavior just don't apply in bridge."

"Did this guy know Smithers before Sunday?" continued Nelson.

"Oh, yes. We all know each other. Nobody liked Bob Smithers. He was the most unpopular guy you could ever find in the world of bridge."

"About Orono," said Nelson.

"Oh, yes. Sorry. He is not that well-liked, either."

"Are there any popular players?" asked Nelson. "Everybody seems to hate everybody else in this game."

"But Lew wasn't the only guy Bob had a run-in with yesterday. Do you want to hear any more of this stuff?"

Wilson rolled his eyes. Fraser said, "Please. Tell us everything you can."

"Well, there's Jack Duffy," said Judy. "He has a temper. His wife, Helen, is a sweetie. She's a good friend of mine." Judy paused to look at the officers. She was satisfied to see that Fraser and Nelson were listening intently and nodding. This encouraged her to continue even though Wilson, who was taking notes, was not showing much interest.

"Go ahead," encouraged Fraser.

"Okay, " said Judy. "Jack gets mad easily, although he seems to cool right down quickly. He had a big argument with Bob Smithers yesterday, too."

"Tell us about it," encouraged Fraser. "I missed that one."

"Well, I just heard Jack yelling at Bob. Then Bob called the director. I didn't hear the whole thing."

"Is there anything else we should know about these characters?" asked Nelson. Wilson suppressed a choking noise.

"This has happened before with Jack. He got a letter from the board of our bridge unit — that's the organization that runs tournaments in this area. I know about it because I'm on the board. We told him that he is on probation for a year and he'd better shape up or we'll suspend him."

Nelson said, "The probation is in effect right now?"

"It's been in effect for at least two months now. I'd have to check my files..."

Oh no, thought Wilson.

Nelson asked, "Tell me about these tournaments. What happens there? You beat your brains out for a couple of days and what? Make a few thousand bucks?"

"A few thousand?" laughed Judy. "I wish. No, there are no money prizes. We play for masterpoints. They're a bridge player's status symbol. You might have fifty, five hundred, five thousand. Three hundred makes you a Life Master, which is basically an expert level player. The top-ranked player in the USA has over fifty thousand. They're a measure of how many tournament events you've won over the years. Take this recent tournament. They schedule events to start on Tuesday night and go on through Sunday night. You could play in the mornings if you wanted to, and there were games that started at midnight. Someone who was really keen could play in over twenty sessions of bridge during the six days. Some people like to play three or even four times a day. I'm a little too old for that now. I'd rather spend the mornings relaxing. And I haven't played in any of the midnight games in over fifteen years. Getting to bed at three in the morning after a couple of drinks always left me with a headache. I'd be numb all over. And I could never focus on anything."

"All for — what did you call them? — masterpoints?" asked Nelson.

"All for masterpoints. The competition at our tournaments is very keen. The old-time players from the Syracuse-Watertown-Utica area — they're great people and they're tough players. We like to beat up on each other. You've got a lot of very good younger players developing. And you get some good Canadian players from Ottawa and Toronto showing up." said Judy.

"Anything else?" asked Fraser.

"That's all I can think of for now," said Judy.

"Russ, give Mrs. Regal your card. Call Detective Wilson if you think of anything, Judy. He'll be delighted to hear from you anytime." Fraser was chuckling to himself as Judy left the hotel.

When the three officers were alone together, Nelson asked, "So, Art, how many of these points do you have, then?"

"Oh, a thousand or so. I don't get to play as much as I'd like to."

Nelson looked at him with a little more respect. "Well, that makes you an expert, I gather. Hey, maybe you could give me and Russ a rundown on this bridge thing. How you play, what it's all about. Do people really get so damned excited over a card game? Especially when there's no money involved?"

"I'd be glad to," said Fraser. He went over the mechanics of the game, dealing out the cards, the bidding and play of the hand, explaining the terms that every bridge player takes for granted, like declarer, defender and dummy. He described the whole concept of duplicate bridge, where every pair gets to play the same set of hands, and the luck factor is reduced to a minimum. He told them about tournaments held every week, all through North America, with hundreds of players participating in each one.

"Boy, there's a lot of people involved in bridge, " said Nelson. "I thought this was a game for eggheads; professor types with enormous brain power."

"We see a few of those," said Fraser, "but we see all kinds. It's a unique culture; different than anything else you encounter. Folks in this world judge themselves and their colleagues, even their wives, only as bridge players. The only thing that matters is the skill that a person shows in the bidding and play of a bridge hand. Looks, age, manners, dress, income, family background, race, religion, education, and all the other normal human attributes we usually judge people by don't matter a damn. A guy could be a millionaire or a janitor and that would cut no ice at the bridge table. No one would care."

"But would people really kill each other over this stuff?"

"Oh, yes, they have; there's been at least one famous murder involving bridge. It was a long time ago, but nothing much has changed."

Paul Walters arrived shortly after, and Fraser introduced him to Nelson and Wilson. "This is a terrible thing about Bob Smithers," said Paul. "Though looking back, I have to say I'm not completely surprised. He was lucky to make it through supper. Oh, I'm sorry, I don't really mean that literally of course, but we had three separate incidents yesterday involving him. You were there, Art. You must have heard them."

"Yes, I played all day. I knew something was going on but I wasn't close enough to Smithers at any point to catch any of the detail.

You say three incidents?" asked Fraser. "Judy told us about two of them: Jack Duffy and Lew Orono. We'd like your slant on them all anyway. Tell us all you can."

"Art, you know Jim Lemone. He was the first of the lot, actually. I thought he was going to clobber Smithers before the game even started. That would have finished Smithers right there; Jim could flatten him without even breaking sweat. A couple of the guys broke it up. Then he had a run-in at the table with Duffy. They got into a fight over a hesitation auction, and Jack called him an asshole. Jack should know better, and he's already on probation for similar stuff. We had a grand finale, too. At the end of the day, we had this committee and they overturned a table ruling and cost Orono first place. Bob evidently made some inflammatory remark about cheating in front of the committee, and when we broke them up, Orono was muttering threats to him. He's another guy who's big enough to snap Bob like a twig."

Fraser said, "Can you tell us who was on Bob's team yesterday? We should speak to all of them."

Walters supplied the names, and said, "You can probably find all three in the phone book. If not, Stewart Appleton will have their numbers."

Nelson and Wilson looked up questioningly at the mention of the new name. "He runs the biggest bridge club around town," explained Fraser.

"When did the bridge game end?" asked Nelson.

"Play ended about eight. The committee took another fifteen minutes or so and we were all done by eight-thirty. The players had pretty well cleared the room by then."

"Any idea what Smithers did after the game?"

"I expect he stopped by the bar with the rest of his team, but I don't know for sure. We have a lot of packing up to do after the game, and I didn't follow what any of the players were doing. You can check with his teammates, though."

The detectives thanked Walters for taking the time to talk to them and sat down with a pot of the Mark's excellent coffee to rehash their progress.

Fraser leaned forward and spoke confidently. "I'm not really surprised that Lemone threatened Smithers. Jim and his wife Muriel are an interesting couple. Smithers supposedly had something going with Muriel. Recently, too. That's the gossip, anyway. I don't know if it's true, but it wouldn't be the first time Bob had an affair with a married woman. We need to look into Jim and Muriel's background and find out what has been going on. I know them both. I'd better touch base with some of my bridge contacts and see if I can dig up anything about their activities."

Nelson asked, "You got time to do that?"

Fraser ignored the question. "We may have to pull Lemone in for questioning. Paul also confirmed that Smithers had a run-in with Lew Orono at the tournament. We need to do some checking on him too. He's a pretty tough nut."

Wilson spoke up. "I can look him up and get some basic info."

"Fine," said Fraser. "What do we know about the murder weapon?"

Nelson replied, "Ever hear of a Buck hunting knife?"

Fraser nodded, "Yes. They're all over."

"Well, Smithers was killed with a Buck Nighthawk. It's a beautifully made black job, if you forget what it was used for. There can't be that many around. It's an expensive item, and we may be able to track it down. Russ is going to look into that."

Wilson nodded. "I'll talk to a couple of sporting goods stores."

Fraser said, "We need to contact Smithers' teammates, too. They may be able to fill in what happened between the time the game ended and the murder. That's critical."

Nelson agreed. "I'll get in touch with them. We haven't said anything about Duffy. He was there, and he had a run-in with this guy too."

Fraser frowned, "He's a pretty good friend of mine. I hardly think he's our man."

Nelson looked at him meaningfully. "So? You never know. We need to talk to anyone who might be involved. A couple hours of my time won't hurt anything. I want to question him anyway."

"Okay, then," said Fraser, recalling Kesten's warning. "Talk to Jack; it's probably better if it's not me who does that anyway. Let's get together, say tomorrow, and share what we learn."

Wilson agreed automatically, but Nelson thought it might be

Thursday before he had time to contact people.

"Okay," said Fraser. "Don't forget that Kesten says this has priority."

"I'm not forgetting at all," said Nelson. "Some of these people may not be in town, that's all."

"The sooner the better," concluded Fraser.

☠ ♥ ☠

Fraser dropped in on Nelson and Wilson again later Monday afternoon. "Here's a little background I picked up. Smithers was a rug retailer and a pretty big operator. Not wall-to-wall stuff – imported Oriental rugs. I have a report from our credit agency that covers some of his financial matters."

He showed Nelson and Wilson a copy of two bank account statements. The murder had taken place December seventh, a Sunday. Five hundred thousand dollars had been deposited on the prior Tuesday morning and another two hundred and twenty thousand the same afternoon. The half million had come from a line of credit at Smithers' bank, and the balance from bonds that Smithers had arranged to sell late in November.

Wilson glanced quickly over the pages. "Lots of money here," he commented.

Nelson whistled. "How'd you get this stuff? The banks don't like to cooperate. Talking to them is like trying to talk to a statue."

"My friend at the agency helped a lot," Fraser said, smirking. "So Smithers had half a million dollars in loose cash sitting in his checking account, earning nothing." He looked at Nelson. "My buddy found this other account too. Almost another quarter million. Close to three-quarters of a million dollars in total. That's a lot of money to leave around earning zip. That money was deposited less than a week before the murder. We need to understand all this."

Nelson said, "So he had three quarters of a million dollars sitting around. The bonds he cashed in were earning a good rate, six and a half percent it looks like. He freed up all that cash for something. The interest on the line of credit will be costing a few bucks too. Maybe he was planning to buy something, then the deal fell apart, or maybe he balked and didn't go through with it."

"Maybe Smithers owed a big bill to someone," said Wilson.

Fraser smiled. "Could be, although you'd think he would have made the payment once the money was in the bank. He could have been getting ready to make a purchase — I suppose a shipment of rugs might run that much. If so, the person he was set to pay will be a bit anxious right now, I would guess. That's a lot of money to be waiting for. And it'll be frozen until the estate's cleared up. Maybe the reason it's there now is that Smithers refused to pay someone, that he screwed someone on some kind of deal. But we have to learn more about his business. We need to find out who was expecting money. Who was leaning on him? Maybe the guy Smithers owed a pile of money to decided to get ugly. Something has to account for the cash appearing in that account. There has to be a tie-in there somehow. Did he block payment? Or get himself killed before he could pay? That much money, just sitting, earning nothing, right around the time of the murder seems like a big coincidence. Maybe."

"The account history helps us a lot. Your contact at the agency gave you that, you said?" asked Nelson.

"Yeah," replied Fraser. "She's been very helpful."

"You like dealing with the agency," smiled Nelson. "She buy you lunch, too?" Fraser turned red. Nelson continued, "You know, just because he was killed at the bridge tournament, doesn't mean there was any connection. This three-quarters of a million in the bank sure didn't come from playing bridge. It would help if we knew more about Smithers' recent deals. Who owed money? Who was in trouble? I'd like to know more about the rug business. None of the three of us is at all close to it. We have some financial information, yes. But we're guessing about how actual operations work. I'm talking about the guts of the business. Where does product come from? China? The Middle East? How does payment happen? On delivery? Six months? We need to get rid of some of the guesswork."

"I agree," said Fraser. "Can you think of someone who could lend a hand?"

Wilson said, "On my salary I don't get into fancy rugs. Cotton from Wal-Mart, that's my style. But my niece married a guy whose family runs a big shop just outside the city. I went to the wedding. Alexander. That's the guy. Nice guy. He'll be happy to talk to us."

Fraser responded, "Go ahead. See what you can turn up. The more we know about rugs, the better off we are."

"Want to come along?" asked Wilson, looking at Nelson.

Nelson sensed a note of anxiety in Wilson's question. "Sure," he said.

"Here's another point," said Nelson. "I talked to a Henry James this afternoon. Evidently he played on Smithers' team on Sunday."

"I know Henry," nodded Fraser. "He's played with Smithers before."

"James says they all went to the bar in the Adam's Mark after the game to celebrate. Smithers bought a round of drinks, and then James bought another. They were there about an hour. Then they all left, at maybe nine-fifteen or nine-thirty. Smithers parked in the cut-rate lot across Bingham Street. The others all used inside parking. After they left the bar, they never saw Smithers again."

"So they say," commented Wilson.

CHAPTER 5

ONE EVENTFUL WEEKEND FOURTEEN YEARS EARLIER, Stewart Appleton had finalized his arrangements to go to Gatlinburg, Tennessee and participate in the most popular of all North American regional bridge tournaments. With its cool, invigorating air and bursting spring flowers, Tennessee is at its best in April. Accommodation in Gatlinburg is inexpensive and of high quality, while the hospitality at the tournament is legendary as being among the best on the circuit. Stewart arranged to play most of the sessions with a friend from Philadelphia, Susan Stiker. Susan was an excellent player and the two had a standing agreement to share expenses whenever they attended a tournament together.

During the week before the tournament, Stewart went through lists of jobs and priorities with all the key employees at the greeting card factory where he was the manager. He was confident everything would run smoothly during the Thursday and Friday that he was taking off to play a little bridge, and Saturday and Sunday belonged to him, not to his employer, in any case. He had thought of everything.

As it turned out, he had not thought of quite everything. The owner of the business showed up unexpectedly on the Thursday that Stewart was in Gatlinburg. Even worse, the owner brought along a grandson who was of the right age and background for a position like factory manager. The owner accosted the foreman in the shipping area of the factory.

"Do you know where Mr. Appleton is today?" he asked.

"Oh, yes sir," replied the foreman. "He's off today and Friday. Be back on Monday."

"I see," said the owner. "Everything going okay?"

"Very well, thanks. We're a little behind on one order because we ran out of that embossed paper we use, but we'll catch up on that next week easily."

"Good, good," said the owner. He decided to spend the next two days looking over the operation, and invited his grandson to join him and, while they were at it, to see the town.

They watched as the workers encountered a few minor problems in addition to the paper shortage. Late Friday morning, a printing press broke down. The operators removed torn paper from the machine and cleaned it up as best they could, but were unable to restart the print job. They left and did not return until after the lunch break. The mechanic they brought with them had trouble locating spare parts. The operators had no useful work to occupy them during this episode and sat idly by, chatting and performing errands for the mechanic. Finally, they finished repairs and got the machine up and running, just before quitting time for the weekend. The owner, fuming, made a note of all this and determined to meet with Stewart first thing on Monday morning.

'First thing' that Monday happened to be eleven o'clock.

"Morning, Raymond," said Stewart. "I wasn't expecting a visit from you this week."

"I've been here since eight this morning. I was here last week as well. Do you often leave the plant with no one in charge?"

"I just took a couple of vacation days. I laid out the work for everyone. We are pretty well organized."

"Do you call running out of embossed paper 'well organized'?"

"There's nothing we could have done about that. There's a shortage all over the country. Everyone in the trade knows about it; we're all on backorder. I covered our customers on the situation weeks ago. They know we'll ship as soon as we get material. They're all happy with our service."

"Your main printing press broke down and the mechanic took hours to fix it."

"I told you last year we needed a new machine. At the very least, we should overhaul that one. It has more downtime than all the others combined. It's obsolete; I told you that. Nobody uses that model any more. Our competitors have thrown them all out and replaced them."

While this was all true, Stewart did not realize that he had just encroached on sensitive territory. Years earlier, the owner had personally overseen the purchase and installation of the equipment in question. The machine had gone on to earn the owner his first million.

"Very well, Stewart, but I'm still not satisfied, and I think it's time to make some changes. I want you to know, that, effective immediately, my grandson is appointed assistant manager here. I expect you will continue to earn your generous salary and teach him everything you know about the operation."

"You really feel we need an assistant manager in a small operation like this?"

"Yes. I really feel that we do,"

It was not a big surprise when, a year or so later, the grandson became manager of the factory, and Stewart was sidelined to a position as a consultant. Six months later, Stewart negotiated a severance settlement and used the money to do what he had really always wanted to do: own and run a bridge club.

He banked what was left of his severance pay after taxes, and drew on it to rent four thousand square feet of building space on the second floor of an older commercial condominium. In a burst of energy, he renovated the premises thoroughly. He also rented a small flat on the same floor and set it up as his home. Perfect, he thought. Flexible hours, no commuting costs.

Stewart's excellent grasp of the laws of bridge coupled with his easy manner made him an outstanding and likable director; the club soon became a popular place to spend an evening. His students, the mainstay of any successful bridge club, enjoyed his teaching and a steady stream of newcomers began taking lessons. He soon had a core of loyal clients who provided him with a modest living, although their reasons for becoming regulars varied widely. A few women came to the club hoping to meet men. Some of the men came to display their mastery of a skill to the women, perhaps the only skill they had. Some clients came to be with friends, some to learn to play, some to improve their game, and still others to find a battlefield where they could feed their egos. For the most part, the players cared little for beautiful surroundings, for gourmet coffee (which he served) or for snacks (which he did not).

Over time, however, Stewart's keenness and capacity for hard work faded, and he became careless in executing some of the details that were essential to running a good business. He delayed paying his bills. He procrastinated in doing simple administrative tasks. He often forgot to place orders for books for his students. He neglected partnership arrangements. The condition of the club itself, so important the first week of operation, went steadily downhill in the fourteen years that followed. The club had a large playing area and Stewart made sure that plenty of ceiling lights were installed. No one had ever seen all the bulbs working at once, but still, no one ever complained about poor lighting. The carpeting began to reveal evidence of Buffalo's winters. Several seasons of tracking snow, salt, and sand into the club imprinted new patterns on the reception area flooring. Players got into the habit of moving quickly over this spot. Even the playing cards were retained for some time after their useful life had expired and they had become grimy and unpleasant to handle. Few of the players minded any of this. It was all part of the atmosphere of the club.

Stewart's appearance was in complete harmony with that of his club. Thin, almost gaunt, he maintained a poor diet. His clothes were old and while not shabby, would never be mistaken for goods recently acquired. A bald patch on the top of his head was expanding and his generous, blond moustache seemed to need trimming more often than not. Without a female partner to cajole him into adopting good habits, and with little surplus income to indulge himself, he found a comfortable rut and stayed there.

At ten in the morning on the Monday after the Buffalo tournament, Stewart got a call from his old friend, Hermann Volcker. Hermann was one of his club regulars and the person with whom Stewart enjoyed playing more than anyone else. Indeed, he and Hermann had once come close to winning a North American Championship. They had ended up fourth, but could have won by a slim margin had Stewart not misdefended a hand near the end of the final round. The experience depressed him and he lost whatever remained of his taste for tough, competitive bridge. Nowadays, in fact, Stewart played very little. In spite of his potential to be a fine player, he lacked the ambition and thickness of skin needed to drive to the top. A few of the very good pros had cultivated him years ago, but Stewart could not stand the post mortems and analysis when things went wrong. The discussions always seemed to strike a personal note, and he withered when he felt he was being criticized. Still, he enjoyed club games with Hermann. Although Hermann's bidding was outdated, Stewart had enough table feel to steer things into the best contract most of the time, and Hermann had always been an exceptional card player. Stewart loved to defend a hand with Hermann or sit as dummy and watch him play the cards.

"Good morning, Stewart," said Hermann. "I was wondering if your game and your party are still going ahead as planned tonight?"

"Absolutely," said Stewart. "I'm just getting things set up now. Why shouldn't they?"

"You heard about Bobby Smithers, did you?"

"No, what about him?" asked Stewart.

"They found him with a knife in his chest, over at the Adam's Mark parking lot. He was killed last night some time, apparently."

"Are you serious? Bob Smithers?"

"Yes. I just learned. You didn't know?

"No. This is the first I've heard about it. A knife in the chest?"

"So I'm told."

"Good God!"

"Your party is still on?"

"Yes. Yes, it is, I guess" said Stewart slowly, stunned by the news.

"Okay, then. See you tonight."

When Hermann hung up, Stewart began to think about whether he should cancel his December holiday party. Annoying as he could be, Bob Smithers had been a regular client. He would miss him, in some ways. More important, he would miss the revenue that came from Bob's frequent attendance at the club. However, as he thought it through, he decided that although all of his regulars knew Bob, few really liked him. Turnout tonight would not be affected by Smithers' death – in fact, it might even improve if people wanted to get the latest gossip. He decided that the wise business approach would be to go ahead with his party as planned: the usual duplicate bridge game, with special prizes, and generous quantities of a party menu. He could say a few words in memory of Bob at the beginning of the game.

As the club owner, and the man in charge of running the game smoothly, Stewart had observed Bob Smithers in action frequently. He had heard the way Smithers spoke to opponents, and even to his partner, and thought to himself, this guy is heading for trouble. There are plenty of people around outside of the bridge crowd who wouldn't tolerate anyone who behaved like that. Try it in a bar on a Saturday night, he thought to himself, and see how they like it.

Appleton himself was neutral. Mainly, he did not either like or dislike the players who came to his club. They were customers, after all. He was providing a service and he did not intend to interrupt the inflow of cash. There were exceptions, of course. Apart from Hermann, he really liked Helen Duffy. She was pretty, and fit Stewart's idea of a perfect bridge player: friendly to everyone, with a wonderful disposition. From the two or three times he had played with her over the years Stewart also knew that she was a capable player. Had he wanted a steady female partner for any reason, he would have picked Helen.

He received several more calls during the day, inquiring about the party. Most of the callers also had ideas on who might have committed the murder. Stewart himself thought that if the crime were in fact bridge-related, there were only three people in the club who could have done it. As the day wore on, he began to wonder whether he should go to the police. Hell, they should come to me, he thought, if they're doing their job properly. And if they do, I'll tell them what I can. If they don't, then obviously it's not important, and I'll keep my mouth shut. What do I know, anyway?

By seven o'clock, he was caught up in the usual bustle of getting the game underway: selling entries, assigning tables and pair numbers, and pairing up any stragglers who arrived without partners. Before play began, Stewart asked for everyone's attention. "I am sure you have all heard about the sudden death last night of one of our regular players, Bob Smithers. I am sad to say that he was murdered. I know Bob would have wanted us to go ahead with tonight's event, but before we do, let us take a minute to remember him." The room was quiet momentarily. Stewart did not add that party night generated the biggest turnout of the season, and that even though he incurred a great deal of extra expense, he also earned a great deal of extra revenue.

Some of his old energy seemed to return on these party nights. While people were playing bridge, he scurried around arranging a buffet table at one end of the room. He set out a cooler filled with ice, and loaded it with beer — the weekly $3.98 a dozen loss leader at the local grocery store. He uncorked wine — whatever California variety the liquor store had on special. Near the end of the game, he began making popcorn, not the microwave kind, but the real thing, made with an air popper, salted, and smothered in hot butter. Some of the ladies had brought along home-made finger foods, and Stewart arranged these into an attractive display.

As usual, two dozen or so bridge players milled around after the game. The group consisted mostly of good friends who came to play most weeks in Stewart's Monday night game. The regulars, the best players in the area, all showed up along with several other Buffalo players and a couple from Rochester. Most of the locals had known each other for several years; some as long as twenty or more, before Stewart first formed his club. Jack and Helen Duffy just liked to see the people and chat with them about anything current.

Betsy Callahan, a middle-aged divorcee who spent a lot of time and money choosing her designer clothes, cosmetics, and occasional facelifts, was among them tonight. Betsy liked to gossip almost as much as she liked to drink wine, but there was no mistaking her main goal, the pursuit of male companionship. At the moment, she had her sights aimed at Charles Werkman whom she had landed as her bridge partner that evening. Charles was a short, powerful, barrel-chested fellow, and while he was never in good physical condition, he was never badly out of shape, either. He wore thick glasses with thin gold frames and slicked his ample brown hair firmly into a part in the middle. His physical attributes met most of her criteria for good looks. He was a quiet member of the group and generally kept on the sidelines, showing little interest in gossip or small talk.

Charles brightened noticeably when Betsy headed over, glass of wine in hand. She raised her glass in the motion of a toast, leaned close, and said, "Thanks for the great game." Charles looked embarrassed but not enough to move out of range of the physical contact that Betsy was offering.

Hermann Volcker picked up a beer, bowed to Helen, and smiled at Jack. "So, what was your best hand tonight, folks?" he asked. Hermann's great interest was declarer play. He liked to hold court on the play of the cards, and to corner whomever he could to review the best hands of the evening. His favorite saying was, 'Bridge is exactly like life. You play the hand you're dealt, never mind how you got there.' Some of the best players in upper New York had gone on to become national champions after they had served an apprenticeship playing with Hermann. Almost everyone in the bridge crowd admired him, but the veterans had learned long ago to be careful what they said if they wanted to avoid lengthy debates on Hermann's fine points. Tonight, Jack did not mind talking to Hermann, but Charles moved to the other side of the room to avoid the cross-examination, and Betsy followed him. Hermann could be interesting, up to a point, but this was not the night.

Helen moved to talk to Art Fraser, who was accompanied by a stocky but striking fair-haired woman. Art gave Helen a firm hug and introduced his companion as 'Karen'; the blonde smiled hello. Helen often saw Fraser in the company of good-looking young women such as the one tonight, and found his touch flattering. He never seemed to grope or do anything she would find insulting. She noticed Jack's careful gaze when Art was close to her, and smiled inwardly at his jealousy. Fine, she thought. Let him stew.

Art Fraser's attitude towards bridge was a puzzle to Helen, though. While obviously smart, with a good natural understanding of the game, he had never shown the ambition to become a top player. For one thing, he always avoided the analytical arguments that seemed to be a habit of better players. He seemed to enjoy the game solely for its inherent challenge.

Fraser himself was feeling awkward, and trying not to show it. Earlier that day, the Smithers murder investigation had become the overriding priority in his life. Nevertheless, he had decided to stick with his plan of attending Stewart's party and playing bridge that night. If the murder did have a bridge connection, it was likely that the murderer would attend the party. If he listened and observed without disclosing his new assignment, he might pick up some useful leads. What if someone connected him with the investigation and asked questions he was not prepared to answer? He would just have to rely on his instincts if that problem surfaced.

To Fraser, any female partner who showed interest in him added to the appeal of the game. Helen was one of those, and he thought her beautiful, charming, and a very good player. It seemed strange that her husband was openly and publicly critical of her play when they partnered one another. Might there be a crack developing in their relationship? It was hard to say. They had played tonight without a scene, but they were not talking to one another right now.

Helen immediately raised the subject he had hoped to avoid.

"Judy Regal tells me you're involved in the Smithers investigation," she said.

"News travels fast," said Art. "I wasn't planning to talk about it tonight." Fraser was thankful that no one except Karen was close by.

"Am I the only curious one?" asked Helen.

"So far."

"Obviously you don't want to discuss it."

"For tonight, anyway. I'd appreciate that."

"Alright, then tell me something else. I've always wondered what got you started in this crazy world of bridge."

"One of my friends at Cornell was a nut," said Art. "I got fascinated right away."

Karen said, "Tell her your friend was a girl, Art."

"That's true. She was a fabulous coach, never critical, always helpful. She taught me a lot." Art didn't mention that his bridge coach had been all for a more serious relationship, but couldn't live with Art's habit of dating two or three other girls every week. Their relationship had never blossomed beyond a bridge partnership.

"When I moved to Buffalo, I took bridge up seriously. I enjoy Stewart's club, play the odd tournament when I can, and I love to read about the game. I have a decent library of books. How about you, Helen?"

"When Jack and I were courting, it was pretty clear that I had to learn bridge. So I did. I'm not a natural like you or Jack; I have to work at it. But I love the game. And the people."

They drifted towards the others in the crowd.

"Horrible about Bob Smithers, but I bet no one's really surprised," remarked Betsy. "He had a real chip on his shoulder. In the Sunday Swiss they had that big row. Smithers' team won by an appeal in the last round. The committee threw out the result of one board, which swung the whole match. They overruled the director."

"Yes, I heard about that," said Jack. "We weren't in contention so it didn't really affect us, but Lew's team were sure bothered. The ruling dropped them from first to fourth. That's tough medicine for a committee to dish out."

"I wish we relied less on committees," said Art Fraser. "They hurt the game. Paul is a fine director. His rulings are usually right on the money. He can play, too."

"Bob was quite a character," opined Betsy. "So unpredictable. You never knew when he was going to start some ruckus."

"He was not a very good declarer," offered Hermann. "He went down in a cold game against us because he didn't allow for a bad trump break."

Helen said, "I didn't mind the man. He was always decent to me."

Karen spoke up. "One of my friends was Bob's partner on that team. I was playing in the B flight so I didn't know anything about it. She really hated to see the bother it caused." This little speech hushed everyone. "She thinks most everybody would have agreed with the committee. The problem was the way that Bob went at it, basically accusing Lew of cheating. That would get my dander up too."

"So you agreed with the committee, Karen?" asked Jack.

"Listen, what do I know about committees? I'm way over my head here. All I can say is, from what I heard it was clear-cut. Lew asked so many questions about the three-club bid. That was just awful. Everyone knew he had clubs. His partner had a decent heart suit, an obvious lead, but he led a club and they won ten IMPs on the hand. After the committee got through, the hand was tossed out, and Bob's team won the match and the event. Lew Orono was really mad at losing first place."

"People need to be careful about the questions they ask. Anyone with any experience knows that someone asking too many questions has values in that suit, and it was Lew's partner who was in the wrong, if anybody was, for not making his normal lead, " said Jack. "But I know what you mean about Smithers. Lew's questions might have been borderline from an ethics point of view. But then Bob publicly accused him of cheating. You just can't do that – use the 'C' word I mean. Lew might have popped him one right then."

Jim and Muriel Lemone came by on their way to the buffet. Muriel was a doll-like figure beside her husband, her blonde hair without a strand out of place. Perfect features framed her perpetual pixie-like smile. Jim, by contrast, could manage only degrees of scowl; tonight, someone who knew him well would have noticed that he displayed intense disgust when the conversation turned to Smithers. Husband and wife were so far apart in size that they could never walk in step; otherwise, they might have formed a decent infantry patrol. Corporal Muriel would decide where to go, and, using body language, would signal starts, stops, and turns; Jim, the bulk of the unit, executed each maneuver with surprising precision. The Lemone procession marched to the wine table, halted, acquired supplies, encamped near the Duffys to remark on the weather and chow down, fraternized with some of the others present and finally retreated to a getaway vehicle in the frozen parking lot.

Charles saw that Jack and Helen were temporarily clear of company and moved over to talk to them. Betsy followed him over.

"Nice game," Helen said to Charles.

"Thanks," Charles replied. "We were lucky."

"Too bad about Bob Smithers," said Jack.

"What? Oh, yeah."

"He made a lot of enemies. Plenty of people will be on the suspect list."

Charles frowned. "I suppose."

"Looks like Bob finally bad-mouthed the wrong person," said Betsy.

Charles said nothing. He just nodded assent to Betsy's remark. The conversation drifted on. Charles made a move to leave earlier than most of the others. He wasn't a big drinker and there was only so much popcorn he could dispose of. Betsy looked his way hopefully as he put on his parka. He nodded to her, and a minute later Betsy was at the coat rack getting help with her winter coat.

With Charles absent, the conversation naturally enough turned to — Charles.

"He looked a little peaked tonight. Edgy, or something," suggested Helen.

"Didn't seem to affect his game, though," remarked someone. "Sign of a great player."

"A pretty good student," conceded Hermann. "He has potential," he added. "He plays the odd hand very nicely."

"The odd hand!" exclaimed the admirer. "I'd say every hand."

"Depends on how you look at it. To be a really good declarer, you have to consider alternatives."

Art Fraser gave his opinion. "Charles is a strange guy. He keeps pretty much to himself. He doesn't really let you in on what he's thinking about anything. Except bridge."

"I know he has a very good job," said someone.

Jack helped Charles with his income tax and knew to the penny how good Charles's job actually was, but correcting the statement would mean divulging client information. The conversation drifted on through speculation on Stewart Appleton's financial problems and the lack of new people coming to the club. All this was punctuated now and then by Hermann bringing up another fine point, or railing at the bridge organization for its emphasis on masterpoints. "You judge a player by the way he plays his cards," said Hermann, "not by how many masterpoints he bought."

The party broke up about three in the morning with hugs all round, except for Hermann. Helen always looked forward to his elaborate ritual of bowing, kissing her hand and saying goodnight.

☠ ♥ ☠

Charles had seen the look Betsy threw his way as he left. He had a lot to think about tonight. Normally he would have nodded to her quickly, but tonight, he was torn between feelings of unease and exuberance. After a brief hesitation, he decided to accept Betsy's invitation for a liaison. They had won the evening's game by several percentage points and the experience lifted both their spirits and fanned the amorous flames that had been kindled over dinner.

Fifty-year-old Betsy Callahan kept herself fit and attractive, and easily passed for someone fifteen years younger. Charles liked her well enough, even though her bridge was not of the quality he expected from serious partners. He had known her for about six years, ever since he moved to the Cheektavia area. Betsy's husband, seriously ill when Charles first met her, had died six months later. She had observed a period of mourning that was somewhere between short and non-existent. The older men on the bridge scene bored her. The married ones, like Jack Duffy, would have little to do with her. Someone like Charles, unmarried, vigorous physically and a good player, seemed like a perfect match. She needed no other qualifications, and began to ask him for bridge dates, and then to pre-game dinners. Tonight, she had in mind a post-game rendezvous. Charles seemed agreeable.

"Why don't we go to my place?" he asked. Betsy hesitated for a few seconds before agreeing. Charles had set up his one-bedroom apartment, in the north end of Buffalo, in anticipation of occasions when a lady friend might accept an invitation. All of his entertaining took place in the living room. The chesterfield had been selected with an eye to the comfort of two adults positioned lengthwise. The artwork was cheap, muted and suggestive.

He showed Betsy his wine selection and, after checking for her preference, poured two generous glasses and turned on some music. Betsy rose and began to float around the room in time with the music.

"My, you're graceful," he commented as he watched her move around the room.

"Finish it," she laughed. "Say 'for a middle-aged widow'."

"I wasn't thinking of that at all," said Charles. "You're gorgeous."

He joined her in the dance, his hands circling her waist gently from behind, and then began to stroke her back gently. When he withdrew his hand, she said, "Don't stop now."

They were both laughing and each sensed that the other shared a ripple of excitement. Charles moved his hands up over her waist and began to caress her breasts.

"Mmm," said Betsy, leaning back against him. "Aren't you bold?" She made no move to take his hands away.

The invitation was clear, and Charles turned her around and kissed her. Putting her arms round his neck, she returned the kiss with as much lust as she received. Their dance had taken them to a carpeted section of the floor. It would have been impossible to say who wrestled whom to the floor, but they sank together to the surface. Fingers now fumbling at his belt and zipper, Betsy worked herself into a position on the carpeting where she could accept Charles' thrusts and respond with energetic moves of her own. The end, when it came, was quick, but surprisingly satisfying for them both.

After a few moments, Charles rolled away, and they both began to tidy themselves up. With their pulses and clothing finally restored to a normal state, they returned to their wine. Smiling at him over her glass, Betsy said, "We'll have to do this again."

"Soon," said Charles.

"Why don't we go to your bedroom?" she asked. "I'm ready for some sleep anyway."

Betsy had no way of knowing that none of Charles' guests received an invitation to visit his bedroom. Not ever. His bookcase held volumes explaining cheating at cards — how to cheat, how to spot cheaters, how to prevent cheating. He had books on magic explaining card tricks and card manipulation. His computer was set up in a corner of the room and he used it to search the internet for information, among other things, on cheating at cards. When he found a good article, he printed it off. The best articles he pinned up on the wall. Others he stuffed into file folders littered around the room. He also had a few very good bridge books. However, a close observer would have noted that the bridge books were in almost new condition. A shelf on his bookcase held an unusual number of decks of cards. Some of these he had bought; some he had acquired by extracting decks from duplicate boards in the tournaments where he conducted his scam.

"Some other time," was all Charles said. She could not fathom his abrupt and awkward response, which broke the mood of the evening. Their feelings towards one another cooled quickly and completely, and Betsy left shortly after.

The next day, Charles took his time getting to work. He was beginning to wonder how long it would be before the police got round to asking him questions about the Smithers' murder. Maybe never, if all goes well, he thought. The murder weapon will be a good red herring. Nobody will ever connect me with that knife. They might trace it to Jack, but he'll never be a serious suspect. Everybody respects him too much. Should I be doing anything to help myself? No, best keep a low profile. Anyway, they have nothing on me. Absolutely nothing. Nobody even saw me leave the tournament. Certainly not the parking lot; there wasn't a soul around when I pulled out. Yes, the best thing I can do is keep my mouth shut. I'll be okay.

CHAPTER 6

KAREN REDMOND, ART'S BRIDGE PARTNER THAT evening, was also a police officer, one of two with whom Art shared an apartment. She was not a bridge expert, but she had become a fair player under his coaching. When the party broke up, the two walked over to Art's garnet-colored Firebird and shared the task of scraping ice and frost off the windshield and rear window. The drive home took almost no time. Both the city and state traffic officers in the Buffalo area knew the car and, even if they noticed it hustling along at twenty miles per hour over the speed limit, they would make no effort to stop it.

Fraser and Karen arrived at their apartment shortly after three thirty in the morning. The car was just getting warm inside as they pulled into their apartment parking lot. They both shivered a bit as Art shared some random thoughts related to the murder. Karen knew him well enough to understand that he was just thinking aloud, not making conversation.

"Lew Orono wasn't there tonight. I wonder if that's significant? He usually comes out on Monday nights. That'll need looking into. Lemone? He was there. He usually looks ugly and he did tonight. Duffy? His wife Helen? Not likely either of them had anything to do with it. Anybody else in the crowd? Hard to tell."

Despite the lateness of the hour, the third roommate, Jill, was in the kitchen making a salad and drinking a cosmopolitan, her favorite drink of the moment. The three had become close friends when they were classmates at the New York State Police Academy. Art's standing as a top student in almost every subject had created many admirers among the group of cadets as well as in the faculty. Among them were Jill and Karen. When the trio discovered that they were all joining the Genessee county section of the New York State police at the same time, they decided to take an apartment together to keep expenses down. The arrangement, on the face of it, seemed precarious.

Varying food tastes, divergent recreational habits and police duties that required strange hours of work might have provided the cause for disagreements within the trio. But a large dose of inertia and just enough satisfaction with the scheme had kept it going for more than ten years. Originally, Art thought that after he earned a promotion or two he might spread his wings in a pad of his own. But even though the promotions came, the urgency to move never seemed to materialize.

Each of them had a private bedroom. They installed an extra large refrigerator after the first year. And after a rocky start, serious negotiation overcame the disagreements over use of the living room. The TV and stereo could be played after midnight, but only if listeners used headphones. Each would take one wall for their own art selections. Fraser liked black and white photography. The center-piece of his wall was a small Irving Penn original he had bought at an auction. He surrounded this with Ansel Adams prints. Karen furnished a wall with Andy Warhol prints and Jill put up a single, modern oil original on a third. The furniture was oak and leather — easy to clean. A thick wool carpet covered the parquet floor.

Art and Karen removed their snow-covered boots and warm coats and greeted Jill.

"You're home late," said Jill, taking a tiny sip.

"Good party," said Art.

"Anyone want some of this salad?" she asked.

"No thanks. I had lots at the party."

"I'll take a little," said Karen, who seldom turned down any kind of food.

"The buzz is you're into murder now," said Jill.

"Lead man, too," said Karen.

"How do you get time to go to a bridge game?"

Art said, "News travels fast. Yeah. Kesten had me take over the investigation. The victim was a bridge player. He thinks my bridge background will help."

"Tell me about it."

"The victim was a man by the name of Smithers. He was stabbed after a bridge tournament. Delivery guy found the body in a hotel parking lot the next morning, frozen stiff. Everybody hated the guy. There are lots of suspects — all bridge players. If the killing did involve bridge in some way, the murderer was probably at the party tonight."

"That's exciting for you," said Jill. "A real change of pace. You hired Karen as a bodyguard?"

"Round the clock. What's new with you?"

"I'm on the afternoon shift," said Jill, who handled domestic disputes. "A husband got beaten up tonight. That was a change."

Karen said, "My partner and I had a quiet day. We had a stolen car and an accident near the airport. Fifteen cars piled up. There was a stretch where the snow was blowing so bad the visibility was down to about fifty feet."

"I'd hate to think of you guys having a busy day," said Fraser. He said goodnight and left the pair munching salad.

CHAPTER 7

RUSS WILSON FOUND HELIOS FINE RUGS LISTED IN the Buffalo Yellow Pages. It was located on the outskirts of the city. He talked to his niece's husband and made an appointment for lunch that same day. "Alexander asked us to come by as early as we could," he told Nelson. "They're having a sale starting today and he expects to be really busy later on."

He and Nelson made the drive in less than an hour. The Buffalo expeditionary army of snowplows had done good work in clearing away the heavy snowfall of the previous night. Traffic was light, the sun was bright, and the clean, fresh snow covering the landscape contrasted sharply with Nelson's black mood.

"Do you think Fraser can handle this kind of case?" Wilson asked.

"Could be," said Nelson. "It's a total piss-off seeing Kesten put him in charge. The guy has no background in homicide. I'd have made him pay his dues before giving him a big one. He should have done a little legwork for someone else so he could learn the ropes."

"It's easy to get mad at the politicians."

"Everyone says that. I guess I have to focus on the positives. We have a job to do. Let's do it. Nobody's any better off if I turn sour."

"That's the old Nelson."

"This Smithers guy sounds like a hard case. He must have hurt someone really badly to warrant murder. The murder could easily be related to money. Like backing out on a payment, maybe. To me, that seems more likely than one of these bridge revenge theories."

Wilson pulled into the parking lot in front of Helios Fine Rugs, and they entered the building in search of Alexander Helios, son of the founder. The one-story building was brightly lit with the floor covered with pleasing displays of several flooring materials — carpets, ceramics, hardwoods and vinyl. Alexander was in his early thirties, with a serious but friendly appearance. Wilson greeted him and introduced Nelson.

"I thought every day was a sale day with you guys," smiled Nelson as he shook hands with Alexander.

"Yes, we do promote a lot. A necessary evil to survive in this business." Alexander smiled back. "But our sales are genuine. We have some real bargains this week. I thought we could walk next door for lunch," he continued. "It's a Greek place, quick, good and cheap."

"That's fine with us," said Wilson, who had prepared Nelson to lay out the money for an expensive meal. "If it's okay with you."

"Sure. They have booths where we can talk privately."

Wilson talked a bit about police business, and told Alexander that he and Nelson were working on an investigation and needed some understanding of the operations side of the carpet business.

Alexander asked, "You're investigating Smithers' murder then?"

Wilson furrowed his brow, and Nelson laughed, "You catch on quick."

"The carpeting business is a small world all its own," said Alexander. "Everybody knows everybody."

"Tell us something about your business," suggested Nelson.

Alexander was delighted to hold court. "We source oriental rugs from a number of places. We buy in the Middle East and the Far East: Afghanistan, Iran, Tibet, Turkey. Seventy percent are from China. They all have a tradition of hand-making rugs. Generations of craftsmen. The people there, poor guys, I don't know what they work for. It can't be much." Nelson nodded understanding.

"We order everything in containers. They're neat. They load the carpets into containers in, say, China, put them on a boat, ship them to L.A. or San Francisco, then a truck picks the containers up at the dock and brings them right here. China to Cheektavia without unpacking until they're in our warehouse. That's the only way to get your costs down."

"So how much money do you tie up in a container load?" asked Nelson.

"It depends. A container of cheap, I mean machine-made, rugs, might run a hundred thousand dollars. A load of good rugs, really good rugs, hand-knotted, fine wool, would run more like three or four hundred thousand. Our cooperative, our buying group we call it, is as big as most wholesalers. And we have the cash to cover everything when we get a shipment. Cash keeps the price down. It takes a lot of cash to operate in this business. If you want to get into big money, and we do a bit of it, you get into hand-knotted pieces. There a good wool rug can retail at five, six thousand dollars for a room size. A silk rug could run three or four thousand for just a scatter mat. Some of these products are beautiful. The artisans have a deep knowledge of dyes, vegetable dyes that produce these bright, saturated colors. And if you know anything about design, many of the figures are meaningful to a connoisseur. Then you can get into quality carpets where a used, say, an antique piece can easily start at ten thousand dollars."

"You have to know what you're doing if you buy in those leagues," suggested Nelson.

"Believe it," replied Alexander. "When we dabble, and we only dabble in the antique types, all of us on staff here consult before we order. And we check every single item carefully when the shipment comes in. We have found a broker we can trust, but we still check everything. There's not much market around Buffalo for the really upscale, pricey products, but we move a few every year, and it's profitable."

"How are the people you deal with? Pretty honest types? Does anybody ever try to cheat you on quality of goods? Do you always get the right amount in the container?"

"We've been with the same guy now for ten years. I don't know too much about the other dealers. You have to be able to trust the guys you deal with. My father has told me stories about problems he had. He got screwed a couple of times. You don't worry too much about your retail customers; those sales individually are all small potatoes. But when you deal with a supplier you can get into big dollar invoices, especially if you buy a full container of carpets."

"Tell me about one of the times you got screwed. Do you remember any of the details?"

"My father told me the whole story. This happened maybe ten or eleven years ago, when I was just starting in the business. Of course, carpets then cost about a quarter of what they do today, so our dollar exposure was nothing like what I've been quoting you. Still, for my father at the time, it was significant. This deal was one where the broker sold us a container of supposed good quality rugs. The agreement was that they were made with the finest wool and the best dyes. If you use cheap dyes, they fade like crazy. When you get a spot exposed to sunlight, you'll have a different carpet in six months. An expensive rug, any rug I guess, would make you sick to look at if they use cheap dyes. What happened on this shipment was that the top quarter, maybe a third of the rugs were all good, as advertised. The rest were crap. Father didn't know, and he wasn't expecting anything like this. We only found out after they had been sold and customers came back complaining. That all happened a year or two later."

"How did you handle the situation then?" asked Nelson.

"We settled with all the customers who complained. That is, we negotiated settlements. We weren't going around offering charity, but anyone with a legitimate complaint got a hearing and usually a settlement. We replaced the rug, or a percentage of the cost of a new rug. It cost us plenty. And the broker who sold us the container load, we never ever did business with him again."

"Interesting," said Nelson. "How well did you know Smithers? He was a pretty big operator, wasn't he?"

"Yes, I knew him all right. Not well. My father knew him better. I met him maybe twice in five years. That's all. He dealt with that same broker I was telling you about. The one who sold us a bad lot."

Nelson said, "Really. He dealt with shady outfits, then?"

"Hey, I didn't say shady," said Alexander. "No accusations. We just don't do business with the guy and never will again. How Smithers handled it, I don't know. From what I know of that broker, he does business strictly on the basis of caveat emptor — let the buyer beware."

Nelson whistled softly when Alexander finished talking. They ordered coffee. "Sounds like Smithers was walking a dangerous line. If he was handling questionable goods, he may have been on the edge of problems. Customer complaints. Settlements. They can add up to a lot of money. I am sure your margins are okay, but if you have to replace an installation, you could more than wipe out your original profit."

"It adds up pretty quickly. Our margins, except for sale items, are maybe seventy percent. But most of our items, you realize, are on sale. Out of that come all of our expenses, and they're pretty hefty, too. We pay a collection agency to handle slow accounts, and we eat a small percentage of bad debts. When we have to replace a few installations, all of those costs are doubled. Our replacements are less than three percent right now. When we had the problem with Smithers' broker, we were up over fifteen percent. One container load was enough."

"That would be a disaster," Nelson responded. "I wonder what he would have done in a case like that? He was known as a tough guy to deal with. You say you pay cash to your brokers on receipt of a container of rugs?"

"That's our policy. That's how we get the best prices. I can't tell you what others do."

"It could be that Smithers bought himself some trouble that he couldn't get out of. Can you tell us the name of Smithers' broker?"

"Sure. His name is Albert Rich. He's active, and very successful."

"Where can we dig up info on Rich? More important, on his dealings with Smithers?"

"Not from me," said Alex. "I wouldn't want to get into that."

"I was talking to Russ. Sorry. That's our baby," said Nelson. "We're not asking you to compromise your ethics, or your business. Let's think for a minute about what we could do here. What I'd really like to know is did Rich and Smithers have a deal cooking about the time Smithers was killed? Smithers had a pile of money, close to three-quarters of a million dollars, sitting in his checking account just before he died. He put it there a couple of days earlier. It seems like he was ready to pay a big bill." As soon as he finished talking, Nelson thought he might have gone too far in divulging information that was confidential. Then he thought, if the kid is as bright as he looks, he won't spread this around.

"Rich and I aren't friends, and I don't have reason to talk to anyone who works for him. There was such a blowup the time he screwed Father that neither side was interested in doing business with the other again. Short of lying to him, I don't see any excuse to start a dialogue. Anything I learned would have to be through some indirect contacts. I couldn't even ask him for a quote."

"If Smithers was in fact paying this guy Rich, and defaulted on the deal, Rich must have a pile of rugs sitting around in a warehouse."

"True. True. That amount of money would buy a full container load. Probably more. That's a pretty big deal. Maybe Smithers was lined up with a building contractor. Perhaps a subdivision or a new condominium somewhere. They usually buy roll carpeting, but an upscale project might use area-type rugs. It's possible."

"Do any of your friends bid on that kind of business?" asked Nelson.

"I can't see it. Real estate has been depressed around here for a long time. There are a couple of dealers around here who might tackle this sort of thing. They'd know some chatter about Rich, probably. And Smithers. It might be worthwhile to talk to them. Come to think of it, why don't you guys talk to Rich? He'd have to talk to you, and you'd bypass a lot of hearsay."

Nelson replied, "You have a point there. Maybe that's what we'll do. We'll keep your name out of it, don't worry. We'd like you to keep this conversation to yourself, as well. Totally."

"That'd be no problem."

Nelson thanked him and reached for the bill, saying, "Russ brings me along for a reason."

CHAPTER 8

RUSS WILSON HUNGERED FOR A CHANGE FROM THE loneliness of his current existence. Not that he regretted his divorce; he had gladly traded the constant complaining of his former wife for the burden of child-support payments, but there were things about married life he missed. Mostly, he missed her cooking, and now sported a slight paunch to mark his habit of high-fat, fast, convenience foods. His suits, never of the latest style although always neatly pressed, had tightened noticeably in the last two years.

He had taken to frequenting bars on Saturday nights and found no trouble picking up singles. For their part, the girls were attracted by his ready, Borgnine-like smile, which displayed even, widely spaced teeth and suggested a friendly person in back. They didn't seem to mind that his diet was slowly transforming his once lean, powerful build into a more pliable, jelly-like form. These easy pickups partially satisfied his physical craving but did nothing to erase his solitude. It was with an eye to something more permanent that he was taking a personal interest in Kathy, the clerk in his and Nelson's office. He saw her as a beautiful and sympathetic young woman who understood police work. That would mean she could understand Russ Wilson. An attachment to someone like her would be perfect.

Wilson handed Kathy a copy of the Buffalo Yellow Pages and explained to her the details of the assistance he needed. "I'm tracking down the murder weapon in the Smithers case. If we can find the owner, we'll be a lot closer to the murderer. Could you get me a list of the stores that sell sporting goods?" he asked. "Especially hunting equipment." He hoped he was making a suitable impression.

"This sounds important, "said Kathy, taking a deep breath and smiling as Wilson's eyes widened. "Maybe we should talk to the maker of the knife. They might know who distributes the product. Is this a Wal-Mart item?"

"He was done in by a Buck Nighthawk. Very expensive. I don't think you'd get one at Wal-Mart. It would probably have to be a specialty store."

"I'd be glad to look into that."

"Terrific. Keep me posted," said Wilson.

In the course of the Smithers murder investigation to date, Wilson had drawn some quick conclusions of his own on who had committed the murder. He felt certain, at first, that the owner of the knife that killed Smithers was the man they were after. After the interview with Judy Regal, when he learned of Lew Orono's run-in with Smithers, it seemed as though Orono had a strong revenge motive. And he certainly had opportunity. These guys are so serious about their game, he thought, they do things normal humans would never consider. So when Nelson asked him to look into Lew Orono's background, he took on the task with enthusiasm. Could this be an opportunity for him to engage in a little sleuthing, on his own, and report back to Nelson with a package all wrapped up and ready to go to the D.A.? Wilson thought so. What if Orono owns the knife? Could Orono physically handle a murder like that? A clean thrust through two layers of clothes. The victim did not fight back. It all must have happened quickly. Whoever did it was strong and quick. How strong was Orono? He'd have to check that out. Wilson thought if he could pin these facts down, he would be ready to talk to Nelson about his conclusions.

Wilson made some inquiries about Lew Orono's background, and found that he was employed as a business manager of a local, small, franchised hotel. The job would not make him affluent but it would give him free evenings and weekends. Lew played a lot of bridge on these occasions. He searched the police records for background, as a matter of routine, and was pleasantly surprised to find a record of a previous encounter between Smithers and Orono. The incident had occurred six years earlier. No charges had been laid. Two officers had responded to a 911 call, complaining of a possible assault. The officers found the two men arguing heatedly, but no physical violence had occurred. So. They had a history, thought Wilson.

Wilson called the Fair Meadow Inn, got hold of Lew Orono, and told him he would be right over. He let Kathy know he would be out for an hour or so.

Kathy said, "You know the info you wanted on knives?"

"Oh yeah," said Wilson.

"There are a few stores that sell Buck knives around Buffalo. Eight of them. I called them all and only one of them sells Nighthawks. They've sold three of them in the past two years, and they've got records of the sales."

"Terrific. Got the phone number and address?"

"I couldn't call them unless I had their number," said Kathy tartly. "They're on Harlem Road, just west of I 90. Look, I typed up the name, address, phone number and the name of the manager. He said to drop in anytime if you want more information."

"You're great," said Wilson, giving Kathy one of his broad smiles. He took the memo with him and went to call on Lew Orono.

The Fair Meadow Inn was an older property, well maintained, just off the New York State Thruway in a low tax area of Buffalo. Wilson's call had not come as a surprise to its recipient. Lew Orono knew that as soon as the police knew about the fracas after the bridge game ended on Sunday, they would be right over to talk to him. The question was, how much else did they know? While Lew was waiting for his meeting with Wilson, unpleasant memories flooded back of the business dealings he had had with Bob Smithers.

At one time, Lew had planned to live out a personal dream. As a young boy growing up in Ohio, he had taken vacations many times with his parents. They made a few trips to northern Ohio and Pennsylvania in the spring and early fall. During their trips, they had stayed mainly in motels and the experience thrilled Lew. The atmosphere of spring and the colors of fall in a rugged countryside gave him memories he would never forget. Apple juice, runny eggs, toast, milk, all chosen exactly as he wanted from a breakfast menu, gave him a novel experience. The sounds, the smells, and the people he met were all new to him. Strangers were friendly, asking his age, where he was from, what he was going to be when he grew up. Motels were part of a perfect world. For years after that, he had dreamed of owning and operating a motel.

He spent a few years in the army and when his parents died, he counted his assets, resigned and took up residence in Buffalo. From money he saved, from the precious little inheritance his parents left him, and with a loan from a local bank, he put together enough money to buy a property. The place was rundown, but Lew could tell that the essentials were sound. He looked carefully at the foundation, at the wiring and at the heating unit, and saw that quality materials had been used and that careful workmanship was evident. He felt he could handle tired paint, old carpets, and worn furniture, in time.

He tackled the painting first because he could do most of the work himself and the cost would be minimal. The motel's fourteen units took him a month to paint, and the lobby took him another week. He undertook freshening the furniture next and applied a coat of varnish to worn-out looking pieces. The chairs all needed re-upholstering, but he knew that would have to wait. He bought a rug-shampooing machine and took it from room to room, energetically scrubbing every square inch of carpet. The results of his effort were disappointing. Caked dirt released its grip but took color with it. Alcohol stains, lipstick streaks, and cigarette burns would never disappear. He realized that he would need new rugs as soon as he could afford them. Until that time, he would have to keep his prices low.

Nevertheless, the appearance of the place after his whirlwind efforts pleased him mightily, and slowly, the stream of customers grew. The first year of his operation was a mild success. After covering his expenses and his scheduled payments on his bank loan, he had a small amount left over. He even had money to take in a couple of bridge tournaments over the winter, although not as many as he might have liked.

By the time the late winter of his second year of operation rolled around, he was exuberant. He told himself he was looking at a very successful business, and decided he would stretch his luck. He would go for new carpeting and that would make the difference between a three-star motel and the marginal place he now ran. He shopped around the carpet dealers listed in the Yellow Pages, and in doing so, realized that he had a passing acquaintance with one of the bridge crowd who was also a carpet dealer — Bob Smithers. Bob carried a line of carpeting that Lew thought was exactly what he needed, and his prices seemed to be as reasonable as anyone else's. Smithers would look after the installation and the disposal of the old materials.

He also agreed to a payment schedule stretched out over twenty-four months with a negligible rate of interest. The agreement they signed made Smithers a secured creditor with a mortgage on the property. Should Lew have to forfeit any of the required payments, Smithers would stand just behind the bank in carving up the assets of the business.

Spring came and with it a prolonged period of icy weather. The following summer was one of the coolest on record. Tourist traffic in Buffalo plummeted with the temperature. A falling Canadian dollar meant fewer cross-border shoppers coming to hit the outlet malls. Worse, it seemed to Lew that every motel franchiser in the USA had made a deal in Buffalo and many new properties were opening up that summer. New competition and a low point in the tourist cycle all but killed his business. During the worst week in this pitiful period, Lew rented no rooms at all. The next week, he rented one room.

Lew lost his appetite and ate only enough to keep alive. He lost weight. His strength and energy diminished. He began cutting his bank payments below the amount he had agreed to pay. Finally, he went to the bank and asked if he could skip a payment. The meeting was awkward and formal. Loan officers did not see their careers advancing when borrowers went into default, and so his loan officer did not like the turn of events any more than Lew himself did. Matters continued to deteriorate as the summer went on. He knew that a meeting with Smithers about payments was inevitable, and after postponing it as long as he could, he finally made an appointment to see him. Smithers heard Lew out, expressed sympathy, and offered Lew an extra week to make his payment.

"A week?" asked Lew. "I need a couple of months at least. I can't believe how bad business is. You can understand that, can't you? Your business must go up and down occasionally too. My business will come back. I know it will. My receipts last year were way higher. I just can't believe this."

Lew thought he saw a trace of a smile flash over Smithers face. "Sorry. A week. That's what I can do. No more. Read our agreement."

"You mean you're going to take my business away?"

"Like I said, read our agreement," repeated Smithers.

Lew was totally stunned. He was ashamed of the tears he had to hold back as he left Smithers' office. The significance of the whole matter sunk in as he drove back to his motel. All his dreams were about to be shattered in one short week. He should never have gambled on the carpeting. Had he not, he might still be solvent and able to scrape by. Why had he chosen Smithers to deal with? My God. There were half a dozen other carpet retailers he had talked to. Or why couldn't he have done one room at a time and paid cash up front for each piece of work? He worried over the affair all night, unable to get much sleep.

The next day, the loan officer called to tell Lew that the bank was foreclosing on the loan, and that Smithers would be taking over the motel. Smithers had agreed to repay to the bank the full balance of the loan that Lew owed. In return, Smithers would assume full title to the property.

That night, Lew became increasingly angry, and determined to visit Smithers the next morning and make a more forceful presentation of his case. He rose, shaved and showered, skipped breakfast and headed for Smithers' office. He arrived at eight-thirty, and found Smithers in his office with only one other employee on the premises. Smithers was surprised to see Orono appear in his lobby, looking haggard and livid. This was not the first time he had encountered an irate business associate, however, and he quickly dialed 911, gave his address and reported a possible assault. He calculated that the police would need about twenty minutes to get to his office. He would have to hold Orono at bay for that time.

Lew stomped into Smithers' office and began to curse. Then realizing that shouting was unlikely to persuade Smithers to cooperate, he stopped himself and begged for one more chance, an extension of the time to repay his debt. "I'll pay double the interest rate. You get your money and more. You've got to let me reschedule the payments." Lew could see that he was getting nowhere. "What in hell do you want with a motel, anyway? You don't know anything about running one."

Smithers was careful to avoid being physically cornered by the larger man in his office. He rose from his chair and stood ready to move around the side of his desk opposite to any advance Orono might take. Orono banged his hands on the desk. "Damn it, man. Say something. Why in hell do you want to ruin me?"

Smithers replied, "Look, my friend. I've been through this all before. Sick businesses don't ever recover. You need to face up to that. I'm taking over that property, paying the bank off, and if there's anything left over, which I doubt, I'll cover off what you owe me. Read our agreement."

After a few more minutes of shouting, a pair of police officers arrived. Smithers immediately asked to have Orono taken out of the building. The constable asked what the call was about and asked for details on what was happening.

Orono and Smithers both spoke at once.

"He's trying to ruin me," shouted Orono.

"He's physically attacking me," said Smithers. "This is my property and I want him out of here."

The officers settled the pair down, asked some questions, recorded the information they needed, and sent Orono on his way.

Orono drove back to his motel to gather his belongings. He was broke, jobless and thoroughly depressed. He did the only thing he could; he began to search for a job working in another motel for one of the owners he had come to know.

His mind snapped back to the present, to the impending visit from Detective Wilson, and Orono wondered exactly what he would want. He told the clerk at the front desk that he was expecting a visit from a police officer any minute, and that the clerk should direct him to Orono's office as soon as he arrived.

"How's the motel business?" asked Wilson, not quite sure how else to start the interview and wishing he had his mentor, Nelson, present to help. He noted that Orono was a husky man, as tall as Wilson himself, but forty pounds lighter. He had a scar on the right side of his face that discolored part of his cheek and gave his mouth the appearance of a constant, twisted smile. Wilson noted Orono's powerful grip and returned the squeeze with a little extra muscle of his own. I'll let this guy know he has to be careful if things get serious, thought Wilson. He eased up only when Orono's head snapped up with a look of surprise.

"Slow at this time of year," said Orono. "We cover our heat and light but don't make much. What've we got here?"

"You knew Bob Smithers?"

"Bastard. Pardon my French. Yeah. I knew him all right. I played bridge against him this weekend. He screwed me out of a championship down at the Adam's Mark – but you probably know that. Listen, he had it coming. You'll have no shortage of suspects; the guy pissed off everybody who knew him.

"Tell me what you know about the murder."

"I don't know a thing. We had this argument at the end of the night. Maybe you heard about that. He wins the damned thing on a technicality. I was disgusted, so I left and came right home."

"Did you drive with anyone?"

"Naw. I drove by myself. I live here, right in the motel. I don't get paid that much, in this work, but the boss gives me a room and meals. Plus I get time to play in bridge tournaments when I want. Not in the busy season. I have to stick around during the summer months."

"So you had an argument. I hear there was a threat."

"A threat? Are you kidding? Who threatened?"

"Did you tell Smithers you'd get him?"

"I don't know, I might have. Listen, I was so pissed off, I could have said anything at that point. I didn't mean anything. I was just mad at getting screwed."

"What time did you leave the Adam's Mark?"

"I don't check my watch every second. I left right after the game and drove right here. We didn't have a victory drink like we should have. Must have been about eight."

"Where were you parked? Did anybody see you?"

"In the cheap lot. Car was frozen solid – took me ten minutes to get the windows clear enough to drive."

"What about here? Anyone see you get in?"

"Yeah. Check with our clerk on duty. He saw me come in. He might know what time it was. It doesn't take long to get here from Adam's Mark when there's no traffic."

"What do you know about carpets?" said Wilson, suddenly.

Orono's scar turned deep red at this remark. "Whadda ya mean?"

"Smithers was in the rug business. You had some business with him a few years back, didn't you?"

"Are you kidding? I wouldn't go anywhere near that S.O.B. for any kind of deal."

"That's not what the police records say."

Wilson perceived that Orono's mind had wandered and repeated his question. "I said that's not what the police records say."

"Huh? Well, okay. I had a deal with him years ago. The son of a bitch screwed me then, too. As a matter of fact, he ruined my whole life. Yeah."

"So you've had more than one run-in with Smithers?"

"He was never my best friend."

"Listen, it's just a formality, but we need you to come down to headquarters to take your fingerprints. For elimination purposes. Can you make it nine o'clock tomorrow morning?"

"That's when I'm on duty here. Eight would be okay. What in hell you going to do with my fingerprints?"

"It's just a routine check. We got to follow through on every lead. Listen. Do you know anything about hunting knives?"

"Do I know anything about knives? Of course I do. I grew up in Ohio. Every kid there knows what a hunting knife is. Tell me you don't."

"Have you ever heard of Buck knives?"

"Sure. If you got lots of money maybe you can afford one."

"A Buck knife killed Smithers."

"So what? I had nothing to do with Smithers' murder. I don't like where this is going. Maybe I better get a lawyer before I come down for any fingerprints."

"We have a number of people coming down for fingerprints. You're not the only one."

"You better not be trying to screw me," said Lew with a scowl.

"See you tomorrow," said Wilson. He gave Orono a card with an address and phone number. Wilson made a note of the name of the night clerk on duty the night of Smithers' murder, and left the motel. Orono could have done it, he thought. He's powerful and he's ugly and he had plenty of motive. Let's see if he owned a Buck Nighthawk.

Wilson looked over the memo that Kathy had made up for him, and planned the route to get to the store. I'll need about an hour or so to get there, he thought, and then I'll have to go through the records with the manager. Better call in and let them know where I'm heading.

When he arrived, he wandered through the store for a few moments, intrigued by the attractive display of hundreds of knives and guns of all kinds — handguns, shotguns, and hunting rifles. When a clerk offered help, Wilson introduced himself and asked about records of sales of Buck hunting knives.

"We have no computerized records of anything, certainly not knives," responded the clerk.

"My office just phoned earlier today," said Wilson. "Somebody told us you did."

"Somebody was wrong," complained the clerk. "We can't spend all our time playing with a computer."

"Then I guess I need to see the manager," said Wilson.

The clerk took him over to a confident-looking, trim man and introduced him. "Big store you got here," said Wilson.

"Biggest dealer in the state," said the manager.

"I understand you sell Buck Nighthawks here?"

"Yeah. I talked earlier to a Kathy in your office."

Wilson nodded. "She said you had some computer records of your sales."

"Not computer, I'm afraid, but we do have records. All on paper. They're well organized, though. Fred here will have to go through the invoices with you. We can go back three years in the store. If you go back further than that, we're in trouble. Older records are in dead storage, and they're not that well organized."

"Okay. Let's get started," said Wilson.

Fred took him to a back room, and pulled out boxes of records. The records were indeed well organized, and they soon found a file with all transactions related to Buck knives. They had sold three Nighthawks in the past year but neither of the first two buyers' names was familiar to Wilson. Then he hit paydirt. The third item was a purchase made just before Christmas the previous year. Helen Duffy. Now we're getting somewhere, Wilson thought happily. Better tell the lieutenant right away. He took a copy of the record, thanked the manager of the store, and headed for his car. As he drove to the police station, Wilson began to think that the new information might well blow up his theory about Orono.

CHAPTER 9

TWO DAYS INTO THE SMITHERS MURDER INVESTIGATION Fraser felt they were making good progress. They had some good leads, though he was not quite sure yet how they were going to translate them into tangible evidence acceptable to the district attorney. Orono was an obvious suspect. Wilson was checking him out. There was the murder weapon, and that ought to help trace the murderer. Wilson was looking into that as well. Now the lab had pulled some prints from the knife too, so even though the database had come up a blank, they'd have something to tie a suspect to when they got close to one.

Fraser thought Jim Lemone might be involved and he was planning to take on that part of the investigation himself. The other prospect was Albert Rich. He was a business associate of Smithers and there was a suggestion of bad feeling between them. Rich had a reputation of sharp, maybe sleazy dealings. Smithers was known to be tough. There was never any talk that Smithers was dishonest, just tough to the point of being unreasonable. Fraser had a sneaking admiration for Smithers as a person who stood his ground in recognizing certain principles even if that meant offending people some of the time.

Nelson and Wilson dropped in at the end of the afternoon, obviously excited.

"Hey, Lieutenant," Wilson said. "Guess what I got."

"Some terrible disease?" asked Fraser.

"No, sir. But guess who bought a Buck Nighthawk knife a couple of years ago?"

"Lew Orono?"

"Try Mrs. Helen Duffy."

"Really? She bought a Nighthawk? I guess maybe she could have bought it as a gift."

Nelson added, "It could well be the murder weapon. Russ has done some good work here."

"Thanks. Kathy got me a dealer that sells them, over on Harlem Road. I went through the guy's records with him. When I found the Duffy name, I quit there."

"This is a big step ahead. We need to head over to the Duffys and ask some questions," said Nelson.

Fraser seemed puzzled and his attitude and frown quenched the excitement that both Nelson and Wilson were showing. "Somehow this doesn't figure. I can't see either of the Duffys involved in a murder."

Nelson said, "All I can say is we have the murder weapon. We know who probably bought it, and the same person probably owns it. We are going to ask the owner some questions. Then we're going to get some fingerprints and see where that takes us. Plenty of people surprise their friends when they commit murder."

Fraser sighed. "I guess you're right. Absolutely. You've got a job to do. It just seems bloody strange to me that Jack or Helen could be involved in a murder."

When Nelson and Wilson were alone in Nelson's office, Nelson burst out. "That son of a bitch."

"What do you mean?" asked Wilson.

"You do a great job tracking down the possible murder weapon and Fraser pooh-poohs the whole thing. 'Can't see Duffy being the murderer.' Gimme a break. Our job is to look into every lead we come across. Damn it, we don't let Duffy off because he's Fraser's friend."

"I think you're right, Bryan," said Wilson.

"I've got half a mind to go over and see Kesten. Tell him the whole story. The guy he appointed is shielding a possible suspect. That'll look awfully bad for Fraser."

"Are you going to do that now, before we look into these other leads?" asked Wilson.

Nelson sighed. "No, not yet, but I'm thinking seriously of doing it. We're not taking Duffy off our list because he's a friend of Fraser's. We're going to call on him and confront him with this. We'll get his reaction, at least."

"Look, Bryan," said Wilson.

"What?" snapped Nelson.

"We got the murder weapon."

"Old news."

"We got the owner, at least the buyer."

"And?"

"Who says the owner is stupid enough to take his knife to a murder scene and leave it there? He lets the whole world know what he's up to. Nobody is that dumb. Unless he couldn't get the knife out of the body, like we thought at first, but the M.E. doesn't seem to think that's too likely any more."

Nelson's face turned red as though he were ready to explode and he seemed on the verge of losing his usual coolness. He sat for a long moment, saying nothing and appearing deep in thought. The redness receded, and he finally regained his composure. "Sorry, Russ. You're absolutely right. I think I let myself get a little carried away. Forget what I just said. Let's just go talk to Duffy."

CHAPTER 10

ART FRASER FELT HE COULD USE HIS RELATIONSHIPS among his bridge-playing friends to break down barriers, and was confident in his ability to uncover information without upsetting anyone. He needed to look into the possibility that Jim Lemone had engaged in an act of passion or revenge. Art often met Jim and Muriel at the Cheektavia bridge club and had played against them several times, but he had never partnered either of them. They were not regulars at tournaments in the upper New York State area.

When Art wondered how he might get more information on the Lemones, his thoughts turned to his roommate, Jill. Her full-time assignment for several years now had been investigating domestic disputes. She was an outgoing person who kept up a network of contacts throughout the city, and probably had a connection with many of the family counselors in the Buffalo area. Although she was only a novice at the bridge table, she had a passing acquaintance with many of the local bridge players. He picked up his phone and dialed her number.

"Hey, Jill," he said. "I'm looking into the background of a guy named Lemone in connection with the Smithers murder. He seems to have a motive and he has this appearance of being a tough guy. He made nasty threats to Smithers the day of the murder."

"Do you want me to arrest him for you?" she asked.

"Later. Right now, I'm looking into whether Lemone had some domestic problems. There's a story that his wife, Muriel, was involved with Smithers. They went off to a tournament together, somewhere in Pennsylvania. The Lemones are sticking together, as far as we can see. I'm wondering if maybe they talked to some family counselor or marriage counselor. This all happened recently and they may still be working with a counselor. Is there any way we could track that down through your contacts?"

"It would be a fluke if we found anything, but I don't mind trying. Do we know where they live?" said Jill.

Art gave her an address in Tonawanda.

"Give me a couple of hours," she said.

Jill called late in the morning to say that she had good news.

"You may have a problem though. Counselors are not required to pass on any information. Not even to nosy police lieutenants."

"Let me worry about that. This is a murder investigation. My job is to be nosy," responded Art. "I can at least give it a try. If he clams up, fine; I haven't lost anything."

"Okay. I'm just giving you the environment you'll face. It's not a he, though. Her name is Celia. She's a friend of mine; I can take you over and introduce you if you like."

"Hey, that'd be terrific. More than terrific. When can we do that?"

Jill called back a few minutes later. "You have an appointment in Celia's office at four this afternoon. We'll have to meet there. I'll introduce you, but I won't hang around." She gave him an address.

"You're a genius," said Art. "See you there."

The counselor, Celia, was a cordial, confident woman in her late thirties. Art liked her immediately. She obviously had a way of quickly gaining rapport with her clients. He wondered if he could find a way to inspire the same trust in her. Art was uncertain as to how much to tell her about the murder investigation. He finally decided to be honest about his interest in the Smithers murder, probe as deeply as he could, and answer any questions she had. He explained the need for maintaining strict confidentiality about their conversation.

"The Lemones knew Smithers," said Art. "Everyone knows that Smithers was fond of women, and he didn't much care about their family attachments. He had plenty of money to finance his own and anyone else's fantasies. Sometimes he invited these women to accompany him on weekends. I'm talking about short trips to bridge tournaments in places like Rochester, Syracuse and maybe Toronto or Pennsylvania. Obviously, nobody cares if unattached women are involved. But when he starts breaking up families, well... There is a story going around that Smithers had his eye on Muriel Lemone. She's attractive. I hear she was receptive to Smithers' ideas. I guess Jim found out about it and threatened Smithers with violence."

"Well, Mr. Fraser," Celia started.

"Art."

"Art. I can tell you that I know the Lemones very well. These things are supposed to be confidential, but I suppose, if there's murder involved..."

Art simply nodded encouragement.

"Well, I'll tell you what I can without stepping too far out of line. You probably know that Muriel is a primary school teacher and Jim works in construction. He's a scheduler or something. They have no children, so their household expenses are not too high. Two incomes keep them comfortable, if not rich. I've seen them three times recently. The last meeting was only a week ago, in fact. We had a long talk. I know that Muriel got herself involved with someone, another man. The whole thing upset Jim terribly. Muriel, too, felt very guilty about it. Somehow she saw it as a failure on her part. And Jim Lemone, have you ever met him?"

"Yes, I know them both," said Art.

"Well this Jim Lemone looks like a house. I guess you have to be tough to survive in the construction business. He's not a laborer, but he used to be. Jim is a big, strong man, but not a clumsy person, as you might expect. He looks like he could frazzle your Mr. Smithers or anyone else with one hand."

"The Lemones both play bridge," said Art, "that's how I know them. They're regular club players, but not tournament players. He's not all that enthusiastic. She's by far the better player."

"They wish now that they could have done more together. I mean after Muriel got involved the way she did."

Art replied, "Nobody can turn the clock back and do things differently. Do you know anything else about Jim Lemone?"

"Only what I've told you. He's quiet. I guess you'd say the strong, silent type. He seems to have quite some temper, although Muriel puts him in his place when she wants to. The school marm is still a disciplinarian."

"Why do you say temper?" asked Art.

"Oh, it's just that I had to keep them waiting for about fifteen minutes one night when they came to see me. He was boiling. I guess when you're a construction scheduler, you expect everyone to be on time. I couldn't help it. We had another case, an emergency where the family really needed help. I had to deal with it right then."

"How did he show his anger?"

"If you can imagine a three hundred pound gorilla who's had his banana stolen by a mere woman, that's as close as I can come to describing him. He said a couple of things before Muriel shut him up."

"It sounds like she's the controller," said Art.

"She's definitely very much in charge of the couple."

"Can you tell me anything else about them?"

"I really believe this was a one-time affair. I don't think Muriel will ever repeat her experiment. She's not that kind of person. But Jim, my God, he could easily be a murder suspect. Wait a minute — he is, isn't he? That's why you're here?"

"At this point, almost everyone is a suspect. We have to look into every lead we come across."

Art thanked Celia for her help, shook hands, and left.

He drove by the Lemone's home after his meeting with Celia. The Lemones lived in a neighborhood of small houses where grounds were mostly neat and not elaborate. He noticed a dark green, almost black Mazda 626 in the laneway and wondered if Jack's neighbor could have mistaken it after dark for a black Chevy Cavalier.

CHAPTER 11

JACK DUFFY KEPT A FOOT IN EACH OF THREE worlds, an unusual accomplishment for a biped. Each was important to him, although at times he temporarily sacrificed one interest in his quest to achieve goals in another. The overriding priority in his life was his family – his wife and two children. In a crisis, he would sacrifice anything for them. Short of a crisis, he gave everything he could to his accounting business, where he was owner, self-appointed chairman of the board, and, surprisingly, a man well-liked by all of his nine employees. In his spare time, he played competitive bridge. He would have liked more spare time.

Neither Jack nor Helen was prepared for the way Tuesday evening unfolded. Nelson and Wilson arrived at their home at five forty-five, just as Helen was about to serve dinner. Jack started to get annoyed when it became apparent that this was not going to be a quick visit.

"Look, guys," he said to the two police officers. "I'm just unwinding after a day at the office. Helen has dinner ready. Can we make it short?"

Lieutenant Nelson stepped up to answer. "Sorry, Mr. Duffy. A Mister Bob Smithers has been murdered. I understand you knew the deceased."

"Yes, we both did. We know about the murder," Jack said. "I never liked him, but I wouldn't wish murder on anyone."

"We were sorry to hear about the murder," Helen said. "He's not a friend of ours, but we knew him quite well. He didn't deserve this."

"We're collecting evidence from all our sources. That's our job. If you have a problem, we can take you down to headquarters and interview you there. It'll be much easier for everyone if you cooperate. I'm sure you'd like to see the case solved as much as anyone."

Helen was right beside Jack, and she spoke up. "Jack, let's help the lieutenant. This was a terrible thing to happen."

"All right," Jack grumbled. "How long do you think we'll be?"

Nelson replied, "We should be done in an hour, max."

"Damn," said Jack.

"It's all right," said Helen. "I fed the children earlier."

It was a chilly December evening and Helen invited Lieutenant Nelson and Detective Wilson to have coffee in the kitchen. They accepted her offer gladly. When everyone was settled round the table, Nelson began the questions and Wilson took notes.

"You knew Smithers pretty well?" Nelson asked.

"At the bridge table. We were never close personally. Helen and I played quite a bit against him. For years. Ten at least."

Nelson asked, "And you have never had any close relations with the deceased apart from competing at the bridge table?"

A red warning light glowed in Jack's mind as he considered this question. "I did a small amount of work for him years ago," said Jack.

"What kind of work do you do?" asked the lieutenant.

"I'm an accountant," replied Jack. "I have my own firm."

"When would that have been, when you did the work for Smithers?" asked Nelson.

"I'd say eight years ago, roughly. When I first met him, I was hungry for clients and used to proposition every businessman I met. He needed some help and I gave him a quote. He accepted. The deal only lasted a few months." Jack left out the fact that after five months of working together and one tax filing, he came across evidence of revenue that was going unreported. That meant that Smithers was breaking the law and that Jack had filed incorrect tax returns for Smithers. If he did not report the situation, he and Smithers could both be prosecuted by the Internal Revenue Service. He brought the subject up with Smithers, who laughed and refused to do anything about it. He threatened to blame Jack for the error and perhaps sue him if it became public. Jack was not quite sure how to proceed and eventually had decided to simply walk away from it. He had always retained a nagging feeling of guilt about the situation. He hoped the officer would move on to another subject.

"Your relationship with Smithers seems to have been one of continuous conflict. The two of you never got along all that well," continued the lieutenant. "Didn't you almost get a suspension from bridge tournaments after an incident between the two of you? Your bridge league has you on probation for a year, don't they?"

Jack reddened, although he actually felt relief at the way the conversation had changed direction. "Yes. I'm on probation for a year. And yes, Smithers and I had a bad argument at the Rochester tournament two months or so ago. But like I said, there was nothing personal in the argument. Just a bridge problem."

"You had another argument on Sunday at the Mark, too? Am I right?"

Jack admitted that he had.

"I'm learning how seriously you guys take this game. Could someone really get murdered because of something that happened at a bridge game?"

"If that's what happened, it wouldn't be the first time," said Jack. "Look up Bennett or Elwell on the Internet if you don't believe me. Bridge players are a different breed. We all know each other — play with and against each other for years, like in this case. I have lots of friends from the bridge crowd. Bob kept pretty much to himself. That was his choice. Many of us are more open and friendly than Bob Smithers was."

"You have a reputation for being a bit of a hothead." This was a factual statement, not a question.

Again, Jack's face turned deep red. He hesitated. Please, Jack, thought Helen, don't say anything stupid.

"Okay, okay," he finally blurted. "I admit I lose it occasionally. But my friends, people who know me, understand that it never lasts long. Every time I've gotten a bit mad, there's been a reason. A damn good reason. Smithers accused me of cheating on Sunday. Wouldn't you get mad at that?"

"That would depend on what the man actually said. I get mad sometimes, sure. We all do. But I keep it under control. We've got indications Smithers' death occurred sometime before midnight Sunday night. That's December seven. We need to know where you were that night, say between eight o'clock and midnight."

Jack was fighting his temper, trying to keep himself under control. He also felt a touch of fear and a need to limit what he disclosed to the officers. "What gives you the right to pry like that? Doesn't a man have any privacy?" he asked the lieutenant.

"These are just routine questions. A man has two serious arguments with another man, and next day we find that one of them has gotten himself killed. You can see why we want to see if you can account for your movements during the time after the game on Sunday. We're going to be thorough in our investigation. If someone close to you had been murdered, I'm sure you'd want to see a careful investigation. We have to do our job, and you can help us most by giving us straight simple answers to all our questions. I'm sure you have nothing to hide."

"I sure as hell don't," said Jack. "Sunday night. Okay. We played in the Swiss at the tournament. When it was over, Helen caught a ride home with a friend and I went to the office for a while."

"Yes," said Helen. "I came home with my friend, Hermann Volcker. He was my partner on Sunday."

"You say Volcker is your boyfriend?" asked Nelson, looking from one to the other in surprise.

Jack spluttered, but Helen laughed and answered, "Good heavens, no, Hermann is almost ninety. My boyfriends are all much younger."

Nelson grinned, then turned his attention back to Jack. "You didn't come right home?"

"Well, no. I slipped into the office for a couple of hours to finish something important. I'm supposed to be off on a hunting trip for a few days, starting Friday."

"Did anybody see you there?"

"No. I have a key to the building, and I can come and go as I like. I just handled a couple of urgent matters and came home."

"Can anyone corroborate your whereabouts after the game? Can you tell us exactly where you went, and who might have seen you? We need this kind of information."

Jack hummed and hawed for a minute, then admitted he had seen no one, had not even stopped to pick up a cup of coffee on the way.

"So you went to your office Sunday night after your bridge game. No one saw you?"

"No, nobody else works crazy hours. But it's my business, and if anything's left undone, I hold the bag. I often go in alone to take care of unfinished details."

"We'd really like some positive evidence that you were at the office as you say. Can you help us with that?"

"I just told you that no one was there. No one saw me. I'm sorry but that's the truth and that's the way it was."

"If you think of anything, let us know. Also we're going to need you to come down to headquarters for some photographs and fingerprinting. Can we settle on tomorrow morning? What time?"

Again, Jack's temper rose towards the boiling point. Lieutenant Nelson opened his briefcase and took out a sealed bag of clear, transparent plastic. "Do you recognize this?" asked Nelson, putting the weapon on the table.

Jack was still distracted by the thought of being fingerprinted. "I have a knife like that — it's in the den. Wait a minute — is that one what I think it is?"

"Yeah, this is the murder weapon. Buck Nighthawk. It came from Smithers' body. There are not many of these around."

"I keep mine in my den with my hunting gear, locked up...," began Jack. Then a terrible realization struck him. "Oh, hell."

"What's that?" inquired Nelson.

"The break-in. A month ago. I came home after bridge. We had a break-in. All the lights in the house were on. Someone took off in a car before I drove up. Nobody got the license number. The guy took off like a scared squirrel. At the time, we didn't believe that anything was stolen. We didn't even think about the knife."

He rushed out, and they heard the noises of a frantic search from an adjacent room. After a few minutes Jack returned, looking sick and clearly feeling much less belligerent.

"It's not there, Helen. Jesus, I can't believe it — is that my knife they've got there? Was Bob killed with my knife?"

"You say there was a break-in?" asked Nelson.

Helen touched Jack's arm but he pushed her away, suddenly regaining his composure. "Hey, I'm not making this up — the police were here. They investigated the break-in. They never found anything. At least, they never told me about it if they did. Your records ought to have a report on the break-in. That must have been when my knife was stolen."

Nelson said, "All right, Mr. Duffy, we'll check into all that. Was there anyone else you can think of who might have had reason to kill Smithers?"

"Not offhand. He upset a lot of people in the bridge crowd, but I can't imagine any of them wanting to murder the guy."

"Let us know if you think of anyone. I'm sorry, Mr. Duffy, but we're still going to need your fingerprints; we need to compare them to the ones on the knife."

"All right," Jack said. "How about first thing tomorrow morning? Say quarter to eight?" Jack felt more nervous than he outwardly showed.

"That's perfect," said the lieutenant. "We open at eight, so don't rush."

Nelson and Wilson thanked Helen for the coffee and left the couple sitting quietly in the kitchen. Helen said, "I gave you that knife for Christmas last year. What a horrible use for it. You won't ever want to see it again."

"I haven't even started to think about it."

"You'd better phone Aaron right now and cancel your hunting trip completely."

"Damn. You're right. Aaron knew Bob. He told me once that Bob was a tough cookie in his financial dealings. He said that a guy owed him money once, and Bob had him bound up in a tight contract. The guy ran into trouble and couldn't pay on time. Bob foreclosed and drove him into bankruptcy. He had a reputation as a hard-nosed S.O.B."

"Make sure you tell that to the police. They need to know about all the enemies Bob made. Somebody out there had it in for him."

"Yes, but think about it, Helen. If someone stole my knife to kill Bob with, it's not a coincidence – it must be someone who knew us both. That means it's got to be a bridge player."

Jack and Helen looked at one another, suddenly aghast.

"I'm going to make some calls, talk to some people," said Jack, getting up from his chair.

Their two children had overheard the conversation with the police officers. Sandra was now fifteen, as sensible and pretty as her mother. Rick had just turned thirteen and showed signs of copying his father's behavior. Now, both children peered into the kitchen as their father left it.

"What was all that about, Mom?" asked Sandra.

"Come on in, you two," said Helen.

When they were seated, she explained the whole affair. She emphasized Jack's innocence, and told them to remember that their father was a man of integrity. Sandra accepted the information gracefully. Rick was another matter.

"How can they pick on Dad like that?" he asked. "Can't he just get a lawyer and get them off his back?"

"Yes dear. But lawyers are expensive, and Dad hasn't been charged with anything. The police have no case at all. They were misled by Dad's knife being the murder weapon. They had to investigate the person who owned the weapon." Helen explained how Jack's knife had come to fall into the wrong hands.

"Yeah, but don't they know Dad's an honest person? You don't go around accusing honest people. I'd go to the commissioner or somebody and complain."

"The lieutenant was just doing his job. He's an ordinary person like you and me."

Rick complained bitterly, "You know what the guys in school are going to say. My father's a murderer. Just wait till he goes to jail. He'll be up for life. Jamie always teases me. He'll ask why I'm not worried. I feel like punching him sometimes. But I can't punch them all. They'd beat me up."

"Oh, honey. I am so sorry. They shouldn't be doing that. Don't worry. It won't last very long."

"But it'll be in the paper. My Dad's going to be in the paper as a murderer."

"No, dear. The paper may say nothing at all. The most they'll say is that he was being questioned. The police have to question people to solve the case; they'll talk to all our bridge friends, we all knew Bob Smithers. Your father had to be questioned, otherwise, the police wouldn't be doing their job."

"But Mom, they'll all be talking about it. I don't want to go to school anymore. I'm staying home."

"Honey, you can't run away. You can't punch people out, either. You just go out there and stand up to these people. Tell them they're wrong. Tell them what I just told you. Dad's knife was stolen and somebody used it. Maybe the person hates your dad and tried to frame him. You have to fight for your family."

"I dunno. I still would rather stay home."

"You're a fighter, I know," smiled Helen as she hugged Rick.

She could not discuss this problem with Jack. His mind would be fully engaged in working out how to divert police attention to the real murderer. Oh God, she thought, he has such a quick temper. I hope he didn't...

CHAPTER 12

HELEN, AT ONE TIME A NATURAL BLONDE, NOW shared a secret with her hairdresser. Dark green was her best color and she wore it frequently, always in the form of dresses or skirts, but never slacks. Her hair and clothing provided a perfect background for beautiful blue-green eyes. Some would say that she became lovelier as the years passed. She bustled through her daily routines, always with details of her day mentally mapped out. She would visit the A&P for groceries, the butcher for a roast for the weekend, the liquor store for replenishment of ingredients for martinis, beautiful martinis, for the next two weeks, as well as a few bottles of wine, red for herself, sauvignon blanc for Jack. Today she thought, no. No wine. No more martinis. Not right now. We're going to cool things for a while.

She thought about what her two children liked best: macaroni and cheese. That's okay if they have a salad with it. I've got to get to the hairdresser by ten. Then I'll go to the lawyer's office. Jack's not guilty. This Nelson has to get off his case. But he's not doing it and it's going to suck away so much of Jack's time, and mine, too. He'll get behind in his work at the office. Nina and Mike are wonderful, but even so... and I won't sleep well until they sort this mess out. I'd better remind Jack of his game tonight. He might not even want to play with all this going on.

Helen sat through her hour with her hairdresser unable to get involved in the chatter, which she usually loved. She kept trying to make sense of the events around her. Oh, if only Jack could control his temper more carefully. She wished with all her heart that he was able to. Every time it happened, he promised not to let it happen again, and he seemed to try. But it always came back to the same thing. Some little incident set him off and he said words that she knew he did not mean. She was learning that she had some control by choosing her own words carefully. But then, out of the blue it seemed, she picked the wrong word, or, at the bridge table, got too defensive, and boom! A big outburst embarrassed them both.

Helen ran an invitational bridge club that met once a month at the golf club she and Jack belonged to. The players out there were not very good and certainly not serious about the game, but Helen liked them all. She took no money for her efforts, but just enjoyed her evening out with the group. She liked the feeling they had that, when it came to bridge, she was on a pedestal all by herself. But how was she going to explain the murder to them? And what about Jack's involvement? She guessed the best approach was to be open and tell them what she knew and how strongly she felt that Jack had nothing to do with it.

Jack — she still loved him, and believed in him, but she wasn't so sure they belonged together any more. She reflected on a trip they had taken in the early fall, one that had been meant to be a lovely holiday built around a regional event in Syracuse. Their plan was to leave on a Wednesday morning, arrive in Syracuse before noon, book themselves into the tournament hotel, and play bridge for five solid days. At least, Jack would play five solid days. She would take a day off on Saturday for some shopping, and they would play again in the Swiss team event on Sunday. Charles Werkman would arrive on Saturday and play with Jack for two days. Hermann Volcker would partner Helen in the Sunday Swiss. They arranged for a baby-sitter to look after the children, and Jack was careful to make sure that everything at work was covered off before he left.

The excursion started well. The drive to Syracuse was uneventful. The sun was bright and their spirits soared as they drove along the New York turnpike. They were taken aback momentarily when they went to check in at their hotel and the receptionist could not find any record of their reservation. She quickly set matters right by offering the couple a suite at the same price, to compensate for their inconvenience. They accepted the offer even more quickly.

The Wednesday game started well for them. They were in third place at the halfway point, within easy distance of the leaders. "Another game like that tonight will give us a good shot at a win," said Jack. "The leaders are not that consistent."

Helen smiled. She could live with whatever happened.

The couple followed their practice of not drinking between sessions. Helen found that even one glass of wine would interfere with her concentration in the evening. Jack would never stop at one glass anyway, and both his bridge and his manners went swiftly downhill after a few drinks.

In the evening session Helen's concentration slipped momentarily and she went down in a contract she should have made. Jack questioned her sharply about her play, and after that she could not bring her attention back to the level she needed to play well. She kept thinking about Jack's criticism and wondering when his next outburst would come. They ended the event in seventh place, just out of the overall standings in the event. Jack said, "What a damned waste of time that was. What in hell did we come here for, anyway? If we can't play any better than that, we ought to stay home."

Helen wanted to say that, if Jack really wanted to go home, they should get in their car and do so right now. Instead, she did her usual thing and tried to placate her husband. "I'm sorry dear. I'll try and do better tomorrow."

The Thursday and Friday sessions were no better. If Helen played well in the afternoon, she was bad at night. One day, she was bad in the afternoon and sparkled at night. She couldn't understand why her game was not consistent enough to play well for two consecutive sessions. Helen started out every session playing carefully and taking her time. But no matter how hard she tried, she couldn't help but lose her concentration for a minute and make some mistake. Probably, had Jack kept quiet, Helen would have recovered and gone on to play well enough for them to place well and possibly win one of the events, but as it was, three days went by and they had not a single overall placing to their credit.

Jack, unfortunately, felt he had to remark on every technical error that Helen made. He did so politely the first day. He became a little testy the second day, and more and more ugly as the week went on. Helen, naturally, threw gasoline on the fire that was smoldering between them. Some of her mistakes gave them good results or mattered very little, and on these occasions she would mutter, "Oh, what's the difference?" or "Worked, didn't it?" When she offered these defenses of her play, Jack exploded. Old Swivelhead, she called him, because he was forever shaking his head in disapproval as they played. Their bickering bothered many of the other players nearby and a few registered protests with the directors.

Jack had to go through the humiliation of being warned by the head director that he must stop his behavior immediately or he would be suspended from the tournament. Jack felt guilty, sorry that he had acted so tactlessly, and agreed that he would accept the director's guidance. However, by the time Saturday rolled around, Helen was glad that he had arranged to play with Charles, and sorry that she had agreed to stay over for the Sunday team game. She could not handle another day of this kind of conduct, at the bridge table or anywhere else for that matter.

She had seriously begun to consider calling it quits with Jack after the misadventure in Syracuse. She was tired of the way he treated her. But once the Smithers murder came up, she couldn't help feeling sorry for Jack because of the accusations that were swirling around. He needed support now more than at any time in his life. Fine, she thought. I'm still mad at him. Let him beg a bit. Then she worried that he might talk to Nina or Betsy or any of the other women with ideas about him. She realized that was inconsistent, but that was the way she felt. In any case, she was going to see a lawyer today and at least discuss divorce proceedings. Maybe she would start them, maybe not. But for sure, she was going to have a plan.

She felt certain that if Jack had any idea that she was seriously thinking about divorce, he would be shocked. Maybe that's what he needs, she thought. Maybe he's a little too darned comfortable with things as they are. Takes me too much for granted. What grounds could she use? Mental cruelty, she thought, even though I don't fully understand what that is. How much will the whole thing cost? How long will it take? She had to know all of the pieces and fit them together. Then she could make a decision. Until then, there would be no more specials for Jack. No more closeness. At one time, she had felt determined to make her marriage with Jack work at all costs. Helen was blessed with a positive disposition that helped her sail over the kind of turbulence that would have rocked most of her friends. She had the capacity to ignore the outbursts that Jack was prone to. Although she made far more mistakes than Jack did at the bridge table, she was still quietly confident in her own ability. Her habit of overlooking the mistakes of others made her a charming person who got the best out of her partners. She was the same with her children. The voice of her mother still rang in her ears, talking to her about marriage and its importance above everything else. She was grateful for many of the things she shared with Jack. But now she was at a breaking point. She was going to act.

Her thoughts drifted back to the murder. Did Lew Orono kill Bob Smithers? Maybe. Orono was a tough nut. Who else was playing bridge that night? Charles? Could Charles want to kill someone? Maybe he could have done it. She shuddered, and decided that she couldn't possibly imagine it. She and Jack had known Charles for seven or eight years. Of course, there was plenty they did not know about him. He and Bob had certainly had words at the bridge table. Not as bad as Jack and Bob, though.

Maybe the murder had nothing to do with bridge whatsoever. Maybe some business associate or some jealous husband just got fed up with Bob Smithers and his self-serving behavior. Bob could easily drive someone over the brink. She could see that happening. If he could do it at the bridge table, he could certainly do it elsewhere. Somehow, the police had to get going and investigate people besides Jack. She wondered about how she might help this happen. Her only connection with the police was through Art Fraser. How far could she go with that friendship? What would Art expect in return? She knew that Jack seemed jealous anytime she was near Art or even mentioned his name. She knew that Art was single and he always seemed to have an attractive girl on his arm. Yet, he had never acted improperly with her. She wasn't sure how she would react if he ever did. What was improper behavior anyway? There certainly were days when she would have welcomed an advance by Art. Tenderness from anyone would have been nice. It would be important to observe proprieties.

☠ ♥ ☠

It's never difficult for a bridge player to find a lawyer. Ray Sternberg was a lawyer specializing in divorce matters and had agreed to meet with Helen at two that afternoon. He was an excellent bridge player and she and Jack had known and liked him for fifteen years. She arrived at his downtown Buffalo office for her consultation with a few minutes to spare, found an empty metered parking spot on a side street, smoothly slipped her car into it, inserted some quarters and went up to Ray's office. He greeted her with the closest thing to a smile that she had ever seen him display, a show of the tips of an upper row of teeth and the absence of a glower.

"How are you doing, Helen?" he asked.

"I'm not sure. All I know is I've got to talk to you."

"Please have a seat. Tea? Coffee?"

"No thanks, Ray. I hope this meeting is confidential. I don't want anyone to know about it except the two of us – especially Jack."

"I never talk to anyone about client meetings. Tell me what's on your mind."

"Okay, Ray." She took a deep breath. "I get fed up with Jack at times. There are days when I can't stand him. I want to look into possibilities of a divorce."

"Oh. This is serious, then."

"I'm not starting proceedings, you understand. I want to find out what's involved, what the costs are, what I have to do, what the process is."

"I can tell you all that. But help me here. Aren't you getting a little ahead of yourself? There are several steps to consider before divorce. Look, I can take you on as a client. Divorce is my business; I do nothing else. But, knowing you and Jack, I can't see you guys separating. Not without trying a few things first."

"What do you mean by that? This sounds like the men's club. Maybe I should see someone else."

"Look, Helen. Forget about a men's club. I have no axe to grind one way or another. I told you I wasn't charging you for the consultation today. We're friends. If I just wanted to run up fees here, I'd take you on as a client and start the clock running at five dollars a minute. That's the way I run my business. I'm talking to you as a friend now. We'll get into the divorce stuff in a minute."

"Okay."

"Let me ask you a few questions first. Do you mind?"

"I suppose not."

"Do you like your relationship with your children?"

"Of course I do! What a question."

"Picture the relationship after a divorce. Have you done that?"

"N-no. Not really. I guess I'd have them to myself."

"Yes, to yourself. Three or four days a week you'd have them to yourself. Do you understand child custody arrangements in a divorce?"

"I've never thought about it, really. Three or four days a week, that's all?"

"That's typical. I've handled hundreds of these cases. Unless there's a real problem with one parent, a real psychopath, for example, or someone with a drug problem; then the children might go exclusively to the other. I don't see how that would apply here."

"Maybe I could make a case for exclusive control of the kids – Jack certainly drinks too much sometimes."

"I have heard that statement a hundred times, and it works maybe ten percent of the time. Think about it. Now, do you like your house? Your car? Your furnishings?"

"Of course I do. I love the house."

"What will happen during the proceedings? Ever think of that?"

"Jack would go live somewhere else, I guess."

"Indeed. And so probably would you. In almost every case, except where someone is very rich, which I don't believe you and Jack are, I mean really rich, the house gets sold and the proceeds are split somehow. Then you have the fun of going out and buying another place with half the proceeds."

"I could buy a nice little bungalow."

"Yes, you could. Do you want to?"

"I'm not sure."

"Now, another question. Have you ever considered a marriage counselor?

"No. Not seriously."

"Let me tell you, they're a lot less expensive than lawyers. I know that some marriages go over the brink, and the best thing in the world to do is for a couple to split. I also see professional spouses. People who run through one partner, then another, with no intention of sticking things out for the long haul. I don't see you and Jack fitting either of those categories."

"No, we don't."

"So, you're mad at Jack. I'm sure you have good reason to be. But I urge you to think these things over before you do anything. Remember that I'm speaking as a friend. I could make a lot of money by letting you go ahead."

"But I want to know how long it takes to get a divorce. And what it costs."

"It varies. Six months. Ten thousand dollars. Twenty if it gets nasty. But look, Helen. Back up for a minute and think this thing through. Have you even discussed this with Jack? Does he have any idea how you feel? The man has a temper. We all know that. Maybe we have to make allowances for that fact of life. But how will he react when you tell him you are going to leave him?"

"Well, I haven't exactly done that yet. I don't know how he feels."

"I can't believe that he wouldn't accommodate you. Why don't you try this? Talk to him. Be open. Then try a marriage counselor. If all that fails, come and see me again."

"Okay, Ray. I'll think over what you said."

"Please do."

"I guess I ought to get going. I know you're busy."

"Never too busy for a friend. I hope I've been of some help."

"I don't know what to say. There are times when I can't stand the man and I feel I have to get out of the relationship. Other times, we have lots of fun together."

"Think over what I said. Be open."

Helen thanked Ray and left. Now she had even more to think about.

CHAPTER 13

THE BIGGEST SNOWFALL OF THE YEAR HIT Cheektavia on the Wednesday morning that Jack was going to have his fingerprints taken. During the night, a northerly wind swept across Lake Ontario from the Canadian side, picking up warmer moisture on its way. As a result, when the cooler air mass in the Buffalo region was encountered, two feet of heavy, wet snow deposited itself, bending branches on trees and dragging many to the ground. Even when the snow stopped, the wind seemed to increase in force, and that spelled ruin for many residential gardens. A birch tree that Jack proudly cared for in his back yard was among those overloaded with beautiful, soggy white fluff. The weight snapped the tree in two and the upper section crashed down into the glass doors leading from their patio to the kitchen. The falling tree shattered the glass with a hideous smashing sound, followed by the tinkle of a million glass pieces falling on the ceramic floor. The leafless, skeleton-like upper trident of the tree finally came to rest quietly on their kitchen table. On its way to earth, the heavy trunk of the birch missile slowed momentarily to destroy the outdoor furniture and barbecue in its path.

At five-thirty, awakened by the noise, Jack went downstairs to investigate the cause of the disturbance and found the wind howling through the opening. The whole kitchen was a mess of birch twigs, bark scraps, the tree trunk, dirty melting snow, and shards of broken glass. Wet snow blew through the opening onto the floor. Jack was furious.

"Son of a bitch. This damned storm had to come up now, of all times. I've got all these things to do today. Now I have to get a crew over and get them started on a cleanup. I've got to call the insurance people and get an adjuster over here right away. Damned birch trees. Damn. Damn."

Helen was not far behind him in his trip to investigate. "I'll get a couple of sheets to hang over the door," she said, "and I'll clean up the broken glass."

The two children were right behind her. "Don't cut your feet," Helen said. "Better if you go back to bed and let Dad and me clean this up."

Jack got his bow saw, cut the tree into a few manageable pieces and stacked them in the yard, while Helen cleaned the floor. The couple sealed off the opening as best they could. By the time they had finished, it was almost eight-thirty, so Jack sat down to phone the insurance adjuster. He was about to pick up the phone when it rang. "Morning, Mr. Duffy. This is Detective Wilson. How are you this morning?"

"About as bad as I can be. I've got an emergency here. Can I call you back?"

"We were expecting you at eight. Did something happen? I have a couple of questions about your break-in – won't take long," said Wilson.

"Look, my house is leaking snow right now. I have to call the insurance adjuster and then get some contractors in. I don't have time for anything else right now. I'll call you back." Jack slammed the receiver onto its hook.

Helen was still cleaning up the debris that had come along with the birch tree. "Who was that?" she asked.

"That so and so detective — Wilson. Has to call me when I'm in the middle of the worst disaster we've had since we've been in this place."

"He doesn't know that. He's just doing his job."

"I told the bastard I'd call him back. 'This won't take long,' he says. Damned right it won't take long. It won't take any time at all. Not now, it won't. I've got to get the repairs organized. He phones me on the worst day of my life."

Helen began to laugh.

"What's that all about?"

"The worst day of your life, my friend, will be the day they officially press charges against you for the murder of one Robert Smithers. Not the day a tree came in the window. Remember, the police are our friends."

Jack's voice softened. "Oh, go get dressed and leave me be. I need to concentrate on my phone calls."

"Here we are, a damned tree on our kitchen table, middle of winter and snow dripping all over our kitchen. Don't you think this is just a little ridiculous?"

Jack was still angry, but he saw that Helen was right. As usual. He picked up the telephone and dialed the insurance adjuster.

Later, Jack phoned his assistant, Nina, to tell her he was canceling the hunting trip he had planned for the following week and that he would be in the office all of the next week. He also told her he would not be in until the afternoon because of a crisis at home. He did not mention that he was also going to the police station to have his fingerprints recorded.

CHAPTER 14

RUSS WILSON BANGED AROUND HEADQUARTERS, disturbing even the usually calm Kathy. "What's eating you?" she asked.

Wilson, in his quest for opportunities to move his relationship with Kathy to a higher, more intimate plane, sensed that his current behavior was not helping. "Sorry," he said. "Somebody just hung up on me and I'm overreacting. People are going to do that every now and then."

"Oh, Russ," said Kathy, "don't let it bother you. People can be so rude at times. Is there anything I can do to help?"

This is not a total loss, thought Russ. "I'll give it some thought," he said out loud, grinning at Kathy.

☠ ♥ ☠

Jack finally arrived at police headquarters three hours later than promised. Wilson was the only person to greet him. Evidently, he did not warrant the attention of Lieutenant Nelson on this occasion. "Is this eight o'clock, accountant's time?" asked Wilson.

Jack went through the indignity of dipping his fingers in ink and recording his fingerprints on the police file. Wilson took photographs and then curtly said he could go. But now he was actually here, Jack had a few points he wanted to be sure were made.

"There are some things you should know about Bob Smithers, detective. Were you aware that he was in the rug business?" asked Jack.

Wilson nodded, looking bored.

"He was a tough customer. A lot of people didn't like him.

Anybody who was late paying him had to watch out. He forced some people into bankruptcy."

Wilson was hardly paying attention. Jack's temper rose again at the thought that the detective was ignoring his statement. He had taken notes of every word during their interview at his home.

"Aren't you interested in more information?" asked Jack.

"We have a file on Smithers," responded the detective. "We know all about his business. More hearsay won't help us solve the case. We've got everything we need from you. You can go now if you want."

"You're mad because I hung up on you?" asked Jack. "Look, I'm really sorry. I apologize for that. I had a crisis at home. The storm did a couple of thousand dollars damage to my house. The place is a mess. I had to call my insurance company, and then I had to get repairs organized right away. What did you call for this morning?"

Wilson looked a little friendlier after this explanation. "I was looking for some information on the break-in to your house. I'd like to check the date, to make sure we have that correct, and run over the details."

"I'd be glad to do that."

The pair went over the file that Wilson produced and confirmed the information that Wilson needed. "The main thing here is the car," said Wilson. "We need to get going on some kind of search for this car. If we can find the owner somehow, we got a big jump on the case. I wonder how sure that witness is about the make and model?"

"Absolutely certain," said Jack. "Harry, the guy that made the statement, he works for General Motors. He sees these cars every day. He was absolutely sure of the model and year. Not the color, though. He could tell it was a dark color, and it looked black. But at that time of night, who could say for sure?"

"Okay," said Wilson. "That's what we'll have to go with."

When Jack left, Wilson was alone with Kathy once again, and found himself very aware of the perfume she was wearing. He found his mind finally relaxing after the unpleasantness of the morning. She was right, he thought, it wasn't that big a deal. I'll get over it. He said to Kathy, "We need a list of owners for Chevrolet Cavaliers. We're looking for all the Cavaliers in New York State, for the 2001 model year only. If you can get us the list, we'll go over it and try to match one up with someone connected to the case."

"How do I do that?" she asked.

"Start with the information desk in Albany. Someone there can direct you to the automobile section. They have records of all the cars licensed in New York state. You'll have to dig a bit."

He missed Kathy's quizzical look at his description of the assignment and went back to his own office.

CHAPTER 15

NINA MCDERMID WAS HARD AT WORK, AS USUAL, when Jack finally arrived at his office. She and Jack had first met as fellow employees in a small regional office of a multinational accountancy firm. They had worked well together on several projects. When Jack bought out the branch from the big firm, he offered Nina tenure for as long as she wanted her job. She was tall and muscular, and her perfect complexion and dedication to physical fitness made her a very appealing woman in spite of less than beautiful features. Although they often found themselves working late together, and the opportunity for a romantic liaison had occurred frequently, they had maintained a close, but platonic, relationship. Nina developed into more than an energetic assistant. She acted as office manager, itinerary planner, and enthusiastic doer of a thousand and one odd jobs. She had tried and failed the professional accounting exams three times, but her years of experience had enabled her to pick up many of the important practical virtues necessary for success in their business, and she was one hundred percent focussed on her job.

"Is anything urgent happening right now?" he asked, squeezing her shoulder as he went by.

"Get your hand off my shoulder," she smiled.

"Sorry. That's as far as I go during working hours."

"Doc Bullow called. He wants the usual," Nina said.

Clients continually pressured Jack and his staff to find them more tax deductions, legal or not. He had carefully trained his people to be prudent about these issues and refer questionable cases to him.

"And you gave him the usual answer?" laughed Jack.

"He wants to see you."

"More likely he wants to see you," said Jack. "But if he needs to talk to me, I'll be glad to. What is it this time?"

"He runs this hobby farm. He thinks all the expenses should be deductible."

"If he had any hope of making money, I could agree. But he's doing it for fun and he knows it. He'll have the I.R.S. on his back if he starts claiming farm expenses against his professional income. When is he coming in?"

"Any time now. I gave him the first appointment this afternoon. Evidently his son is out of work and is going to move in and run the farm. He thinks that takes matters out of the category of hobby."

"Maybe. Well, we'll see what he's got."

Nina was one of nine employees, all of whom got along well together and admired Jack. When Jack had bought out the large accounting firm eight years earlier, the staff had all elected to stay with him even though the national firm had offered them jobs. The income from his practice, serving local professionals, small businesses and institutions, was adequate to pay his bills, cover future college expenses for their children, and to finance his and Helen's competitive bridge habit. He charged less than the large firms, and found he always had more business available than he and his staff could handle. It was tempting to add more staff and take on more customers, but Jack preferred to keep the business small.

Nina showed Elmer Bullow and his son into the conference room and took orders for coffee. The accounting question was routine, as Jack had expected, and they dealt with it quickly. Jack outlined clear-cut steps for dealing with the issue, and Elmer nodded while his son took notes. On the way out, Elmer mentioned the death of Smithers. "You knew him, didn't you?" he asked.

"Yes, at the bridge table," Jack replied. "We were never close friends, but I played bridge against him often enough. He was a serious player."

"That was a violent way for the man to go. He was a contributor to our hospital in a big way. We are going to miss him. Not that he left a lot of friends behind, even at the hospital; he couldn't help wanting to tell us how to run the place. He figured if he gave all this money he should have something to say about the way we do things. He put a lot of people off."

"I guess he was hard-nosed in a lot of ways. I know he forced some business associates into bankruptcy. Slow payers didn't have a chance."

"I'm not surprised. But he helped our cause over the years. We need more people like that. And he left the hospital a good sum in his will."

"Really? It's hard to understand a guy like that. That's good for your hospital, though."

When Bullow and son had left, Jack reflected quietly in his office for a while. He saw clearly now how a good reputation could be taken for granted, as a natural, God-given right, and how easily it could be lost through what seemed to him a series of chance events. He felt tension mounting, tightening his chest and his stomach. He was going to have to talk to his people about the murder, before they heard from someone else that he was being questioned – or read about it in the newspaper. They needed to be able to deal with any clients who called with concerns, if nothing else. The way to start would be to level with Nina and Mike. He could gauge their reaction and go on from there. Jack was not sure how they would take the news, but he hoped they would cooperate and help to clear his name. They could certainly help if he explained matters properly.

Finally, he got up and called Mike and Nina into his office and shut the door. Mike Secord, a little older than Jack, was a capable accountant who liked the suburban life of Cheektavia.

Nina said, "Looks like some sculptor hacked a furrow in your brow."

Jack looked from one to the other. "I've got a problem and I don't know what to do about it. What I know for sure is that I need help. From you guys."

"Tell us," said Mike. "That's what we're here for."

"There's been a stabbing, a murder. Guy by the name of Smithers. He was a bridge player. I knew him fairly well, as well as anyone knows anyone in the world of bridge. Helen and I saw him all the time at club games and tournaments. I never got along too well with him. He always liked Helen. Of course, he was a womanizer and went after anyone in a skirt. I honestly don't know how far I should go in talking about this whole affair. My problem is that I'm being questioned in connection with the murder."

"Nothing bad about that," said Nina. "I'm sure you'll help the police as much as you can."

"I wish it were that easy," said Jack. "But it goes deeper. I'm involved circumstantially. I had an argument with the guy the day he was murdered. Stupid, but just one of those bridge things; nothing serious really, but it looks bad. Then, Sunday, the night he was murdered, I left the tournament about eight-thirty or so and came down to the office to clean up a few items. There were no witnesses, nobody saw me, so I have no alibi for the critical time. We have no cleaning or security staff on the weekends. I didn't even stop on the way to pick up a coffee. The worst part of the whole affair is the murder weapon."

Mike and Nina looked puzzled at this remark.

"He was stabbed, wasn't he? Some kind of knife, I guess," said Mike.

"You're right about some kind of knife," said Jack. "It was *my* knife. My bloody hunting knife. Can you imagine?"

The room went silent for a few moments.

"You're kidding!" blurted Nina.

"I wish I were," Jack responded. "It'll kill me if you spread this around. The police were over last night and let me know about the knife. I think it must have been taken a few weeks ago when we had a break-in, but I'm not sure the cops are convinced yet. Lieutenant Nelson, the S.O.B. in charge of the case, he hinted they may even charge me if any more evidence points my way. I had my fingerprints taken this morning. I'll bet they're all over the knife."

"That's awful," said Nina. "Somebody out there has a serious grudge. Oh God. I don't like this at all."

"You and me both," echoed Jack.

Mike whistled softly at the end of Jack's explanation. "I don't like it. News like this won't be good for the firm. But they've got no case against you. None at all. Don't worry about that for a second. It's all circumstantial."

"I'm going to have to spend a lot of time over the next week answering questions and doing whatever I can to clear my name. I want the damned police deflected from me entirely and pointed in the direction of the right suspect. I can tell you, I'm worried," continued Jack. "The idea of bad publicity over this just kills me. You're right, the business doesn't need this. We'll be lucky if the news doesn't turn away some of our clients."

"I agree," said Mike. "I still think you've no cause for real worry. They don't go round pinning crap on innocent men. Your reputation round town is too good. But I take your point about publicity. It'll set tongues going. And take time to erase after."

"That's what I don't want," said Jack.

Nina was thinking hard. "You know Sunday night? The night of the murder? You said you came to the office after the game?" she asked.

"Right," answered Jack.

"Did you turn on your computer? Do any work with it at all? Send any emails?"

"I might have. Why?"

"That might give you an alibi. A lot of things done on a computer, especially emails, but even letters and spreadsheets are saved with a date and a time on them. That's done automatically."

"That's an interesting thought. No, I didn't send emails though. I tried but our server was down that night. I'll look through my other files and see if there's anything there."

"I can do that for you," offered Nina. "I can just do a search for the date and time. That's a snap."

"I don't know if that would serve as evidence, but it might." remarked Mike.

"It's absolutely worth a try," said Jack.

"It'd be best to do it as soon as possible. That might be all it takes to get the police off your back," said Mike.

"Our next problem is the staff. Obviously, I haven't told anyone in the firm except you two. Not yet. I'm shocked, embarrassed, all mixed up over this. I'm not exactly sure what to do."

"If you want people on your side, you're going to have to take them into your confidence," said Mike. "You'd do best to let the others know right away. You don't want them to hear second-hand. Much better for them to hear the news from you. They'll believe what you say to them. They'll all be supportive if they know the facts."

"How can we be sure of that? The more people that know, the sooner it gets around town."

"True. But that's one thing you can count on — it'll get out anyway. This is a small burg. News travels."

"Okay. I hear you. I'll tell everybody."

Nina added, "I'm glad you're going to tell them. You might even do that today. I don't know how gossip spreads so fast, but it does. Policemen's wives, crime reporters. News always gets around quicker than you'd ever think."

Later in the afternoon, Jack called a staff meeting. He included Nina and Mike in the meeting, although they knew the whole story. He related the circumstances of the murder and his own personal connections with the deceased and the crime. He gave details of his interviews with the police.

"I can tell you I'm damned upset over the way the investigation is headed. I have no choice but to dig into the whole affair myself and try and find something that will help get the police on the right track. I won't be able to do my regular job while this is going on. You folks are going to have to pick up the slack for me."

Nina said, "Don't worry. You were planning to go on a hunting trip next week. You've canceled that. Just take the time off anyway."

Mike addressed the group briefly to mention how important it was to communicate carefully with customers about the issue. He said, "We've all got to be completely open about the whole thing. Don't hedge one bit. We all know about the murder. Now we know the truth about any rumors of Jack's involvement. We know he had nothing to do with it. Our best approach here, and this is just common sense, is for us to answer all questions. Don't bring the subject up, but answer questions openly." There was general assent that everyone was willing to help.

Jack felt better after hearing Mike support him. He spent the rest of the afternoon trying to catch up on some files that had gone lagging. He reviewed his correspondence, which Nina had left neatly organized on his desk. The tasks went quickly without any interruptions, and he was able to scan and organize most of the items he had to deal with for the week. He knew that he was leaving a huge burden on the rest of the staff by only giving instructions about what was to be done. He believed they would learn a lot by actually doing the work. They might not like doing it but they'd learn. Collections were the most pressing item. The little firm had to have cash to survive. New customers and money owed were fine, thank you, but money collected was the real thing. None of his staff liked to call a customer to collect money; Jack had always done that. He had developed a knack of talking politely, joking with people, and finally getting around to putting the bite on them, asking for a specific amount on a specific date. He was good at it, and now he had to turn over the task temporarily to Nina and Michael. He left cryptic little notes with each collection notice.

"The Doc always has the money somewhere."

"Remind him that we are not a bank."

"Laugh when he threatens to take his business elsewhere. Tell him we know all his secrets."

CHAPTER 16

JACK RETURNED HOME LATER THAN USUAL ON Wednesday evening. Rick and Sandra had eaten at the usual time of six and were busy with their homework. "No martinis tonight?" he asked.

"Help yourself," came the cool reply. Jack absent-mindedly felt that something was changing in their life. The couple sat and talked about the murder and about how to proceed in gathering evidence to support his defense.

"Remember the tournament the night of the murder?" he asked. "Bob Smithers' team won after a committee overturned the director's ruling. Remember the team that lost? Who were they? I think Henry and Tom were playing on it."

"Yes, Tom was playing with his girlfriend."

"So Lew Orono must have been Henry's partner."

"Lew Orono. What a pet. That scar on his face makes him look like a pirate. All he needs is a cutlass and an eyepatch. He's not anybody's favorite bridge player."

"There aren't many who like him a whole lot. He could be the killer. Sure as hell Henry and Tom had nothing to do with it. And Tom's girl wouldn't kill a spider if it threatened to bite her."

"Oh. Do you think Tom and Henry are suspects?"

"No, no. Of course not. I'm trying to think of ways to deflect the police away from me. I had nothing to do with this blasted murder. But here are the police, wasting their time, wasting everyone's time in fact, by investigating me. They've got to look at other people. Lew Orono may have had something to do with it."

"That's obvious. Don't you think they're looking into his activities?"

Jack said, "I know it's obvious. So why do they keep bugging me?"

"They have to cover all the angles. You're an angle, in case you didn't know."

Jack said, "At least the people in the office are being supportive. Nina and Mike were absolutely great. The bad news is that there is not much they can do."

"Can we possibly get something to show that you were at the office right after the game on Sunday? That would clear everything up. No pretty girls doing caretaker or cleaning work on a weekend?" asked Helen.

"Nobody is scheduled for Sunday. And I didn't even stop anywhere on the way over. I just went to the office and cleaned up a few small, urgent things. There is a ray of hope, thanks to an idea Nina had. She's going to look through my computer files and see if dates and times are recorded. You know, every time you save a file, the software automatically records the date and time of the save. If she can find some kind of record, that might get the police out of my hair."

"Someone should bug the people down at the police station about the break-in. That must have been how the killer got your knife. They haven't gotten anywhere with that case. Maybe I should drop over and try to get some action on it."

"Not likely, since we didn't report anything stolen. They wouldn't treat it as a priority unless there was a serious crime."

"But now we know your hunting knife was stolen. The murder weapon. That makes it a priority to us, I'd say."

Jack said, "I know they're looking for the car, Wilson said so this morning, but how many black Cavaliers are there in the area? Must be hundreds if not thousands. What I don't understand is why anyone would choose to take that one item and nothing else. I didn't even know it was missing until we found out it was the murder weapon."

"We didn't even look for it."

"Yeah — you know it was sheer chance my knife was in the den at all. It was only there because I had all my hunting gear laid out ready for the trip with Aaron. It's really diabolical — steal my knife and then use it to frame me. Who would do that? Lots of people we know had it in for Bob, but I can't think of anyone with a big grudge against me. I wish we could give the police some leads. They've got to move off the idea that I'm a hot suspect because my knife was used and I didn't like the guy."

"Umm. We keep wondering why anyone broke in. If we're right that the murderer is a bridge player, someone who knows both you and Bob, then here's a crazy idea that occurred to me today," said Helen. Jack looked at her. Helen continued, "When the break-in happened, that was the day before the worldwide pairs contest. We were storing the bridge hands in the den. Remember, the sealed hand records for the game I run at the golf club?"

"Sure I remember. But they weren't in the den; UPS delivered the carton of hand records and booklets to the office and I stored them there overnight in the office safe. I never even brought them home. So what?"

"Oh, that's right. You kept them at your office. What I was wondering," continued Helen, "was whether someone could have thought that maybe they were in our house. Maybe somebody thought they were going to be here overnight. Some people would do anything to win one of these worldwide events. Lots of people would like to look at the hands before game time. They might try to copy them, or memorize them if they had the mind for it."

"Okay, but I put the box in the safe. I took it out myself. When I gave you the carton, it was still sealed. Nobody looked into the box I gave you. That's bullshit."

"Whatever excrement you like best. What I am trying to say is, there has to be a reason for the break-in. It doesn't seem reasonable that someone would do it to steal a hunting knife that they had no reason even to know would be there. It was worth quite a bit to you, but it's not the kind of thing people break in to steal. It may have been just accidental that someone picked it up while he was after something else. When I shouted and turned on all the lights, he took off like a jet. He didn't find what he wanted in the house. He didn't have time."

"Okay, I see where you're going. Plenty of people knew that you were having a game. They could figure that you had to have the hand analysis booklets. And the person who broke in thought, for whatever reason, that we had them at home and maybe locked them in the den overnight. That could be."

"Keep going."

"So let's say our caller drives by, makes sure that the place is deserted, and breaks in. He picks up my knife for some reason. He gets disturbed in the middle of whatever he's doing, and takes off with the knife."

"That's what I'm thinking," Helen replied. "It's possible. He broke into our house because he wanted something. Maybe he didn't know exactly where to look, and when he saw the hunting knife, he picked it up. He had to leave in a hurry, and taking the knife may not have been planned at all."

"Yeah. I guess so. If he wanted a weapon, he could have taken my shotgun and some shells. There was plenty of gear there, and it was all out in the open. And the only marks showing a forced entry were splinters around the washroom window. The frame is made out of cedar — pretty soft stuff. It would be easy to chisel an opening or just force it. Then he panicked and took off when you started to holler."

"It's hard to imagine anyone out there stealing a knife with the idea of trying to lay the blame on you for a horrible murder. They would have to be really sick."

Jack said, "The whole thing is depressing."

"What has happened, deliberately or accidentally, is that the murderer has created a smokescreen. He has turned the police investigation away from himself, at least for a while. And sometimes a trail goes cold, after a couple of weeks or so."

"Inspector Helen Duffy speaking," laughed Jack.

"Laugh all you want, mister. I've read that somewhere; most cases get solved in the first few days, or they never get solved at all."

"There were plenty of people who disliked Bob Smithers," said Jack, "but I can't imagine anyone hating him enough to want to kill him. I should have a talk with Charles. He might have some ideas about who could have been nursing that kind of hatred for Bob."

"Lots of people hated Bob more than you did."

Jack reddened. "I didn't hate him," he blustered. "Bob was a jerk, that's all. We just had different ideas on what's right."

Helen just rolled her eyes. "What kind of work did Bob do?" she wondered.

"He was a rug dealer. He sold rugs from Asia and the Middle East."

"The kind you wear on your head or put on the floor?"

"They start at about fifty pounds. I suppose a person with a strong neck could wear one."

"There are a few bridge players who might qualify."

"In any case, he came to me professionally a few years ago, but I didn't like his creative approach to accounting. I decided to drop him as a client."

"Probably a good thing, the way you two got along. Your hunting trip is all messed up, too."

"It'll be next year before I can get out."

"I'll miss plucking and cleaning all those wild Canada goose carcasses. Oh well. I know how much you and Aaron love your outings in the rough," she replied, smiling at her own last remark. Jack and Aaron went to a very upscale hunting camp, with guides, dogs, open bar and sumptuous meals provided as part of a package. Aaron was Jack's biggest customer, and Jack provided this treat each year as a perk.

"I just got my hunting stuff out of storage and had it all packed. Damn."

"At least you'll be able to move around your den after you put it away again."

CHAPTER 17

ON THURSDAY MORNING, CHARLES WAS SURprised to get an early morning call from Jack before he headed off to work. Jack asked if they could meet for lunch and Charles agreed readily. Just before noon, he jumped into his red Hyundai Sonata and drove the nine miles to the coffee shop where he had agreed to meet Jack. Traffic was heavy and it took him over half an hour to get there from his office. I'll have to be a little careful, he thought. I'm sure Jack doesn't suspect anything, and it'll just be business as usual, but I can't have any slip-ups.

Jack was waiting. "Hi, Charles."

"Greetings," said Charles, thinking that Jack looked grim and cool.

"We can get a sandwich here. Their selection is limited, but everything's fresh." said Jack. "My treat."

Charles began to realize that Jack did not suspect him at all. "Never too proud." They ordered sandwiches, tea for Jack and black coffee for Charles. Jack couldn't wait to begin talking about his problem related to the murder.

"You know the Bob Smithers murder? Here's the damnedest coincidence. What do you think was the murder weapon? It was my bloody hunting knife. A present from Helen, for God's sake. It was stolen when our house was broken into few weeks ago."

Why is he talking to me, Charles wondered. Charles felt sure the blood was leaving his face as Jack talked, and he wondered if Jack would notice.

"The cops are asking me for an alibi for the time of the murder. Of all the damned things. They connect the knife with the fact that Bob and I had a public argument. You know that incident we had at the tournament when you and I were playing against him? The man practically accused us of cheating after your so-called hesitation. This whole thing burns my ass something fierce. I want to try to turn up some information that'll get the cops off my back, but I don't know where to start. It's terrible. If I can't stop them laying charges somehow, it'll have an impact on my family and my business. You know, it's scary when you get involved in something like this. I've had a high opinion of our legal system all my life, always thought it was foolproof. So much for boyhood idealism."

Jack didn't notice that Charles sat tight-lipped through this monologue. Charles, in fact, was paying attention with only one quarter of his mind. He wondered if he could get Jack away from the subject of the murder. Maybe they could talk about some bidding nuances he wanted to introduce into their partnership.

"That's really bad luck, Jack," he commented.

"It's more than bad luck," said Jack. "It's a career-threatening situation now. At least until I get them off my back. I can't focus on a damned thing. Not my business, my family. Not even a game of bridge."

"That does sound serious," echoed Charles. "Not even bridge."

"I'm dead serious," said Jack. "I wish the cops would do their job properly. Until they do, I'm hung up. I feel I want to do as much as possible to clear my name, but I don't know where to start."

"How can I help?" asked Charles.

"I wanted to run over just who might have had it in for Bob. Who might have had a reason to kill him? Any ideas? And this connection with my hunting knife. My knife! How the hell could that possibly happen?"

"Bob had a lot of enemies at the bridge table," responded Charles. "The list is pretty long. Not just you and me. You could run through all the good players at the tournament and I'll bet ninety percent of them have had a run-in with Smithers. I'm not just talking ancient history, either — even during the last six months it would be a long list. You know he won the Swiss teams that day in committee? Lew Orono was mad as hell at him. I bet Lew's teammates were, too. We know who they were. And even the director, for that matter. How would you like having someone question your rulings all the time?"

"Okay. Those are all people who have a grudge against Smithers. But is any of that enough to want to kill him?"

"I know what you mean. But it doesn't stop there. Think of all the players at Appleton's club. You have the same thing. Most of them are happy that they won't see Bob Smithers around anymore. He made more enemies in a week than most of us make in a lifetime."

"He was the least popular guy in the crowd," agreed Jack. "From that point of view, it could have been any one of a dozen bridge players. But someone obviously has gone off his rocker here. The police will eventually narrow it down, I suppose. I'd just like to get them off my back, right now."

They finished their lunch and walked out to the parking lot together. Jack noticed Charles's bright new car. "How d'you like the Hyundai?" he called.

"Great car," answered Charles. "Great price, too. They've come a long way in the last couple of years." He drove off with a mild feeling of satisfaction over the way he had handled the conversation. He'd been right all along; there was no reason at all to worry.

CHAPTER 18

THE POLICE OFFICERS GOT TOGETHER AGAIN briefly to review the case. The first question Fraser asked was, "Did you have any luck on Orono?"

"I got a lot on him," Wilson boasted. "I can picture him doing the job. He's a big, strong guy and as ugly as everybody says. I'd guess he's capable of handling someone like Smithers very easily. There are some questionable incidents in his background. I found an incident in the police file that ties him to Smithers a few years ago. A squad car was called to Smithers' office on a possible assault alert, although nothing came of it. Smithers and Orono were having an argument when the officers got there. The patrol guys might have prevented an actual assault by being prompt.

"I had a good talk with Orono. His alibi the night of the murder seems to hold water, but I need to do some more checking. He says he went right home after the game. He works at a motel and the owner lets him live in a room there. I still have to talk to the clerk he says saw him about an hour after the Sunday game wrapped up. If it checks out, it doesn't leave much time for him to murder anybody. The interesting thing he told me was that he feels Smithers ruined his life. He owed Smithers money, and Smithers foreclosed on a motel that Orono owned. Ever since then the guy has had to work for someone else instead of running his own business. He's still pretty bitter about it all."

"You'll stay with it until you track down the alibi?" asked Fraser.

"You bet," answered Wilson.

"Okay," said Fraser. "Let's leave him for a while. Now this guy Rich. Do you have anything more you can tell me about him? Your report suggests he's into some borderline deals. Can we get a better understanding of his business?"

"You're asking me?" wondered Wilson. "You're the genius in this area. I got a few things here. It's not hard to get the basics on Rich.

He's a well-known guy around town. I got a blurb on his company, and our agency pulled out some financial stuff. It seemed almost too easy."

"He probably lets out exactly as much information as he wants, and deflects questions on all the rest," said Nelson.

"Sure," said Wilson. "The guy is no dummy. He's built up a good-sized business over the years. Right now, he must be worth over ten million. And his record shows no criminal charges, let alone convictions. Nothing I can find anyway. So he's stayed on the right side of the law."

"You checked his record?" asked Nelson.

Wilson's smile brightened. "You bet."

Nelson said, "Some of these guys, like Rich, are smart as hell. They have good lawyers, and they know how to keep their records clean. Still, if we have nothing on him, that's as far as it goes. He must have plenty of influence around town. He didn't pile up all that dough over many years by making enemies among the politicians. We run the risk that Rich may send up some flak if we're not careful."

"Is this Lieutenant Nelson advising caution? I'm not used to this," smiled Fraser.

"All I mean is, we have so little to go on, let's not upset this guy. Not yet, anyway. We'll nail him if we get a case on him."

"Remember the information I got from our credit agency about Smithers?" Fraser asked. "He had all that cash just sitting in an account. It looked like Smithers didn't like a shipment and refused to pay. It's possible that he and Rich had something in the works. Your friend says they did business together. You'd better visit Mr. Albert Rich and see if there was a deal that went sour."

Nelson added, "And we've got to find out Rich's whereabouts on the day of the murder. Even if he's not involved directly we ought to pin down his activities."

Nelson and Wilson left headquarters to head towards Rich's business address. In the car again, Nelson asked, "So we focus on Rich for the moment. How you think we ought to approach the guy, Russ?"

Wilson relished the idea of consultation on such an important matter, and responded, "When I talked to him to set up the appointment, he seemed okay. There was no problem talking to him. The only thing is, he's smooth. You never know what's underneath.

Maybe we just ask a few easy questions first off and get on his good side. We might get more out of him if he's our friend. We don't need him mad at us first thing. What we really want is information."

"Yes. Our friend." The pair drove silently for a few more minutes and arrived at the building where Albert Rich had his offices. "This sure is nothing to look at," said Nelson.

"You'd never know anyone here had money. The place could stand a going-over with a fire hose."

"And a coat of paint. I guess some people just don't have to show off how much they're worth."

They walked around a pile of fermenting garbage bags and entered the building. The inside was a pleasant surprise, with polished granite floors and clean, well-maintained furnishings. The officers took a lumbering elevator up to the second story where the name ALBERT RICH, FINE IMPORTS loudly proclaimed the location of the business they were looking for. "He ought to import a fine motor for that elevator," suggested Wilson as they walked down the hallway.

Rich kept them waiting only a few minutes. He had three people at work besides himself, in a set of spare, open-area workspaces, which passed as offices. Everyone was actively engaged, either on the phone or staring into a computer screen. Rich came over, tie loose, sleeves rolled to his elbows, and greeted them in the brisk, genial voice of a businessman who avoids making enemies but has few real friends. "What can I do to help? You fellows are out of your territory."

"Thanks for seeing us," said Nelson. "Can we talk privately?"

Rich's fixed, meaningless smile beamed at them. "We can talk right here at my desk. Don't worry about these folks. They've been with me for years. Every one. We trust each other." He winked at Nelson, as his smile widened. "They're so busy they won't pay any attention to what we're talking about. I keep everyone here totally occupied, myself included. We go hard all day. If I take an hour out of my day, I get a backlog. Have a chair." He motioned the plainclothesmen to a pair of wooden captain's chairs beside his desk. The chairs could have come from a used furniture sale at police headquarters. "But before we go anywhere with this, you've got to tell me what it's all about. If you're recording our talk, I need a lawyer. If I find I need a lawyer, we won't be here long. Shoot," said Rich.

"Okay on that. No tape. But Wilson here has to keep notes," began Nelson. Rich paused momentarily and then shrugged assent. "We're looking into the murder of Robert Smithers. I believe you knew him. He was killed last Sunday."

Rich nodded again. "I knew Bob well. I'll be going to his funeral."

"You're in the rug business, Mr. Rich?"

"Imports. Rugs are the biggest part. But we bring in related products. Tapestries. Woven textiles. Fine art from the same countries that we buy rugs from. Afghanistan, China, Turkey. Some of the items are treasures."

"Your office hides the treasures pretty good," remarked Nelson.

Rich's eyes narrowed. "I'm not a man who needs to impress anyone. The people here are the most knowledgeable and dedicated that you could find in their field. I pay them well. They're not here for show. Now, what exactly can I do for you?"

He's all business, thought Nelson. "Smithers was in the rug business as well?"

"We've done business for years."

"I hear he was a hard man to deal with. He was the kind of guy who made enemies pretty easily."

"A hard man? You bet he was. So am I, I hope. You don't survive in this business by bowing down to every person you deal with. If he didn't like a deal, he'd put the boots to it in short order. There was no fooling around with Bob. We definitely had our problems from time to time, but we could always talk things out."

"Put the boots to it? That's pretty tough talk."

"That's a figure of speech. What I mean is, he would have certain expectations about a deal and if he saw they were not being met, the deal was off, right then. That's the way he operated. That's the way I do business, too. We understood each other."

"Tell me about the recent deal that got canceled at the last minute."

Rich raised his eyebrows. "You know about that? We worked on that deal for several months and then Bob canceled the whole thing ten days ago. He wanted a bunch of high-class Afghan rugs for a housing development in Florida. Some ridiculous place called Himalayan Meadows. Can you believe that? Anyway, I came across a deal on a lot of rugs, used rugs, from Afghanistan. They are real treasures, and when I say treasures, I mean it. These items are pure gold. I got them and arranged to pass them on to Bob as part of our deal. His end of it was about three-quarters of a million."

"Used rugs? You tried to get away with that?" asked Nelson.

"Now look, lieutenant. Let's be careful here. The general public, and I include you in that group, knows nothing about the rug business. These old rugs come from castles in Afghanistan, and other countries as well, like Turkey and China. Some of them were made a couple of hundred years ago, and they're so well-made they'll never wear out. They'll last literally hundreds of years. They are treasures in the pure sense of the word. The dyes are wonderful. Very fast. You seldom get a chance at them. That's what I came across, and I wanted to use them for Bob's Florida project."

"Okay. And what happened?"

"When Bob realized the rugs were not new, he told the guy running the development down there – fella named Duster. This guy hit the roof, and Bob canceled the whole deal with me on the spot. Said he couldn't expect his customer to accept second-hand goods when they were promised new material."

"Then what?"

"I told him these Florida so and so's were getting a real bargain. They'll never see rugs like those again. All they know is nylon, polyester, and olefin. They never heard of wool and silk, or knots per inch. I talked to Bob and explained my thinking on the whole deal, and in the end, he agreed with me. But he couldn't get the client to agree, so I went to Sarasota to talk to Duster personally. That was the day of poor Bob's murder. I got nowhere talking to the man. And I realized that I had no comeback to his objection. So, the Himalayan Meadows people are ignorant; there's no law against that. They don't have to accept the arrangement if they don't like my goods."

"And you take a big loss on the deal. That must hurt. And Smithers was responsible."

"Look, in the first place, Bob only did what I might have done myself. And in the second place, I'll say it again, lieutenant: you don't know the business. What big loss? Sure, I brought these goods in as part of a deal which fell through. But I won't lose money on them. I can sell these rugs through my regular outlets. My people out there will have them all moved in a couple of months, and at better prices than Smithers was paying. Sure, my inventories tie up money for a while. But lose money? No, sir."

Wilson wrote steadily during the whole interchange. Nelson was nonplussed by the open, rapid-fire delivery that Rich displayed. He had come to the meeting expecting to have to pry, threaten, use court orders to extract information. Yet here was Rich, telling him almost everything Nelson wanted to know about his association with Smithers. He seemed to be hiding nothing.

"Now, lieutenant, if you have no more questions, I'd better get back to work. If you think of anything else, I'd be glad to help."

"Can you give us the name and address of your Sarasota customer? You said his name was Duster, I believe."

"Charley Duster," said Rich. He searched for a file, scribbled the name and address on a pad and handed it to Nelson.

"One last question," said Nelson. "Do you play bridge?"

Rich threw back his head and laughed. "No, not me. I tried it a couple of times when I was at college. A huge time waster, if you ask me. Oh, it's a great game. It's just that you have to spend so much time at it to be any good. I know Bob was a nut. He talked about it sometimes. But I never had any interest."

The two detectives thanked Rich and wandered back to their car. "At least we confirmed our suspicions about a deal between him and Smithers that got cancelled," said Nelson.

"We were right on there. Rich is either very honest or very smooth," said Wilson.

"Smooth for sure. Time will tell about his honesty. But he doesn't seem to hold anything back. He comes across like a trained seal. He puts all that information in your lap before you even think up the questions. I have to say I was a little worried when we went in. I didn't know how I was going to start the questioning."

"Yeah. He seemed to know what he was going to tell us. It was almost as though he practiced before he talked to us."

"He may be smart enough for that, too."

"After we came away from talking to Alexander, I started to feel like Rich was guilty before we met him," said Wilson.

"He's not off the hook yet, as far as I can see. We have to track down this Florida alibi and confirm it."

"For sure. But who says Rich did the murder himself? A guy with all that dough could have hired someone."

"That makes more sense. He could easily have connections with the kind of people, killers, that are available for hire. And then again, following up on him may get us nowhere."

"At least, we can confirm where he was on the day of the murder. Rich has to be a pretty good actor if he killed Smithers. He didn't show any sign of nervousness, of trying to hide anything," said Nelson.

"We need to work on who Rich might have hired. If he hired someone to do his dirty work, he's just as guilty as if he used the knife himself. There are two things we got to do. One is to try and trace the guy who used the knife. The other is to check out Rich's story. That's the easy part. You need to get down to Sarasota for a day and do that. You can get a night flight down and come back the next day."

"Florida, eh?" said Wilson.

"Rich and Smithers had a fair-sized deal going on down there. We need to understand it better. According to Rich, it was just a million-dollar deal that went sour. Normal business. But was it? Didn't seem to bother him at all. Was Rich trying to screw Smithers? Maybe Smithers got himself in over his head. He played the tough guy for a long time. It worked for him too. Then he found someone who was just a little bit tougher. Rich is as tough as they come. The whole story could stand checking."

"Yeah. That could be a bit tricky. How do we know that Rich won't set somebody up, a friend down there, say, to tell us what he wants?"

Nelson continued, "We'll have to work around that. We need to organize the information we think we're sure of, write it all down, and then we check it out. You go down there and ask questions. Nobody can lie all the time. I know an officer on the city police down there. His name is Klaus Eckert. He's a great cop. Smart as hell. He owes me a couple."

"That'd help," said Wilson.

"Rich gave us the name of Smithers' customer, the guy who was going to buy the goods. Rich said he met with him on the Sunday of the murder. Klaus could give us some background on the guy. A few facts would help us confirm our whole theory," said Nelson.

"Sarasota. That's a nice place," muttered Wilson.

"Have you been there?"

"Only once. It's great for golf and sunshine," said Wilson.

"You could get on a flight tonight and be back tomorrow night."

Wilson was delighted at the idea of a Sarasota visit. He tried not to show too much enthusiasm. "I don't know if I could get ready that fast," he complained.

"Bullshit," laughed Nelson. "You're dying to go. Kathy can get you a special to St. Petersburg for a hundred dollars return this time of year. You'll have a ball tracking this down. I can handle the call on the Duffys tonight. And I'll let Fraser know what we're doing."

The arrangements were duly made, and when Nelson called on Wilson to drive him to the airport, he was surprised to find Wilson appear wearing sunglasses, with a bright yellow Hawaiian-style shirt showing through his open parka. His frame dwarfed the golf clubs hoisted over his shoulder.

"What in the hell are you thinking of?" laughed Nelson. "You're going for a couple hours, not a month."

"I can get an early morning round in," protested Wilson. "If I tee off at six-thirty, I'll finish by nine o'clock. Eckert won't want to see me before nine anyway."

Nelson shook his head, laughing, and drove his friend to the airport.

"I phoned Klaus. He's a German guy and you'll find he's all business. He wants to meet you in his office tomorrow morning. He'll spend most of the day with you. You be there by nine-thirty, then. Take him out for a good lunch. Go easy on the booze; you're an officer, remember. And don't show up dressed like a damn tourist."

Wilson gave solemn assurance that he would do as asked. Nelson shook his head again as Wilson trudged to the check-in counter.

CHAPTER 19

FRASER LOOKED UP THE NAME OF THE COMPANY where Jim Lemone worked: Rittenhouse Construction. He was sure he knew someone there. Who was it? He finally remembered the name of a girl, Donna Trope, who had been a witness in a major traffic case that he had investigated a few months ago. The case involved a death and several tens of thousands of dollars of property damage. The investigation took several days. Donna had seen the whole accident from start to finish. Fortunately she had escaped injury, although her car was totally destroyed. He and Donna had had a number of long interviews as he gathered evidence. They had got along quite well, but Fraser, as usual, had no interest in a long-term relationship.

She was glad to hear from him and agreed readily to a meeting. "The best time for me is lunch or dinner," she said. "We are busy at work right now and I don't want to take time off."

"How about meeting me for lunch tomorrow at the Fish Market?" Art asked, naming a restaurant right across the street from her office.

"Perfect. Twelve on the button?"

"I'll see you then."

☠ ♥ ☠

On his way from the parking lot into the restaurant, Art had to side-step a truck delivering fresh fish to the back door. The Fish Market was crowded at lunch, as usual. A strong smell of fish and an interior that bordered on dingy didn't stop customers from flooding in to enjoy the brisk, friendly service and excellent food. Donna was waiting in the reception area, and the maitre d' quickly assigned them a table. They both ordered halibut and salad and a glass of wine.

"Only one glass," said Donna. "I don't want to fall asleep on the job."

"Same for me," said Art. "Just a little muscle relaxant."

They chatted until the food came and dug in. "Have you been with Rittenhouse long?" Art asked.

"I've been there eight years. It's a good company. I think I'll stay as long as they want me. The owner is a terrific guy. He treats us all so well."

"He's not a slave driver?"

"We get busy sometimes. He expects us to put in the overtime when that happens. But he always pays us fairly."

"Have you ever run into a guy called Jim Lemone?"

"Oh, yes. Everybody knows Jim. He's a gorilla, but I like him. Why?"

"We're running an investigation now and there might be a connection. I'm trying to get a little background on some of the people close to the incident."

"'Investigation' and 'incident'. You're really blunt, Art."

Fraser laughed. "When it's all over, I'll tell you the whole story. Right now, you don't want to know. We go up so many blind alleys in police work you'd probably find us ridiculous."

"Okay, I hear you. Well, Jim started a couple of years after I joined the company. At first, he did odd jobs, pouring cement, setting up forms, that sort of thing. He always seemed like a smart guy and he always worked hard. There were a lot of things he did that impressed people. He dressed neatly, and he was well-spoken for a manual worker. It wasn't surprising that he caught the eye of Mr. Rittenhouse himself. We needed a scheduler and he was an obvious choice. Jim got to know the workers and how work gets assigned. Mr. Rittenhouse put him in there to learn. And he is so good at it. Our schedules often got screwed up before, but we almost never have a screw-up now. The only time we have a problem now is when the client changes something at the last minute."

"That's an accomplishment."

"Jim's only difficulty is his temper. He was pretty humble when he first started in scheduling. Now, people think he walks on water and he knows it. He doesn't put up with little annoyances the way he used to, and if you cross him, he'll tear a strip off you."

"You'd want to be careful of a guy like that."

"Tell me about it. But I'm careful with him and he treats me fine. I've met his wife. She's a cute thing. There's no question who's the boss in their relationship. She has him by the nose. But still, there are these rumors you hear, about his background."

"Really?"

"There are stories, and who knows if they are true? He's supposed to have got into a fight at a construction site years ago. They say he hurt the other guy so badly he spent a long time in hospital, and was off work for over a year."

Fraser whistled.

"But I haven't heard anything but good reports on him since he's been with us."

"A reformed sinner. Who did he work for before? Do you know?"

Donna agreed to look into the matter and phone him the next day.

"He was lucky that Mr. Rittenhouse would give him a second chance," continued Art. "Now tell me. What kind of projects is Rittenhouse into these days?"

"Our big thing is commercial projects. Shopping centers, strip malls, and industrial condos. Those kinds of projects have been hot for several years now. We're good at them and we're usually low bidder when we see a project we want. Part of our success is the scheduling system we use."

"You don't do any residential building, then?"

"Very little. Upper New York hasn't seen a residential boom for years."

"And 'very little' means how much, exactly?"

"We did one project in Buffalo. It was just a favor, really, for a friend of Mr. Rittenhouse himself. We built a great big house. It was a fun project. A few of us had a tour when it was finished, before Mr. Rich moved in."

"Did you say Rich?" asked Fraser, working to conceal his excitement.

"Yes, he's a big importer, I think. He's been a friend of Mr.

Rittenhouse for years. You should have seen the place. Spa. Beautiful ceramics all over. And the carpets. Of course, there was no wall-to-wall. Just the most beautiful oriental carpets you've ever laid eyes on. It was a thrill to take that tour."

"And the guy's name was Rich. Was that Albert Rich, by any chance?"

"He's the guy. Why? Do you know him?"

"I think I've heard of him. Did you have any contact with him, or get to know him at all?"

"No, not at all. I shook hands with him once. But Jim got close to him. When we got near the end of the project, Rich wanted a few changes. Changes are death in a construction project — I mean, changes after the work has been all scheduled. Materials get ordered in advance. Work crews are given advance notice of the schedule, they're told how long they'll be at a certain job and exactly when it starts and ends. Everything has to be done precisely; otherwise, nobody knows what the costs will be. Jim is the key there. I guess Mr. Rittenhouse just told Rich to go see Jim. He'd be the only person on earth who could steer through a bunch of changes and then still have the project finish on time."

"What kind of changes are you talking about?" wondered Art.

"Oh, Mr. Rich found some exotic bath fixtures. Marble. From Italy, I think. Then he got hold of some fabulous flooring. Mahogany from Honduras. I've never seen anything like it. Rich paid for all the waste — all the materials we ordered and couldn't use. I hate to think of it. To a guy like Rich I'm sure it was pocket money."

"Interesting. And he and Lemone got on quite well? There was no friction between them?"

"They were like brothers. That was strange, too. Jim usually gets pretty worked up over last-minute changes."

"A little extra cash lubricates most deals," laughed Art.

"I guess that's it."

Art gave the waiter his credit card, and he and Donna prepared to leave the restaurant. "Thanks for the lunch. I'll call you tomorrow. And anytime you want to do it again," she smiled.

"This was great. You've been a big help," said Art. He gave her a warm hug and they parted.

On the way back to his office, Art mulled over his conversation with Donna. Lemone and Rich knew each other. It wasn't impossible that they were connected to Smithers' death. Rich could even have hired Lemone to do his dirty work for him. How could I sort that out, I wonder, he thought. I need to find out about Lemone's activities at the time of the murder, and whether he has an alibi. If he doesn't, then maybe I'm on to something.

CHAPTER 20

DONNA CALLED HIM THE FOLLOWING AFTERNOON and told him that Jim Lemone had previously worked for a plumbing company that specialized in septic tanks and sewer connections. Fraser called the company and made an early morning appointment for the next day with the owner, Nate Crestor.

Nate was a burly man, dressed in stained grayish overalls, obviously a working owner who did many of the physical tasks himself. He was pleasant enough, although obviously in a hurry to get the interview over with and get on with his day. "There's lots of sewer connections waiting out there," he smiled as he shook hands with Fraser.

"No doubt. I won't keep you," responded Fraser. "I'm looking for a little background on Jim Lemone. I understand he used to work for you."

"Oh, my old friend Jimmy."

Fraser nodded positively.

"Yeah. He worked for me all right. He was a damned good man, too. Have you got something on him?"

"Right now, this is just a routine investigation. I need a little background on Lemone."

"Is this off the record?"

"Absolutely off the record."

"He can scare a guy. You know that?"

Fraser could not imagine anyone or anything scaring Nate. "Tell me about him."

"We worked together for about three, the better part of four years. We could've gone on longer, too, but we hired this little helper. Work was gettin' too much for the two of us. So we got this guy to handle phones, make appointments for us, look after office stuff. Bright kid, too. But you know Jimmy. He's no slouch, neither. And he's always been a stickler for schedules. Guess that's what he's doin' now over at Rittenhouse."

"So I understand," said Fraser.

"I'd bet he's damn good at it, too. Anyway, this young kid, his name was Nate, same as mine. Little Nate, we called him. Guess that'd make me big Nate. This happens in the middle of summer, when we're really busy. That's our peak. Everything dies right off in winter. But in July and August, we got more work than we can handle. So little Nate, he's makin' up these schedules, and we're doin' fine. He seems to have the hang of it. But then one week, early in August, he doesn't just double-book work, he triple-books us. He lines up three jobs all to be done the same week. We can usually handle one in a week, but almost never two. Three's a joke. So here we are with three jobs on the books this week, and we're trying to figure how to soothe the customers and try to pick the two we're goin' to cancel out, when little Nate sees somethin' funny in the whole mess. It is funny, after the fact, but right then me and Jimmy didn't see it. I could live with little Nate laughing, but Jimmy sure couldn't. He saw red. Just got madder'n hell, picked the kid up and slapped him silly. He ruined a few of the kid's teeth, and broke his nose. I got them apart, but it all happened so fast I couldn't stop him soon enough. Jimmy got mad at me then."

"Our Jimmy seems to have a vicious temper."

"You said it. We was done right then. Forget one customer. Forget two or three customers. I had to fire him on the spot, right in the middle of our busy season. I had to tell the customers we had an emergency and were canceling a lot of our jobs."

"What happened to Lemone and the kid?" asked Fraser.

"The kid was laid up for about three months. The police investigated and pressed assault charges against Jimmy. They finally dropped the case because of lack of evidence. The kid wouldn't testify."

"How about you? Weren't you a witness?"

"Was I?" smiled big Nate. "You said this is off the record."

"I did. And it is," sighed Fraser. "Lemone was out of work for a while then?"

"His wife, Muriel, was a schoolteacher. She had to go back to work. Jimmy lay around for a few months, trying this and that. He finally landed a job at Rittenhouse. They're equal opportunity or somethin'. I was glad to see that."

"So little Nate refused to testify?"

"He was plain scared. Jimmy almost killed him. I paid all his medical expenses, helped him get another job, gave him some dough to help out."

"That was the end of it?"

"Yep. Little Nate's doing good. Jimmy's never had another problem, far as I know. That's the whole story. Now I gotta go."

Fraser thanked big Nate for his help, and left for police headquarters wondering how to deal with this information. And what was the connection with Muriel Lemone? He could picture Jim Lemone finding out about Smithers and his association with Muriel, and in a fit of temper, dealing with Smithers in the most violent way.

CHAPTER 21

AT SIX O'CLOCK, RUSS WILSON PEERED OUT OF THE window of his motel room in the dim morning light. The day showed every sign of gloom, with the Florida sun in total hiding and clouds threatening constant drizzle. Perfect, thought Russ. Nobody'll be out on the course at this hour. He shaved and gulped down the coffee he had made in his room. He donned plain purple trousers, a purple and pink checked shirt, and somewhat sadly, a worn black rain jacket that covered up the most resplendent part of his outfit. He grabbed his clubs and drove his rental car to the public course he remembered from playing it five years earlier. The pro shop was closed when he arrived, but he knew that by the time he donned his shoes and carried his clubs over to the bag loading station, someone would be opening up. Sure enough, as he trudged over, a car pulled up in the lot, and an elderly man shuffled along.

"Mornin'," said Russ.

"Not the best day for golf," responded the old-timer.

"You're not going to be crowded."

"You going to play?"

"Soon's I can get off," said Russ. "I need a cart, too. How much is that?"

"I guess you qualify for the early bird special. Thirteen dollars."

"How much for the cart?"

"Thirteen dollars is everything."

"Deal," said Russ. In a few minutes, he had his clubs loaded on his cart and was patrolling the rough and sand traps, ignoring the odd drop of rain. True to his word, he finished eighteen holes, got back to his motel, cleaned up, attired himself in conservative dress, and arrived at Sarasota police headquarters just before nine-thirty.

Wilson and Eckert shook hands as Eckert said, "Not the weather we usually serve up for northerners."

"Still beats Buffalo, anyway. Did you talk to Bryan at all?" Wilson asked the last question hopefully.

Eckert replied, "Yes. He covered me on the background. You have a homicide on your books."

"That's right. One of our suspects claims he was here the night of the murder. I need to check out his alibi. We got a couple other background items we could firm up too."

"The place we want to visit is called Himalayan Meadows. Priceless name. Only in Florida," laughed Eckert. "Not far from here. Look," he said, showing Wilson a promotion brochure that included a map. "Read this. Plain, classical ceramics covered with spectacular oriental carpeting. Does that turn you on?"

"Just what I had in mind," said Wilson.

"You may find these places a little outside your budget. They start about seven hundred thousand. Some places run over a million dollars. Here's one for a million fifty. But it's fun to see them, apart from the evidence you need."

Wilson laughed, "Who says they're outside my budget? You probably don't know how much a New York State detective brings in."

"True."

"Himalayan Meadows. That's the place Rich was talking about. There's a guy there, Charley Duster, that he says he was visiting. He's Rich's alibi. Did Bryan mention that name to you?"

Eckert said, "Yes he did. We're going to take a run over there. I've got Duster lined up for two this afternoon."

"This fellow that was murdered, Smithers, was into pretty expensive rugs. Imported oriental rugs. Two thousand dollars and up. Some of them ran to ten times that."

"You won't see those installed in the average Sarasota subdivision," said Eckert. "I pulled together a list of major developments here. There are only a few of them. All the prime waterfront land is taken so you don't see many condos being built any more. Golf villas are the big thing today. You buy one and you get a golf membership. A couple of them are really upscale. I have some flyers to show you. This one's from a development called Southern Dornoch, and it's hot right now. Duster is running this development, too. He reclaimed some swampland at the southeast end of Sarasota, and built one heck of a golf course there. These places are cheaper than Himalayans. The homes start at three fifty."

"Do any of them throw in carpeting? Rugs, I mean? At those prices, it sounds like they could afford it. But I wonder if they're popular down here."

"We'll find out."

They located Southern Dornoch and Himalayan Meadows on their map.

"This sounds good. I've always wanted to see the Himalayas. You say you made us an appointment for two o'clock?" asked Wilson. Eckert confirmed that he had, and then suggested they take a drive around some of the other developments first. Wilson continued, "Sounds good. Then do we have time for a snazzy place for lunch? My treat."

A good lunch was near the top of Eckert's list of favorite pastimes, especially a free good lunch. "We've got plenty of time to stop by a good place on the way."

The pair arrived at a restaurant called Catfish and More at noon. Business was brisk even at the early hour they arrived. Eckert was obviously well-known. He decided not to tell Wilson that his meals there were usually free. The tables were solid pine, covered with a thick, transparent plastic coating that made for a cheap, glitzy, yet attractive atmosphere. As they sat down, Eckert asked Wilson what he would like to drink.

"Draft, I guess. Light beer maybe. If they have it."

"They have it, all right, but listen, try this instead. They make rum martinis here. That's the best drink you'll ever have. The bartender mixes amber rum and lemon rum with a bit of orange something. You'll never go back to gin."

I never was on gin, thought Wilson. He considered the offer for perhaps a millisecond before consenting to the choice.

The bartender rolled his cart over to their table and made the drinks with a flourish, pouring ingredients from three bottles simultaneously into a cocktail shaker, rattling the ingredients and ice around vigorously, and filling their glasses to the brim. He left the shaker on their table with a grin. "A small refill there for somebody," he said. Klaus evidently had influence in the place.

Wilson remarked, "These chairs are about as comfortable as mine back in the office."

"You have to bring your own cushioning," laughed Eckert. "If you like seafood, this is the place though."

"No hamburgers?" asked Wilson. "I don't know if my system will take fish."

Eckert was surprised at this comment, and more surprised a few minutes later when Wilson ordered the giant seafood platter.

"Our man at Himalayan Meadows, Charley Duster, he seems to be okay. On the surface, anyway. I ran a background check and he has no offences, no charges, and no convictions. I talked to a couple of other officers who know him and they all say he's straight. No problems they ever heard of."

"So we can rely on what he says about meeting Rich. If he says anything, that is."

"I'd say so. Tell me about your murder," suggested Eckert.

Wilson drained his martini glass. "Not much in these things."

"Slow down. There may not be much in them but they are potent."

Eckert drained the cocktail shaker into their glasses and motioned for another round. Wilson took a sizeable sip. "That's more like it. Now, this guy Smithers, the victim. He was a rich guy. Fancy rug dealer. Also a tournament bridge player, which if you're into that stuff is apparently a big deal; they take the game very seriously. Nobody liked him, not in business, not in bridge. Somebody stabbed him after a bridge game and left the body under his car in the parking lot of the Adam's Mark hotel in Buffalo. Russ and I got a call at five in the morning when the temperature's ninety below or something. Smithers gets killed at a time when he has three quarters of a million in his checking account. The dough's just sitting there, drawing no interest, and it turns out he was ready to pay this guy Albert Rich for a big shipment of rugs. They were supposed to come down here to Himalayan, but the deal went sour and he backed out."

"So Rich is in the frame right now?"

"It's not clear. He says he was down here meeting with Duster the day it happened, and that he won't lose money on the rugs anyway. Right now, we're spinning our wheels. We have nothing solid to go on. The murder weapon belongs to a bridge player. His fingerprints are all over it, of course, but the guy's a straight arrow as far as we can see. Another bridge player had a run-in with Smithers the night of the murder. He has an alibi of sorts, not cast-iron, but fairly solid. That leaves us with Rich. Bryan and I are thinking there may be a connection somehow. All that money. They're both in the rug business."

"How did the murder weapon get out of the hands of the owner?"

"Duffy — he's the owner — he says it must have been stolen during a break-in a few weeks ago."

"Sounds pretty thin; was there a break-in?"

"Oh, yeah. Duffy's wife reported it, and a squad car was there that night. They said there was nothing stolen, at the time. Then this knife turns up in the body of Smithers, and now they say it must have been taken that night."

"So, if that's true, whoever did the break-in stole the knife and committed the murder," said Eckert, with finality.

"Easy, ain't it? Hey, these things go down okay," said Wilson, tapping his glass.

"The bar is closed," smiled Eckert. "We have work to do this afternoon." He waved for the waiter to bring the bill.

"The thing is, we got no idea who did the break-in."

Klaus Eckert leaned forward intently. "But you and Bryan must know that whoever stole the knife is the murderer. That narrows it down. You must have a clue or two about that. What about the break-in? How did he get in? Was the house locked?"

"Oh, yeah. There is one clue, come to think of it. A neighbor spotted a car pulling away just before the patrol car got there. He swears it was a black Chevy Cavalier, 2001 model."

"There you go," said Eckert. "Find the car and you've got your murderer."

"Pretty simple, huh?" said Wilson.

"What does Rich drive?"

"Rich drives an El Dorado. The theory is he could have hired somebody to do his dirty work."

"How about your other bridge players? What do they drive?"

"We should hire you to come up and solve the case for us."

"I'll settle for a consultant's fee."

"The weather's great at this time of year. You'd love Buffalo."

"Snow changes my personality."

"You like the rain better?" asked Wilson.

"Definitely. Have you considered the question of motive?" asked Klaus.

Wilson replied, "We're wondering about all this money sitting around. Three quarters of a million dollars. We think that has to be tied in somehow."

"You have a lot of pieces to fit together," said Eckert.

"It seems that way to us, anyway," said Wilson.

"We better go. We're meeting Duster in a few minutes. How was your Florida hamburger?"

"I love that stuff."

They reached the Himalayan Meadows development and parked the rental car outside a building marked with dual signs of 'Model Home' and 'Office'. A handsome, tanned young man who introduced himself as Jim Regan greeted them inside. "What can I do for you gentlemen?" he asked in a beautiful baritone. Wilson had a strong dislike for salesmen in general, and for the smooth-talking species in particular.

Eckert asked, "Can you show us where Charley Duster hangs out, please?"

"Charley. The boss himself," Jim declared. "Right over there." He pointed to an office with a closed door. "He'll be free very soon. Can I show you anything?"

"He was expecting us," growled Eckert. "Okay. Give us the spiel."

"This structure you're in right now, as we speak, is a base model and you can see the quality everywhere. Top materials are used for everything: floors, countertops, roofing. Everything's the best. Of course, you can upgrade to an even higher level if you want. We have access to all the best suppliers."

Wilson spied some interesting-looking carpeting in the living room. "Do you use that kind of carpeting in all your houses?" he asked.

"Well, actually, that's an option that we can get for you if you want it. That particular carpet would run you about eighteen or twenty thousand dollars extra. Of course, we can supply cheaper ones. That one is an authentic Chinese wool rug, imported specially from China."

Where else would you import a Chinese rug from, wondered Wilson.

"To be honest, we're having a little trouble with our supplier. There's a wait right now of two or three months. But if you like that particular design, we will do everything we can to accommodate you."

"Who do you buy your rugs from?" asked Wilson.

"We have an importer who brings in these products for us. A specialist who knows everything about carpets. He's very good at his business."

"Is he a well-known name around Sarasota?" asked Eckert.

"Oh no. This guy is a big operator and we buy in bulk. He doesn't have a showroom around here. He's from Michigan, I think."

"Not New York state, by any chance?" asked Wilson.

"Yes, come to think of it, it is. I remember a reference to Buffalo. That's in New York, not Michigan, right?"

Wilson rolled his eyes at Eckert. "I think you're right about that. Yes, I think Buffalo is in New York."

"There's Mr. Duster right now," said Regan, as a door opened.

They thanked the salesman and moved into Duster's office.

Charley Duster greeted them cordially and motioned them to comfortable chairs. He took coffee orders and then joined them. "You're interested in Albert Rich, I hear," he said.

"What can you tell us about him?" asked Wilson.

"Not a whole lot. I met him through Smithers. Bob Smithers. I was shocked to hear about his murder."

"That's what we're looking into. How long did you know Smithers?"

"Oh, about seven or eight years. He was a supplier to another project I worked on, and we've been doing business ever since."

"Do you know any reason anyone might have wanted to kill him?"

"I didn't know him that well outside business; he didn't spend much time down here. He's a tough guy to deal with, but I've always found him honest. I've never had a problem I couldn't sort out."

"How about this recent thing with the second-hand rugs?" asked Wilson.

"Second-hand rugs. Yes. I had a deal worked out with Bob. Rich was in on it – he was the importer. The way it turned out I couldn't use the rugs. I had to cancel the contract."

"Weren't you a bit surprised to be getting used rugs?"

"Like I said, I couldn't use them. I told Bob I was calling the deal off. Then Al came down himself. Al Rich, I mean. He tried to get me to change my mind. We had a good talk on the subject. I almost bought his line. No doubt, those carpets he showed me were gorgeous, and they probably were worth what he said they were, but there is no way I'd put up a million or so for second-hand goods. I'm no carpet expert. If I was in the business and knew what I was getting into, I might think about it. But I rely on the brand names, maybe the odd oriental product if I'm sure it's genuine. Second-hand goods? No thanks."

"When did you see him?"

Duster checked his desk diary.

"He came down Sunday morning, December seventh. He flew back on Monday morning. I drove him to the airport."

"How'd he get over here?"

"A limo brought him over. He called for an appointment. I said sure, I'm not that busy on Sundays. I ordered him a limo at the Bradenton airport. Here's their card. I'm sure they'll have a record of the trip."

Wilson inspected the business card that Duster handed him. "Was anybody with Rich?" he asked.

"No. He came down alone. Look, if you want to call the limo owner, I know him. I can give you his cell phone number. That'll save you time checking your facts."

Wilson accepted Duster's offer and he was soon able to confirm all the details of his account of Rich's arrival. Assuming they could trust Duster, Albert Rich was fading fast as a suspect.

Nelson met Wilson's return flight at the Buffalo airport. The evening was cold and starry. "At least the driving is good," Wilson remarked.

"Perfect. Thank goodness. This isn't like the other night when you couldn't go anywhere because of three feet of snow. You know the city had to borrow equipment from Toronto to get all the streets plowed and cleaned up?"

"Yeah. Just like Sarasota," laughed Wilson.

"Oh yes. Eighty degrees and snow on the streets."

"We dressed for it."

"Did you find anything?"

"Rich seems clean. The guy down there confirms Rich's alibi. I'd say it's cast iron. In fact, he confirmed the whole rug deal. They made an agreement quite a while ago. Duster called it off when he learned about the carpets not being new. If Rich is involved in the murder, he hired somebody to do the dirty work."

"Did you get your golf in?"

"I broke a hundred," said Wilson. "Hey Russ?"

"What?"

"Eckert and I had a long talk about the case," said Wilson.

"A long, sober talk, I hope," said Nelson.

"Well, it seems to me we're not paying enough attention to the murder weapon."

"Yeah."

"I know Duffy's alibi isn't very good, but I just get the feeling he's not our guy."

Nelson seemed interested. "Right," he said. "But you're going to say there's a connection."

"Exactly," continued Wilson. "I'm thinking the guy who did this was the same guy that broke into the Duffys that night and stole the hunting knife. If we find him, we got our murderer."

"We've always known that."

"Yeah, but we're not doing anything much about it. We gotta talk to Fraser about this."

Nelson shot him a dark look.

CHAPTER 22

HERMANN VOLCKER WAS A SPRY EIGHTY-THREE. He loved to play bridge — especially when he got to play a hand himself. His reputation of being a very good declarer indeed was justified; perhaps aided by the fact that his prodigious memory carried several thousand hands, all available for instant recall. His problem, some thought (although not Hermann), was that his bidding was a little old-fashioned, if not downright archaic. To Hermann, bidding was a simple proposition: "When you got something, you bid. When you want to be in game, you jump. Otherwise, you just shut up." He would add, with a twinkle in his eye, "Naturally, at the right time, you chuck in the odd stink bid." He believed every word the great Ely Culbertson had ever written back in the 1930s, and had a collection of Culbertson's works, including the Gold Book, the Blue Book, the Red Book and others. He disliked Culbertson's later book on point-count bidding, because 'it was probably ghost-written, not written by Ely, and prostituted the principles of quick tricks which Culbertson stood for.' Not having the same familiarity with bridge before 1960, nobody else knew what Hermann was talking about.

Nonetheless, Hermann could play. There were days when he would show up at the local duplicate club and lap the field by several percentage points. Of course, there were other days as well, not quite as good. But Hermann loved the game, and loved to play with different partners. He would play with anyone in the club, regardless of their experience or their ability, and was always polite and, in his own way, charming. He especially liked to play with a beautiful woman. She did not have to be young, just beautiful, and Hermann thought that most women were beautiful.

Although he was a gracious partner, and polite to everyone, he did have a habit of pointing out, on every hand, no matter who played the hand, how it should have been played, and why. If he played a hand and missed his contract by several tricks, he explained why he had gambled on a finesse for an overtrick when he could have settled for a sure thing. If an opponent or a partner misplayed a hand, no matter whether they made the contract or not, Hermann always had his analysis ready. If they played it right, in his eyes, he always congratulated them. Hermann was quick in his analysis, and usually accurate. Oh, he had been wrong on occasion. Once, in 1975, he made a mistake in his analysis playing against one of the national champions he had coached. But no one had caught him in an analytical error since that time.

Hermann was not quite as competent in running his personal affairs. His wife had died in her sixties, leaving Hermann living alone. He ate poorly and his wardrobe had not been updated for decades. He always showed up dressed neatly with a white shirt and a tie. His suits were made of finest wool worsted and twist fabrics, cut in styles that had not been seen recently. They showed little sign of wear, although some had been purchased fifty years ago. He had seen no advantage in new-fangled zippered flies, and he had ordered all of his trousers made with the old-fashioned buttoned design.

To his chagrin, Hermann found that he had to visit the bathroom at increasing frequencies — on his worst days as often as four or five times a session. Occasionally he arrived back at the table with not just one, but two or three buttons unfastened. This was embarrassing to his partner when he was playing with one of his lady friends. It was even more embarrassing to Hermann when he found out himself. Seven days a week, however, at least once a day, he showed up at local bridge clubs and all of the local tournaments, and was usually rated as the opponent to beat for the day.

On the Thursday after Smithers was killed, Helen had a date to play with Hermann, who was her very favorite partner. All of Hermann's little remarks fed her ego and buoyed her spirits. When he liked what she wore, he complimented her. That in turn prompted her to choose carefully when they had a game together. He often mentioned her hair, and so she made a point of going to her hairdresser before a game. Sure, he pointed out mistakes she made during the play, but he did that to everyone. And he told everyone when they had made a good play. When he occasionally returned to the table with his fly unbuttoned, she avoided looking at him, and sought out Stewart Appleton to confide in, and to relay the problem to Hermann.

Helen and Hermann were having a fine game that night. Helen loved it. She could hardly wait to brag to Jack about how well she had played, and how she had fielded many of Hermann's old-fashioned bids. On a night like tonight, she seemed to understand everything that Hermann was trying to communicate. Helen expected to win easily, but that all changed during the last round.

They were chatting as they waited to move to the last table where they would be playing against Charles Werkman and his partner. Helen said, "I love playing with you, Hermann. You make your bids so easy for me to understand."

"Everything is natural," Hermann said. "Nothing fancy."

"Tough round coming up."

"Who've we got?"

"Charles and his partner."

"Not a good declarer. Just let him play a hand or two. We'll be okay." The table became open and they sat down and greeted their opponents.

"Big game tonight?" Helen asked Charles and his partner.

"Not bad, not bad," answered Charles in his high-pitched voice.

Hermann looked up, startled. "That's who it was," he said, sharply. "Cards in the pocket. You were the one talking to Bob Smithers in the washroom." Hermann was quite agitated now.

"I don't know what you're mumbling about," responded Charles.

Hermann seemed to go into a trance as he spoke. His eyes glazed over during the three hands they played, and Helen's spirits sagged as she realized that their game was being destroyed. He misplayed two easy contracts that he normally would have made. Hermann was far off somewhere. For once, bridge was the last thing on his mind. After apologizing profusely for his errors on the first two hands, he misbid the last hand and they ended up in fifth place.

☠ ♥ ☠

At five o'clock on Friday morning, the superintendent of the apartment building where Hermann lived responded to heavy banging on his door. Two uniformed police officers appeared and one told him that there was a dead body in his parking lot and asked if he knew anything about it. He put on his leggings and parka and accompanied the officers to look at the body. "It's poor old Hermann," he said.

"You knew him?" asked one of the patrolmen.

"Hermann Volcker. Sure did. He's one of our old-timers — was. Lives on the ground floor in the back; I've known him for years. Poor old guy."

"It looks like he had a heart attack or a stroke," suggested one of the patrolmen.

"He might have slipped on the ice and banged his head as he fell," said the other. "Maybe he hit the side of the car or the pavement."

" He was a healthy old bugger. Never heard he had a heart problem. That's a strange welt on his head there," said the superintendent.

"We better call the coroner," said the first cop.

"Does anybody live with him?" asked the other officer. "We need to let his next of kin know."

"He didn't live with anybody," said the superintendent. "His wife died years ago. He's been on his own ever since."

"We'll need you to sign a statement that you identified the body. We'll need a key to his apartment, too. Did he have visitors?"

"Every day, he went out to some club and played bridge. That's all he ever did. You oughta talk to some bridge players."

CHAPTER 23

ON THE MORNING AFTER HE KILLED HERMANN, Charles rose and mechanically put himself through the motions of shaving, showering, and dressing for work. He didn't feel much different than usual, except for a certain tightness in his chest and perhaps a heart that beat a little faster than normal. Work itself, most days, was mainly a series of unconscious actions. Today, he was glad of that, because he could focus most of his thoughts on assessing his position and doing some planning.

On the drive to his office, he reflected on his chances of getting caught. Art Fraser is a smart cop, he thought. Not as smart as I am, though. I beat him most of the time at the bridge table. Still, I'll have to be damned careful. I can't afford any slip-ups. How will they ever tie me to Smithers' murder? Not through the murder weapon. That could never be traced to me. He smirked to himself as he thought about the police bothering Jack and Helen in their effort to gather evidence. Tough luck. They can put up with a little inconvenience for a good cause. The longer the police spent on false leads, the colder the trail would become and the better his chances of evading suspicion. He hadn't even been questioned yet! He thought of poor old Hermann. The way he dispatched Hermann reminded him of his first killing, when he was still a schoolboy. He had gotten away with it and no one had ever found out.

At age twelve, his parents had allowed him to have a cat as a pet. He named it Peanut, and for a time was delighted with his new toy. But he soon tired of cleaning her litter tray and setting out her food and water. He detested the way the cat presented him with her hunting trophies — birds, chipmunks, mice — always delivered to Charles, in his bedroom if possible. Disposing of the dead animals revolted him. His biggest mistake was to overrate the degree of domestication of the cat. Her wild streak was barely concealed beneath a veneer of playfulness. He tickled the cat's stomach one day, and both seemed to be enjoying the fun, but the cat suddenly turned vicious and sank her claws deeply into his forearm, removing most of the skin and producing an ugly, painful wound that required a trip to the hospital.

One of the boys at school had demonstrated the use of a snare for catching chipmunks or squirrels. "If you're going to catch a squirrel," the friend said, "You got to use strong cord. Nylon or something. Chipmunks are easier." Charles listened carefully and watched his friend demonstrate the technique. He felt sorry for the chipmunk and had to look away as the friend killed the little animal. Charles left quickly and cried most of the way home. His mind buried the details of the incident deeply in his memory.

The details all came back to him when his anger rose at the way Peanut had hurt him. He schemed for a few days, then went out and bought himself a roll of stout cord. He waited for an opportunity when his mother was occupied with household work. Charles put his cord in his pocket and let Peanut outdoors onto the patio. He tied a slipknot in the end of the cord, as per his friend's demonstration, and formed an opening in the end that was plenty large enough for Peanut's head to enter. He played with the cat first, and as usual got her excited with his little game. He began to move the cord around furiously, becoming as keyed up as the cat. He dangled the cord over the cat's head, and as Peanut tilted backward in the fun, slipped the noose over her head. He jerked the cord tight and he had her. Following his friend's instructions, he took away the slack in the cord and ran with it, lifting the cat off the ground. He ran around the yard this way for a few moments as the cat fought an enemy it could not understand, furiously at first, then spasmodically, until it finally expired. Charles exulted. He had his revenge. He dragged the corpse of Peanut into the garage and found a heavy plastic bag, opened it and inserted the still warm, still soft body. He tied the bag up and stuffed it into the garbage pail.

The garbage was picked up next day, and Peanut the cat was gone forever. When his mother asked where the cat was, Charles lied. "I don't know, Mom," he said. "I haven't seen her for two or three days. I've looked everywhere."

"Maybe a fox or coyote got her. That's too bad."

Yes, that's too bad, thought Charles.

His thoughts returned to the two murders he had committed and how there was no sign that the police connected him with either death. His spirits rose as he thought about how easily he had outwitted everyone so far. Murderers who got caught were just plain dumb, he thought. He became almost carefree as he went into his office to begin his daily tasks.

CHAPTER 24

MID-MORNING ON FRIDAY HELEN ANSWERED THE phone and, after the usual greetings, heard Art Fraser introduce himself and ask, "Did you hear about Hermann?"

"No," she replied. "What about him?"

"He was found dead in the parking lot at his apartment."

"Oh no. Don't tell me," said Helen. "I played with him just last night. What happened?"

"They don't really know, but it seems like a heart attack or something. Must have happened as he was getting home after the game. Poor old guy."

"I can't believe it. He seemed fine last night. He was such a dear. His usual bright self, except..." Her voice trailed off.

"Except what?" asked Art.

"Let me think. He acted a bit funny during the last round. His mind seemed to wander off. His eyes glazed over and he played terribly the last three hands. He is usually so good. Especially when he plays the hands."

"Oh, I know."

"He seemed so distant, as if he were in another world. He must have been having an attack, maybe a stroke right then. Our evening went into a tailspin right there."

"We'll all miss Hermann. Mind you, he was in his eighties."

☠ ♥ ☠

"Fraser called," Nelson said to Wilson. "He wants to talk to us about the Smithers case. He's coming over to see us."

Nelson was interrupted by his phone. Shortly after he answered, he called to Wilson to pick up an extension.

Nelson explained into the phone, "I've got my colleague here, Detective Wilson, on the line. Okay Russ, this is Miss McDermid from the Duffy accounting firm on the line. She tracked down the work Duffy was doing the night of the Smithers murder. You know, when Duffy was supposedly in his office. Miss McDermid, can you repeat what you just told me?'

"Sure. Please call me Nina, by the way," said the confident voice at the other end. "I looked up the files that my boss Jack was working on that Sunday night. I have a list of them. I can find four. They include the date and time he saved the work. The first time shown is a word processing document at eight twenty-six, December seventh. The last one was saved at ten fourteen. So they prove Jack was here that whole time. I can print these out and mail the list to you or you can drop in and see them for yourself. I recommend you drop over."

"Okay," said Nelson. "And what time do you suggest?"

"It would help us if you wouldn't mind avoiding interference with our customers. Early some morning. It won't take long."

"How would seven-thirty tomorrow work?" asked Nelson.

"That's perfect. I'll be here."

"Great," said Nelson. "Thanks for your help, Miss McDermid. We'll need your address and some directions."

Nelson made a note of the information, hung up and asked Wilson, "Wanta come along? We might as well both look at what she's got. Her office is not far from here."

"Fine. If Miss whoever has what she says, it'll pretty well clear Duffy.'

"Yeah. This information all ties in with his story, and it pretty well supports everything Duffy said."

"This damned case is driving me nuts. We get what seems like a good lead, on the surface, anyway. Then it fizzles out. They all fizzle."

"Yeah. Rich, Orono, Lemone. All possibilities, but we can't pin them down. Duffy looks clean now. You going to tell Fraser?"

"Naw. Not yet. Let him figure it out. Maybe Duffy can turn up something useful for us. You never know. We'll just leave him itch a bit, trying to clear himself. He might help."

"I suppose," said Wilson. "It must be hard on his wife and kids, though. What's Fraser got?"

"Fraser wouldn't say anything over the phone, so I'm in the dark like you. He's a good friend of all these bridge players. Maybe one of them passed on something useful. When are we going to get done with the car ownerships, the Cavaliers?"

"We got a list of Chev Cavaliers in this area and I had a quick look. I'll get it out again."

Nelson said, "We know all of the bridge people who could be involved in the murder. Maybe we can match a name and a vehicle. Let's look at it together. We're sure that it was a Cavalier?'

"We have that statement in the file from the night of the break-in. The neighbor works for a GM dealer. He said he could tell absolutely that it was a Cavalier, and definitely 2001."

Wilson reappeared after a few minutes with a file containing a thick pile of paper. He said, "Here we are. This is what Kathy got for us. All of the 2001 Cavaliers in New York State."

"The whole state?" murmured Nelson. "Seven thousand of these damned things." He was looking at pages printed with two columns each in ten-point type, thirty-five addresses to a page side, and roughly fifty two-sided pages.

"This is taking a lot of Kathy's time," said Wilson.

"We'll fall asleep reading this. Listen, Fraser is big in cars. He handled a lot of theft cases. Maybe we ought to talk to him about it."

"I never thought of that," said Wilson. "You're right. He has a reputation as a sharp operator."

Nelson scowled at this comment. "What I was thinking is, he has access to all kinds of information on cars and ownership tracing, all that stuff. Why don't we explain our problem to him and ask if he can help us?"

"Can't lose nothing by trying," responded Wilson.

Art Fraser walked in at that point and greeted the two homicide officers. "Glad we're able to get together on short notice. Anything new on the case?"

You know damned well, thought Nelson. "We're following all the leads we got so far. We're not even close to an arrest yet. We talked to Rich, and he gave us a story about a rug deal he had with Smithers for a Florida housing development. Russ checked the story with Rich's

Florida contact, and the whole story hangs together. I'd say that, at the moment, Rich is a dead end. His story explains all the weird balances in Smithers' bank accounts."

Fraser said, "Interesting. I got thinking about Rich more and more. He and Lemone know each other. Quite well, evidently. I was beginning to wonder if there is a link between the two. Rich the mastermind and Lemone the man doing the dirty work. He's capable of it. Lemone and Rich go way back. And they both had reason to kill Smithers. It's possible that they worked out a deal," said Fraser.

"That connection may still be there," said Nelson. "But the financial angle seems to be clear. Rich is either a very good actor or his story that the deal fell through but he had no problem selling the left-over rugs is a true one. My gut says we ought to believe Rich."

"Just a minute here, guys," said Wilson. "Something bothers me."

"Spit it out," said Nelson.

"The guy we're looking for drives a Cavalier, broke into Duffy's house, stole a knife and killed Smithers. That's what we're assuming, right?"

"And?" said Nelson.

"Everybody says what a big bugger this Lemone is."

"So?" asked Nelson.

"If he is so damned big, how in hell did he get in the bathroom window at Duffy's place? To get the knife, I mean. That window is maybe twelve inches high by two feet wide. I can see him pushing his head and arms in and then getting stuck halfway."

Nelson thought about this and burst into a gale of laughter. "Arms dangling inside, feet waving around outside. My God. What a sight." Wilson joined in the laughter. Fraser sat quietly.

"I think we better wipe Lemone off the list of suspects," said Nelson, still choking intermittently.

"Maybe he shoved Muriel through the window and had her open the patio door for him," said Wilson.

"That's not nice, Russ," said Fraser, and all three enjoyed another round of laughter.

"I've got some news for you guys," said Fraser. "I wanted to let you know that another bridge player died last night."

"Is he another one of those bridge players nobody liked?" wondered Nelson.

"Not poor old Hermann. Everybody liked him. His name was Hermann Volcker, an old guy in his eighties. They found him dead early this morning in the parking lot next to his apartment. There was a big red welt on the side of his face, but the doc says no reason to suspect foul play. Looks can be deceiving, but everybody said Hermann looked so well and never complained of any bad health. We're going to have to look into the death of Volcker."

"If the Volcker case was a murder, too, we've got work. Lots of it," said Nelson.

"Wait a minute here," said Wilson. "We don't have no Volcker murder on the books. What's all this?"

Fraser answered. "What I'm saying is there's been another death, another bridge player. It looks to me like a possible homicide. We need to look into it. The victims are both bridge players, so I'm wondering if there is any connection."

Nelson turned to Fraser. "Did you see the body?" he asked.

"No, I didn't. But when the building superintendent identified the body, he saw something queer about the appearance of Hermann's face."

"Did someone pass this thing off as heart failure when there was a wound on the guy's face?" asked Nelson.

"Not so much a wound as a welt," answered Fraser. "If you're not looking for foul play, you assume something natural happened."

"But could a guy take a fall and bounce off his face? If he had heart failure, he would be more likely to sag. And if it's an old guy, this is not like he was running and tripped, bang."

"That's what makes me think we should look into it," said Fraser. "If the two deaths are related, it'll help us track down the guy who did it. On the other hand, the local bridge players are going to get a little nervous about their own safety."

"They'll want this thing wrapped up pronto," said Nelson. "The first order of business here is to take a good look into Volcker's death. We can move on to theories when we have that figured out. What exactly does Wilbur say? I've never seen him screw up," said Nelson.

Fraser answered, "Wilbur was out of town for a day. You can't blame a guy for taking a day off. He asked another doc as a favor to stand in for him. The doc did screw up, but not as bad as you think. He doesn't know much about homicide or examining bodies. But he agreed to take over just as a good turn. One thing this doc did do for us — he did take a lot of pictures of the body. And he kept a good file on the condition of the body and symptoms he saw. Wilbur looked at the pictures with me. The welt was not on Volcker's face. It was on the top of his head, and there was a crease in his skull. That's gotta be from a blow, not a fall. It looked like a rod or something caused it. The cross-section was round, but it was bigger at the end. It looked like a mark from a tire wrench – you know, the thing you use when you change a tire to take the nuts off. And another thing, it looks like Volcker's jaw was broken. Hermann was an old guy and his bones were pretty fragile, but you don't get that from a fall either, especially after a heart attack, where the body just sort of sags. The pictures were good. When we blew them up, you could see the damage to the skull and the jaw pretty clearly."

"Yeah?"

"And the doc made notes on the body. After a heart attack, you'd get maybe a different look to the corpse. Like I say, a sag to the pavement. Not a quick fall and a sharp hit. All the signs on the corpse are consistent with a hard smash to the jaw, a fall backwards, and another smash over the head with a weapon shaped like a tire wrench."

"Okay. Now we've got ourselves a pair of victims. But was it the same murderer?" asked Nelson.

Fraser said, "I'll bet it was. Too much of a coincidence for there to be two bridge-playing killers in the same town at the same time. Let's see where that takes us."

Nelson asked, "What about finding a blood-soaked tire wrench for a murder weapon?"

"That would help, but we'll be lucky to find it," said Fraser. "The strange thing here is that this is exactly the opposite of Smithers — everybody liked Hermann. I can't think of a single exception among all the players I know. Figuring out a motive is going to be tough. Maybe it's time we all paid a visit to Stewart Appleton at his bridge club. He always has good insight into these things. Volcker's murder happened shortly after the game in his club."

"Can we see him today?" asked Nelson.

"He has a game on this afternoon. I'll call him right now." Nelson pushed his phone over to Fraser. In a few minutes, Fraser hung up the phone and reopened the conversation. "He said to come around at four-thirty. He'll have everyone out of the club by then and we can talk privately."

"Sounds good," said Wilson. "Do all three of us need to call on Appleskin, or whatever?"

"Appleton. Yes, we do."

Nelson continued, "All right. Now Russ and I got one for you. We need to track down a certain car and we could use your help." Nelson explained the incident of the black Chevrolet Cavalier, and asked if Fraser had any ideas on tracking it down. "We got all the Cavaliers in New York state. But who's got time to go over the whole list with a magnifying glass? You know a lot about cars, am I right?"

"That's my bag, for the past seven years, anyway. Cars and ownership. The state has access to a huge database on cars and ownership. I can easily get someone in the traffic section to do a search. There's an officer in traffic named Karen. She's the best we've got on working the data. She can pull out information from a specific region, say Genessee County. The more specific you get, the more she can help."

Wilson said, "All we know is it was a 2001 Chevy Cavalier. A General Motors sales manager identified the model and year. I suppose that's as reliable as you get. The color is presumed to be black, but the car was spotted at night, so it could be any dark color."

"That won't matter much," said Fraser. "We don't have color data anyway. But by the time we narrow it down to models in this area, you won't have too big a list to look at. I would guess that General Motors make between two hundred and two hundred and fifty thousand Cavaliers a year. New York state gets about six or seven thousand of those."

"Seven," interrupted Nelson. "We already got that from Albany. Seven thousand damn cars and owners on the list. You'd go blind trying to read it."

"Okay, seven," said Fraser. "We ought to look at the counties right around Genessee here. These counties might get ten percent of all of New York state's shipments, say four or five hundred. The black ones would total about fifty."

"Do you mean you got a way to boil the list down to fifty cars?" asked Wilson.

"No," responded Fraser. "We can narrow it down to a list of five hundred. I told you, we can't get a color breakdown. Don't forget my mental arithmetic can be off a bit. But if it's two hundred or six hundred, so what?"

"I see what you mean," said Nelson. "Okay. When could you have that?"

"I'll get it started today. Can you send a clerk over to help, and pick up the list when it's all ready?"

Wilson volunteered immediately. "Oh yeah. Kathy would love to come over."

"Give me until tomorrow morning to brief Karen. I'll tell her to expect Kathy then."

"I'll get on to Kathy right away and let her know what's needed," said Wilson.

"I'll bet you will," smiled Nelson.

CHAPTER 25

WHEN ART FRASER FIRST CALLED STEWART Appleton and told him that he, Nelson and Wilson wanted to drop over and talk for an hour or so, Appleton could see an interruption to his afternoon game, and he was hesitant. A visit from three police officers at four-thirty in the afternoon was an imposition, and he had suggested they call the next day. Fraser insisted, mentioning that they were looking into the death of Hermann, possibly his murder. When Appleton heard this he resolved to help as much as possible.

Stewart made sure that his session finished just before four, and he had the scores all ready a few minutes later. He checked for possible errors as quickly as possible, and then made sure that all of the players were gone when the police officers arrived. They climbed the rickety wooden stairs at the back of the building housing the Cheektavia Bridge Club and found Stewart waiting for them. His hot, very good coffee relaxed everyone considerably.

Fraser thanked Stewart for accommodating the request of the police officers. "You finished your game in good time," remarked Fraser.

"Yeah, I cut out the last round. We played twenty-four boards anyway. Nobody seemed to mind," answered Appleton. "You're investigating Hermann's death? Does that mean it was another murder?"

"At the moment, we're not calling it a murder. We're just investigating. There may be a connection with Smithers' murder, but right now, that's all speculation. We'd like you to tell us what you know about Hermann. Especially what went on last night. As a matter of fact, we'd like to know anything you can tell us about Bob Smithers, too. Any piece of background might help us," said Fraser.

"Hermann and Bob were both regulars here," responded Appleton. "They're as different as you can get. I could name ten people who had it in for Bob, but not a single one who disliked Hermann. He was in his eighties, you know, but a very healthy guy. He was the type who wouldn't hurt a soul. I hate to think that he's dead."

"Did Hermann play in your game last night?" asked Fraser.

"He was there playing with Helen Duffy," said Stewart.

"Who else was here last night?" asked Nelson.

Fraser interrupted. "The important thing would be who was still here at the end of the game. The ones who left about the same time as Hermann."

Nelson gave him a sharp look and asked, "Okay. Take us to the end of the evening when the game breaks up. Right?"

"Right."

"People start to leave. Does everybody rush out at once? Do people stay around for a beer or coffee? What does everyone do at the end of the game?"

"No beer. I don't have a license. Sometimes I..." Appleton caught himself, remembered he was talking to police officers, and stopped for a second. "The coffee's all gone by then. What happens is, most people leave. The serious players and any who think they might have done well stick around and wait for the scores. The last round score slips have to be collected after the game. I put the scores into the computer and work out everybody's matchpoint total and then announce the winners."

"Okay. Now let's go back to last night. Who was still there waiting for the scores?"

"Let's see. Charles Werkman was here, and Jim Lemone and his wife were too. Lew Orono was here. I forget his partner. But it's in the computer if we need it."

"Was Jack Duffy here last night too?" asked Nelson.

"That's right, the Duffys were both here. But surely neither of them was involved in the murders. Those two wouldn't harm a mouse."

"I'll put you on my list of folks that know that Jack Duffy is innocent. It's a long list. I don't wanta hear anymore about how the Duffys are innocent," snapped Nelson.

Appleton continued, "Muriel Lemone's a school teacher and she keeps Jim under pretty good control. I can't see him being involved in anything violent when she's around. Jim's a big bruiser, though. Big as a house. You don't ever want to cross him up."

"Oh, I don't?" asked Wilson.

"No, you don't, Russ," said Nelson. "He's a tough guy, is he?"

Appleton answered, "He doesn't act tough or anything. He's just big."

"Okay. And then there was this guy, Orono?"

"Lew Orono. He was one of the last to leave also. He's a pretty good player and he usually waits for the scores."

"Is there anything special about him?"

"Not really. Some people think he's a bit of a rough customer, but I get along with him fine. The only thing about Lew is that he was on a team in the tournament last Sunday that lost in a committee to Bob Smithers. Lew was very upset by the whole thing."

"Yeah. We heard all that. Orono had a big grudge against Smithers."

"Only a bridge grudge," said Appleton, torn between wanting to be fair to people who might or might not have been involved in the murder.

"You mean a bridge grudge is good?" asked Nelson.

"No, of course not, but I think of Jack Duffy as a good example. He gets real mad at the bridge table, but his anger disappears as quickly as it comes. That seems to be the way with bridge players. However seriously they take the game, it has nothing to do with real life. Bridge life might as well take place on another planet."

"You said there was another guy waiting right to the end," said Nelson.

"Yes. You know Hermann stayed around. And Werkman. Charles Werkman. He was one of the last to leave too."

"Is there anything you can tell us about him?"

"He's just a quiet guy, a very serious bridge player."

"Was he at this tournament last weekend too?" asked Nelson.

"Yes, I think he was playing with Jack Duffy – they're a regular partnership."

"Did these people all go out together last night? Did anyone leave with Volcker?"

"I honestly can't say," said Appleton. "I had to gather up the boards and clean the place up. There's always a certain amount of litter after a bridge game. I could hear people muttering as they put on their coats. I didn't pay attention to them leaving."

"Okay," said Fraser. "Thanks for your help. Anything else you guys can think of?" nodding at Nelson and Wilson. They shook their heads, and Fraser said, "I'd like to ask you a small favor. Do you mind keeping the Volcker investigation quiet? At least until we tell you differently or you see it in the paper? It may be useful to have the killer in the dark about our suspicions. He is more likely to be careless if he feels we're treating the death as one from natural causes."

Appleton readily agreed and Fraser thanked him for his cooperation. Nelson echoed Fraser's thanks and the officers shook hands with Appleton and left.

☠ ♥ ☠

When the officers returned to headquarters, they found that Kathy had left a list on Wilson's desk. The list included all the 2001 Chevy Cavaliers in the immediate area, condensed into only two pages of information, and they scanned it quickly. "There's nothing interesting here," said Wilson. "None of the owners has a name I'd recognize. And none of the owners is from this area."

Nelson showed Fraser the disappointing news.

"Are any of the cars owned by dealers, or registered under used car lots?" asked Fraser. "Your problem here may be that you've only got individuals, not companies. We need to check car rental agencies, too."

"Yeah. I see what you mean. A couple of these cars are owned by dealers. And some by used car people." Nelson went down the list, marking some of the names. "And here we got a couple of rental agencies. Yeah. We can check all this out."

"You've got several possibilities. A rental. A trade-in. A loaner. The car couldn't just disappear off the face of the earth. At this point, we have to assume the car has a New York state license. If not, we've got a huge problem. We'll just have to start all over again."

Nelson looked at Wilson. "Did you get all that, Russ?" Wilson nodded. "Tell Kathy thanks and get her to make us a new list of business owners only. I'm talking dealers, rentals, and all the businesses you can think of. There won't be that many."

"Got it," said Wilson.

CHAPTER 26

THE THREE OFFICERS MET BACK AT THE STATION JUST after lunch. Nelson unloaded some of his frustration. "Whoever did the job on Volcker was at that bridge club. But you know what it takes to get the D.A. even interested in talking to you — a hell of a lot more than opinion and hearsay. Appletree hasn't given us a thing that will stand up as evidence."

Fraser said. "We don't have a picture that ties everything together. Motive, opportunity, the physical act of what happened. Say our murderer had a reason to kill Smithers. From the motive angle, we've got Lew Orono and Jim Lemone."

"I thought we threw Lemone out for size," said Nelson.

"You're right," said Fraser.

"And we got to drop Duffy from our list after what little Miss Nina told us," said Wilson.

"I agree with that. Let's forget about Duffy. He had nothing to do with murder," echoed Fraser.

Nelson scowled at his colleagues and replied, "Okay. We leave Duffy out for now," he said. "This Werkman guy's a new name. Between us, we haven't done a thing about Werkman. I say we got to pin down what the two possibles were doing at the critical times: Werkman and Orono."

"Let's talk about Orono for a minute. He was around for both murders and has a possible alibi for the first one — we don't know about the second yet. How would his alibi stand up if we put heat on it?"

"I looked into Orono some," offered Wilson. "I talked to him. His story seems to check out. But his problems with Smithers go back a few years. He swears that Smithers ruined him."

"I'm wondering if we have questioned the people giving him his alibi all that closely. Somebody at his motel saw him after the murder," said Nelson. "But it was a long time after."

"I spoke to the guy that was supposed to see Orono. His story checks out," said Wilson.

"I mean really put it to him. What exactly was he doing? What makes him so sure he saw Orono? And we ought to double check all the times."

"I put it to him pretty good," said Wilson. "But we can go back there any time you want. I got the name and phone number."

"We may do that," said Fraser.

Nelson said, "We're missing something here, though. It's easy to find a motive for killing Smithers. But what about Volcker? Nobody had anything against the guy, as far as we know. And as far as Werkman is concerned, he has no motive that we know about for either murder. He had the opportunity to commit both murders. He was around for both, anyway. Those are the leads we got. No real evidence pointing to one person, no real alibi clearing a guy for sure," summarized Nelson.

"Right," said Fraser. "Maybe it's time to sit down with Mr. Orono. Let's see if we can find any holes in his stories."

Wilson agreed to line up a meeting for the three of them with Orono.

☠ ♥ ☠

Nelson, Fraser and Wilson got to the Fair Meadow Inn at six-thirty, a time when Orono said he would be finished with his daily shift. The officers waited for half an hour in the lobby. Nelson was close to his boiling point when Orono appeared.

"Sorry," Orono said. "A guy checked out without paying. I had to fix it. Come on into the bar and I'll buy you a drink."

"Skip it," snapped Nelson. "We don't drink on duty. Let's go somewhere private."

"My office is being used by the night man," said Orono. "The bar's the most private place we got here."

"You have rooms, don't you?"

"Okay. If you insist." Orono went to the front desk and got a key from the clerk, motioning to the officers to follow him. He opened the door of a neat room containing a small conference table surrounded by half a dozen comfortable chairs. The men sat down.

"There was another death in the bridge crowd yesterday," began Nelson.

"What are you talking about? Hermann?" responded Orono.

"That's right."

"I heard he had a heart attack. Everybody loved the guy. He talked too much, but the whole crowd loved him."

"Not the whole crowd," responded Nelson. "Maybe one person didn't. As of now, we're simply investigating his death."

"My God. He was murdered too?"

"Maybe it was murder, maybe not. You were there at last night's game, I hear? Tell us about it."

"What's there to tell? I played in the game. I didn't win. I left after the game. What makes you think his death was murder?"

"We have certain evidence. Get one thing straight here. We're asking the questions, not you." Nelson paused for a moment to let this sink in. "Did you wait for the scores after the game?" he asked, using his newfound knowledge in what he thought was an expert way.

"Last night? I guess I did. I always do. So what?"

"Who else was there?"

"Hermann. Let's see. Stewart. He runs the club. The Duffys were both there. Charles was waiting. Werkman I mean. I don't know who else. Maybe the Lemones."

"Who left with you?"

"Nobody as far as I know. We had a poor game and as soon as I saw we weren't in the running, I put on my coat and left."

"What did you do right after the game?"

"The usual."

"Meaning?"

"I got in my damn car and went home. It was zero degrees and snow was blowing. Do you think I waited around looking for three more players to set up a game in the parking lot?"

"I told you before, I'm asking the questions," said Nelson. "More smart remarks and we'll all go down to the station. You can spend the night there if you like. My treat." Orono looked miffed at this outburst, but sat quietly.

"Was there anybody else in the parking lot?" asked Nelson.

"I wasn't paying attention. All I did was start my car, scrape the frost off the windshield, and take off."

"There were no other cars in the lot?"

"I wasn't looking."

"You're not helping much. Did you see a Chevy Cavalier? Black one?"

"I told you I wasn't paying attention. All I was trying to do was get out of there."

Fraser asked, "What kind of car do you drive?"

"Pontiac."

"What make and year?"

"Sunfire. 1997."

"I see. What color?"

"Dark blue."

"How long have you had it?"

"I bought it second-hand in late ninety-nine."

Nelson said, "And what time did you get home?"

"I got back to the motel here about midnight."

"Did anybody see you?"

"The night clerk might have seen me. I don't know. I hope to hell you put all those others through the third degree, not just me."

"We have a murder here. Maybe two murders, in fact. You were around when both deaths occurred. We're just collecting facts, right now. We're not accusing anybody of anything."

"You keep talking like that and I'd better get me a lawyer before we go any further."

"You won't need a lawyer if you have nothing to hide," said Nelson.

Wilson asked, "Was this the same clerk that was on duty Sunday night? The one who saw you come in late after the Smithers murder?"

"No. This was a different guy." He gave Wilson the name.

"You knew Smithers, didn't you?" asked Nelson.

"Sure. We all knew him. He was the ugliest guy in the bridge crowd. I told him before," Orono said, nodding at Wilson. "Smithers stole a team game off me last weekend."

Wilson said, "You knew him more than just at bridge. You had some rug problems with him too, didn't you?"

Orono's face flushed. He hesitated for a while before answering. "I told you that last time. Maybe I better call my lawyer."

Nelson said, "You can make this as tough as you want for all of us. If you want a lawyer, you get to spend a lot of your dough and we get to make four or five trips instead of one. Right now this is just a routine call. We're checking out all the people at the club, and the people at the Adam's Mark the night of the tournament. Just give me the dope on this old stuff between him and you."

Orono again paused to consider Nelson's words. "Okay. Smithers and I had a rug deal. Smithers screwed me totally. He took away my property and every cent I had. That's why I have this bullshit job now. You can check my story in the police records. You probably have already."

Wilson nodded.

Nelson said, "Okay. What about Volcker? You knew him, I presume?"

"Sure. We played against each other for years. I played with him once. He was old-fashioned as hell. But we never had a grudge against each other."

Nelson said, "If we need more from you, or if Wilson finds a problem with your alibi, we'll be back to see you."

On the way back to the station, Wilson said, "Something about that guy gets to me. I find his behavior very erotic."

Fraser and Nelson looked at each other, puzzled. "I didn't know you felt that way," said Nelson.

"You never know what he's going to do next."

The two lieutenants choked with laughter.

CHAPTER 27

JACK ARRIVED HOME AT SEVEN THAT NIGHT. HELEN gave him the coolest of welcomes, just brushing his lips when he offered a kiss. A red head peered around the doorway into the living room. "When are we eating?" it demanded. "I'm hungry."

"Everything's ready. Come on."

Sandra and Rick joined them in the dining room and sat down to one of Helen's gourmet meals of poached salmon and a Caesar salad. "Hey, this is great," said Jack. "Sockeye?"

"Not fish again," complained Rick.

'Yes to both of you," laughed Helen. "It's good for you."

"That sauce is cool," remarked Sandra.

"Your little fish market comes up with great stuff," said Jack.

"He always sells me twice as much as I ask for. I order for four and he seems to double it. There's lots left if anyone wants seconds."

"He sees you coming," said Jack.

"It's good cold. I can't remember you turning down a salmon sandwich."

"You just haven't the heart to ask him to cut what you really want."

"He's not doing that well. He needs to build up his clientele, but I like him. I love his stuff. He's so good with special orders too. Oysters and scallops. Everything's so fresh."

"What a softie."

"I hope you get some bologna one of these days," complained Rick.

"You're full of it now," said Sandra. "Can I have more?"

In spite of his protests, Rick cleaned his plate. Helen asked the children to clean up the kitchen and, as usual, Rick complained and Sandra agreed immediately. They left Helen and Jack with some privacy.

Helen told Jack about Hermann's death.

"I'm sorry to hear that," said Jack. "You're going to miss him. We'll all miss him. He always seemed in good shape for his age; I wouldn't have expected this. When is the funeral?"

"I don't know," answered Helen. "I don't even know where he lived. I feel very sad. I loved Hermann. Art Fraser seems to think there's something strange about his death. Hermann was so healthy-looking, Art can't believe he had a heart attack."

"Art Fraser. How the hell does he come into this?"

"He phoned this morning to tell us about Hermann. He's in charge of the Smithers' murder investigation."

"Your friend Art," said Jack.

"That's right. Everybody knows we're an item now." Jack did not know exactly what to make of this remark. "Art is nice to his partners, I'll say that for him."

"Huh? Oh." Jack began thinking aloud. "Yes, he is nice. You say he's been assigned to the case. I thought he was in traffic or something?"

"He was. A full-time traffic specialist. He looked into stolen cars, theft rings, and so on. Not right now, though. He's assigned to homicide investigations."

"You'd think our brilliant detectives could make something out of the break-in incident. There has to be a connection with the car that Harry spotted that night. He identified the model and year positively. I suppose if anyone can make something out of that information, Fraser should be able to."

"It might help if I pay a visit to my policeman boyfriend tomorrow," Helen grinned. "I can talk to Art. He'll help me. I know he will."

"You played with Hermann last night. It's hard to imagine that we'll never see him again."

"I've played lots with him over the past few years. You know, something really funny happened at the end of our game last night."

"What was that?"

"We sat down to play against Charles and his partner, and as soon as we said hello, Hermann started to get very excited. You know him, he never raises his voice. He said something garbled to Charles about 'cards in the pocket' and 'you were the one'. Then he lost his concentration and seemed to drift off. Our game was wrecked. I wonder now if he was having a stroke or something right then."

"Did you say anything to Fraser about the conversation? He might be able to make something out of it."

"No, I didn't. I wasn't thinking about that when Art called to tell me about Hermann. But maybe I should. That phrase 'cards in the pocket' makes you wonder. At the time, I thought Hermann was just talking about the duplicate board on the table, but now I'm not so sure."

"Come on, I've played with Charles for years — are you saying he's been switching decks or something?"

"I don't know what I'm saying. Maybe Hermann was just having some sort of attack and it was crazy talk. But I think I should tell Art. At least he's one policeman who's going to be favorable to our side. Nelson and Wilson don't have much sympathy with us."

"Maybe meeting with Fraser is not such a bad idea. Could you do that?" asked Jack.

"Absolutely."

Helen was not quite as sure about an encounter with Art Fraser as she had made out in her talk with Jack. She decided the best way to approach Fraser, if she ever worked up the courage, was just the same way she always had. They were friends, they played the odd game of bridge together, and they met only in public places. She knew Art realized that she was the better player, although he occasionally commented on some of her decisions. He apologized for every error he made, although Helen could tell that he was not aware of all his mistakes. She did not bring them to his attention. He played with her only once or twice a year, but every time they played he complimented her on her play and told her that she was one of his favorite partners. What was in it for him? Friendship? Unusual for a man. She knew she was attractive, and men often had sex in mind when they pursued a relationship with a woman. Well, too bad. She felt that a discussion with Art right now was vital and she would have to overcome her uncertainty. She would have to go after him without knowing exactly what he wanted.

Helen's phone rang at nine the following morning. "Hi, Helen," said a business-like voice over the phone.

Helen's heart pounded when she recognized the voice. Please don't do anything stupid, she thought. "Hi, Art. How are things?"

"Fine. We're working our way through the Smithers case, but we're not breaking any speed records. It must be bothering you and Jack a lot."

"You can say that again. Jack seems to be really depressed by the whole thing."

"I called to ask if we could get together and go over a few things related to the case. Maybe you can help us."

"I'd be happy to do that. Your guys Nelson and Wilson just don't seem friendly. They haven't said a kind word to either Jack or me on any of their visits."

"They're good officers, but I'm not surprised at your comment. Bryan Nelson is known for being brusque. I've known him for a long time. What I was thinking, Helen, is that you may well have some information that we don't. If I went over the events of the past few days with you, I could understand what you've picked up and see what's important to us. We may find something we could use."

"I'd do anything to get them off Jack's case and on to the right track. In fact, I was going to give you a call." Helen hoped she did not sound too anxious.

"We could meet in my office. I could spare an hour, some time this week. The sooner the better."

Helen was relieved at the suggestion of a meeting in Fraser's office. "What time have you in mind?" she asked.

"To be honest, today some time would be best."

"I could do that, " said Helen, thinking that Sandra and Rick were away until four. "Actually, right now would work for me. I could be there in half an hour."

They agreed and she arrived just after ten at police headquarters. A constable handling reception directed her to Fraser's office. He was on the phone when she arrived, and motioned to her to take a seat. She was happy to have a few moments to gather herself before talking to him.

After exchanging greetings, Helen said, "Art, I know in my heart that Jack didn't commit that murder."

"I can't imagine Jack murdering anybody. Actually, we've gathered enough facts now to clear Jack completely, in my opinion. I'm not a judge, and I have limited influence, but if I can do something as a friend, I will. The investigation will bring all the facts out, I'm confident of that. The odds are good that we'll get the person who did this, but there are no guarantees in this business."

"That's reassuring," said Helen. "I guess I was confident it would turn out all right for us in the end, but it has been very upsetting."

"I'm sure it has. Look, the reason I called you was to explore any information you may be able to share. We need everything we can get. You never know what little details might be important. Let me get my notebook out."

"Okay," said Helen. "The big item that bothers me, one that nobody seems to be following up on, is the fact that someone broke into our house a month before the murder. And the person that did the break-in stole Jack's knife."

"Slow down a minute here," said Fraser. "We do know about the break-in, and we are investigating it."

"Don't you think that the person who stole the knife just might be the murderer? Find that person and you've solved your case."

"That may be a little simplistic. I'm not saying you're wrong. Maybe we're not as fast as you might like, but don't forget that we only just found out that Jack's knife had been stolen. That wasn't clear, at first. The police don't have unlimited manpower to go into all these petty crimes. And we don't even have a plate number from the car involved. All we have is a firm maybe on the kind of car, the year, and the color. That's not a heck of a lot to go on."

"But our neighbor, Harry, says it definitely was a 2001 model of a Chevrolet something or other."

"We know all that," said Fraser. "There are thousands of Cavaliers in New York state. It'll take time to track a specific car down."

"You have to get started, don't you?"

"Believe me, we're started," said Fraser. "It's a major job and we're giving it priority." He assured Helen that they had just agreed that morning to use a better method in tracking down the Cavalier. "I'm sure if it's a New York car, and if it belongs to someone we recognize, someone close to our bridge scene here, we'll find it. If it's an out-of-state vehicle, then we have another problem."

"Okay. I didn't realize you were actually doing anything with the car investigation. Now the next point is about my bridge club. You know I have this little bridge group at our golf club?"

"I guess I've heard you mention it."

"It's an invitational group and we have a game once a month. The ladies love the worldwide matchpoint game, so I always run one once a year. They like to see their names in print if they have a good game."

"Like the rest of the world."

"Exactly. Here's my point. The infamous break-in happened the day before the game."

"And?"

"Jack and I think whoever broke in could have been after the hand records for the worldwide game. The burglar, whoever it was, might have thought we stored them at home."

"I see. Your theory is that the motive for the break-in was hand records."

"Yes. Exactly."

"Did the burglar actually get anything? I thought all he took was a knife."

"That's right, he got nothing else. My point is that he was after bridge hands. Hand records, I mean. Whoever it was really liked to cheat. He thought he had an opportunity to get one of those booklets and look it over before the game."

"You're saying the intruder may have been looking for hand records that he thought were in your den. You interrupted his search, and all he got was a knife for his trouble."

"That's right. Jack actually had the hand records in his office safe. But the guy must have thought we had them at home."

"Is anybody in your club that keen on winning?"

"No way. They're all pussycats. There's not a serious player in the lot. They love to win but they'd never do anything like this."

"Okay. So if there is a connection between that worldwide game and your break-in, the person is not from your club."

"That's what we think. The women in my club are smart in many ways, but they can't remember a hand for five minutes after playing it. I can't imagine any of them studying records of hands they had never played. Now, there's one more thing."

"Just one?" smiled Fraser.

"The night Hermann died, or maybe was murdered, he and I were playing together. He had a run-in with Charles Werkman just as the last round started. They had an argument before the first hand was played, and then Hermann seemed to be off in space all through the last round. He was fine up to that point."

"That's odd. Hermann was one of a kind — such a gentleman. Everybody will miss him. Tell me about the run-in with Charles."

"Let's see if I can remember the details. We sat down and said hello, and then suddenly Hermann started talking to Charles about 'cards in the pocket'. Hermann got more and more excited. He raised his voice, and almost shouted, 'You were the one. Talking to Smithers in the washroom.' And Charles didn't seem to know what Hermann was talking about. That was exactly when Hermann went into his trance."

"Now that is interesting," said Fraser. "Could there be a connection here, between Werkman and Smithers, and then Werkman and Hermann? This may be worth looking into."

"Do you think Hermann stumbled onto something that might tie Charles to Bob Smithers' murder?"

"Could be. Could be."

"But that could make Charles the..." Helen interrupted herself and shuddered.

"Exactly. It's a horrible thought. Let's not get ahead of ourselves, though. What we have to do is to use all of our modern tools and go over the evidence systematically. You've passed on some useful facts. Do me a favor, though, Helen – don't repeat what we've said to anyone, even Jack." Fraser now realized that all of their other leads might have been red herrings. He was not going to admit to Helen that the police had not looked into Werkman's activities at all.

When Jack arrived home that night, Helen told him about her meeting with Fraser. Her eyes twinkled as she voiced the policeman's name. "Art is putting more priority on trying to investigate our break-in. They all agree that the matter needs looking into. I went through the story, your missing knife, the murder and all. Art was apologetic.

He says they've already got a major investigation going to find the car and the owner. And he agreed that the chances are good they'll be able to pin down a few vehicles in the area and check them out."

"That's a step forward," said Jack.

"At least we've got someone in the police force on our side," said Helen.

CHAPTER 28

THAT AFTERNOON, THE THREE OFFICERS MET IN Nelson's office to review the case.

"I had a good talk with Helen Duffy this morning," said Fraser. "She tells me that Volcker had a run-in with Werkman the night he died."

"If all these bridge players keep running into one another, somebody might get hurt," said Wilson.

"Somebody did," said Nelson. "Two people, in case you forgot."

Fraser continued, "She told me the strangest damned story about the night Volcker died. He was playing bridge that night with Helen. They sat down, near the end of the evening, to play against Werkman. Volcker blurts out, all of a sudden, 'Cards in the pocket.' Nobody knew what he was talking about. Then Volcker gets all red in the face and says, practically shouting, 'You were the one talking to Smithers in the washroom.' Hermann totally loses his concentration and plays the last few hands like a beginner. The guy was a very good card player. One of the best, in fact. Next thing we know, he turns up dead in a parking lot."

"So he and Werkman had a big argument. These bridge players ought to form a debating club," said Nelson. "We haven't paid much attention to Werkman so far."

"That's what I've been thinking, too. I'm wondering if somehow Werkman has been cheating, and that's what the 'cards in the pocket' was all about. If Hermann somehow knew, and was going to report him, it would devastating – he'd be banned for life. This would give him a motive," said Fraser. "In fact, it ties him in to both murders, since Hermann mentioned Smithers too, so maybe Smithers found out and had to be silenced, or maybe he was even involved somehow and they had a falling out."

"It has possibilities. There's nothing here that's solid enough to go to the DA with. But we may be getting warm."

Kathy knocked on the door and flashed a file. Wilson was quick to invite her in and make her welcome.

"Here's the work on the Cavaliers that you were in a hurry for, Russ," she said.

"Oh, yes. Thanks Kathy," Wilson said, taking the file. He looked it over quickly and a broad grin appeared on his face. He moved over to the table where they were gathered, doing a few steps of a heavy-weight hip-hop on the way.

"We've got something for the D.A. here, I bet," he said.

"And?" replied Nelson, gesturing him to get on with matters.

"You're going to like this. Guess who owned a black Chevy Cavalier and traded it in two days after the date that Duffy reported the break-in in his garage? Charles Werkman."

"Well, now," said Nelson, his impatience changing to a tone of interest. "Tell us more."

"That's it in a nutshell. The car's at a Hyundai dealer now. The dealership is listed as the owner. Werkman traded it in on a new Sonata. But he owned the Cavalier at the time of the break-in. There is no doubt about that."

"That's a good piece of work. Werkman, eh. Good work."

"Damned good," Fraser said in hushed tones. The three detectives realized that this was the break they had been waiting for.

"So much for all the other crap," said Nelson. "We can forget Orono and Duffy. Werkman is our man. Now we get Werkman to tip his hand, open up a bit, and give us something solid without him getting advance wind of our suspicion."

"Are we going to arrest Werkman?" asked Wilson.

"We can't," said Fraser. "Not yet, anyway. We need to tie this up in an airtight package so the D.A. will jump on it. The D.A. should buy our case on motive and opportunity, but we need a little more."

Wilson beamed, "I like that. I say we get Werkman in here and work him over for a few hours. I bet he'll crack."

Fraser responded, "When you say 'work him over', I assume you mean verbally."

"Oh, yeah," said Wilson. "If we bring him down here and question him for six, eight hours, don't you think he'll cave in?"

Fraser replied, "We can't count on it, but that's what we're going to have to do, I suppose. We're going to do it at the right time, though. We need to think the thing out several steps ahead before we pull him in."

Nelson outlined the chain of events relating to the break-in, identifying the car driven by the person breaking in, the information they had on car ownership and how that tied Werkman in to the acquisition of the murder weapon and the crime. "This is a lot of theory, so far."

Fraser said, "It explains a lot of things, though. See, let's keep the theory simple: Werkman was accused of cheating by Smithers. Werkman's reputation as a bridge player would have been ruined if he were convicted of cheating. He might be out of bridge forever. I've heard of cheating cases where guys have never been allowed to play again. For some people, this doesn't matter, but in the case of a really serious player, or a professional, proof of cheating can be the end of a guy's career. It would have affected his reputation in other ways, too. Someone in the company he works for would be bound to hear about it. He would have faced ridicule, maybe even have lost his job. Possibly forced to leave town. He had to have it covered up. He had to have it covered up so badly that he was willing to kill Smithers to make sure it stayed hidden.

"That would be a murder motive. No doubt in my mind. Then you add in the fact that Smithers was easy to hate. Three quarters of Smithers' acquaintances hated him. He could start a row just by opening his mouth."

Nelson asked, "And what about a motive for the Volcker murder?"

"That all ties in with the information I got from Helen Duffy," said Fraser. "It sounds to me like Werkman was fiddling with bridge hands – maybe keeping pre-dealt decks in his pockets. Let's say that Smithers caught on to Werkman and accused him openly of cheating; Volcker overheard the conversation. Werkman disposed of the problem by killing Smithers. But the night Hermann played with Helen, he brought it up to Werkman's face. When Werkman found out that Volcker knew all about it, Werkman decided he had to get rid of him as well. Two hours later, Volcker was dead in his parking lot. I'll bet that's what happened. We know that a second murder is always easier than a first."

"It fits," said Nelson.

"We can tie in the reason for the break-in at Duffy's and the theft of the murder weapon. If Werkman is a real cheat, and the facts certainly point that way, he was after something in Duffy's home the night he stole the Buck Nighthawk. Helen thinks he was after a set of hand records. There was a big game the next day, and Werkman wanted to get his hands on information that would let him win."

"I have no idea what you're talking about," muttered Nelson.

"Me neither," added Wilson.

"Don't worry about it. In a bridge sense, all of our facts fit the theory that Werkman committed both murders. We have some good points all round," continued Fraser. "You guys have done a heck of a job turning up what we've got so far. We're almost ready for the D.A."

"Almost?" said a disappointed Wilson. "Too bad we couldn't make more use of some of the bridge crowd."

Fraser said, "We've got Duffy totally pissed off at being a suspect. We won't get much help from him."

Wilson continued. "Maybe not. But he'll be happy as hell to know he's off the suspect list. He must know it anyway, deep down. But his wife and kids are involved as well. I wonder if we could involve him and get Werkman to spill a little more. They're good friends."

Nelson broke in. "Here's a for instance. We need to know more about Werkman's activities at the time of the murder. You won't get that by direct questioning. He'll just clam up and work out a way to cover his trail. But say we involve the Duffys. Maybe they could pry something out. Maybe even get the solid stuff the D.A. wants."

Fraser said, "Werkman is pretty cagey. If he knows we are on to him we make it easier for him."

Nelson went on. "Let him go on as he is until we're ready. We don't have all that much to confront him with, not yet anyway. You never know what makes a guy crack. Sometimes the smallest bit of hearsay gets a guy feeling guilty and he opens up. Suppose we work on the guilt angle. Nobody outside this room needs to know what we're doing. Let's say we arrest Duffy. And then use that somehow to upset Werkman and get him to break and confess, or at least do something stupid. This might be a case where a little psychology helps us out. We need to get Werkman feeling a little sorry for his friend and then trip himself up."

"I'm not sure we ought to involve the Duffys. You think a guy who kills two people has got feelings for friends? Hit me again," said Fraser.

"Everybody has some feelings."

Fraser was about to launch a sarcastic analysis of Nelson's logic, when he remembered Kesten's words. Make peace with him and treat him with respect. Fraser persevered. "I still don't think Werkman will show us a guilt trip. He's a hard nut. And look at the bad publicity Duffy gets. Not just him. The wife and kids too."

"Okay. I'll back off the arrest angle," said Nelson. "But how about setting Duffy up as a suspect – a straw man. We can make Werkman think Duffy is under serious suspicion. We might have more luck getting Werkman to open up if he's distracted. How could he know the difference?"

"That might work. I could drop the word to Werkman's girlfriend about Duffy being under suspicion. She'd get the news to Werkman in an instant. That might help set him up to talk more easily," said Fraser.

Nelson continued. "A small point. I wonder if he was driving the Chevy or the Sonata when Volcker was killed?"

"Definitely the Sonata," said Wilson. "The dealer record shows he traded two days after the date of the break-in. I told you guys that before."

"That's right, you did," said Nelson. "So we know he was driving the Sonata when he killed Volcker."

"For sure. I got a new tire wrench from the Hyundai service manager and took it over to the coroner's office. We took some measurements, length, diameter, angles, and the coroner thinks it's a good fit with the wound on Volcker's head."

"Good work, Russ. Some days you show potential," said Nelson.

"Gee, thanks."

Nelson said, "We need to find that tire wrench. It's gotta be our murder weapon."

Wilson replied, "Right. But ow'm I supposed to look in the back of Werkman's Sonata without him knowing?"

Nelson said, "You're going to the dealer. Ask if the service people know anything. Start there, anyway. He might have been back for a service call."

"Yeah. They know me over at the dealership there and it won't take a minute. If that don't work, I'll get a warrant, go over to Werkman's place and have a look."

Fraser asked, "Hey, you know the people at the dealership, you say?"

"I met them the other day."

"Get them to call Werkman. Pull the car in on some pretext. They have recalls all the time. They're a routine sort of thing. All car dealers, not just Hyundai."

"That might work. It'll keep Werkman from knowing our game, anyway," said Nelson.

"Here's something we ought to do," said Fraser. "We've got to get the D.A. to give us a warrant to search Werkman's place. If we can find some decks of cards, maybe even a pair of trousers or a jacket with cards still in the pockets, we'll have a good piece of evidence. Could be the scabbard for the knife is lying around. Maybe even bridge books marked up with the hands he used. I'll bet we find something useful there. It's possible Werkman has been careless and not gotten rid of those items. We should get the warrant pretty quickly, too, before he knows we suspect anything."

"I'll look after the warrant," said Nelson.

"Another angle here," said Fraser. "A witness would be worth a lot. I'm wondering if one of Smithers' teammates didn't see someone hanging around after the game. Smithers' team all went for a couple of drinks after the game. They stayed for almost an hour in the bar. Werkman must have noticed what they were doing and waited around. Then he followed Smithers to the parking lot. How did Smithers get there? If he went outside, he'd have to go through the lobby of the hotel. Someone might have seen Werkman following him. There's an exit to the parking garage right near the bar. If he went out that way, it's dark there and he could have been followed easily. Smithers' team all went to the hotel lot, not the cut-rate lot. They parted company with Smithers somewhere in the hotel, but one of them may have spotted Werkman tailing him."

Nelson said, "Maybe we ought to get a mug shot of Werkman and show it to the hotel staff that were on that night."

"Yeah. The bartender, doormen, people like that," added Wilson.

"We're on track now," said Fraser. "We better check with the staff in the restaurant while we're at it. Werkman could have hung around in the restaurant — it's an open concept design — there are no walls to block your vision. He could have sat there and kept an eye on the bar planning to follow Smithers after he came out."

"I can talk to them too," said Wilson.

"And the cleaning staff," said Fraser. "He might have hung out in a washroom and been spotted. Can you look after that, Russ?"

"Be glad to."

"It's probably best that I talk to the players on Smithers' team. I know them all and can probably find out what they know without mentioning Werkman by name. Away we go," said Fraser.

"A witness would sew this up," said Nelson.

"That's what I think," said Fraser. "And if you get anything at all talking to the staff, call me right away."

"I'm off," said Wilson.

CHAPTER 29

CHARLES WERKMAN LEFT WORK THAT SAME DAY with a feeling of satisfaction. He had been in contact with one of his firm's largest customers, and nailed down an order for over a million dollars. That's a lot of paint, he thought. The customer's agent had phoned in and asked to be connected to the salesman responsible for the account. Charles lied, said the salesman was not in, and asked if he could help. The customer's agent had relayed all the details of the order and Charles recorded them and confirmed quantities and dates. The customer was solid, and although the order was spread over two years, his company would appreciate the revenue. Instead of phoning the salesman and telling him that the order had come in, Charles was mean enough to try and undercut the salesman's commission by letting the sales manager know right away that he was responsible for the deal. It's not as if he did anything for it, he thought, but I'll send a note to the salesman to cover myself.

After work that day, he went to his apartment to clean up before heading to the restaurant where he was meeting Betsy. They planned to have a quick dinner before a game at Stewart's club, and had made a vague commitment to a post-game rendezvous. Charles had planned to discuss their bidding agreements over supper, but Betsy was full of gossip about Jack.

"I think the police are going to arrest him," she said.

"Oh, no. That can't be right," replied Charles.

"I've heard it," insisted Betsy. "It's all over town."

"What's all over town is totally wrong," said Charles. "I know Jack's hunting knife was the murder weapon, so someone had it in for Jack and for Bob Smithers. But there's no way on earth I could see Jack pulling a stunt like that. Murder? Somebody is nuts. Tell me another, Betsy. Jack and Bob had their disagreements, but Jack's not a man to murder anybody. Verbal fights. Cuss a guy down. But never violence."

"That's not what I'm hearing. I have pretty good sources."

Charles slammed the door on Betsy's line of conversation. "Let's talk about Blackwood. You know that mix-up we had when hearts was the agreed suit, and we got to slam missing two aces?"

"Yes – the hand where they misdefended and I made six anyway."

"That doesn't make it right. Here's what we have to do when hearts are agreed." He explained his ideas for dealing with the problem.

As they finished their meal, Betsy reminded him of the starting time for the game, and they had to hurry to make it. During the evening, neither concentrated to their capability. Betsy saw that Charles' play was not up to its usual standard and knew that something was bothering him. They finished below average, and although Charles was not showing outright animosity, neither was he radiating warmth. They drove to Charles' apartment in silence. Charles showed her in and opened a bottle of cold wine.

"Sorry we had such a rotten game tonight," she said.

"It happens. No one is perfect every session. I could have played better, too."

"Here's to your good health," she said, raising her glass in a toast. "This is lovely wine."

"From California. I'm glad you like it."

"I'm not sure what threw me off. The second table we played at — Harold made a silly overcall. I never thought we had a slam."

"Six spades was cold," he said. "In fact you could even make seven if he didn't cash his ace of clubs. I had no idea your hand was that good."

"I was going to make a slam try," said Betsy. "I didn't quite know how to do it and then, I thought, if Harold has a good hand, we couldn't make a slam anyway."

Their post-game amusements were usually thrilling when they followed a successful bridge session, but tonight Betsy sensed that she had a challenge to meet. She knew that her tight-fitting sweater and skirt outfit was Charles' favorite, and she made sure that there was plenty of physical contact as they sipped their wine on his chesterfield. After kicking off her shoes and putting her feet in Charles' lap, she could feel that a few touches were stirring the senses of both of them.

"Why don't we go to your bedroom?" she asked.

The question distracted Charles completely. "Let's just finish our wine," he muttered.

Betsy had no option but to comply with her host and leave when her glass was empty. As she drove home, she had a numb feeling that she had done something totally wrong. She recalled that the same thing had happened the previous time she had suggested that Charles take her into his bedroom. He had turned into a cold frog, and she could not understand his behavior then, either.

At home after Betsy left, Charles reflected that a week had passed since the murder of Smithers, and three days since he had bludgeoned Hermann. His emotions were on a roller coaster. One moment he was feeling tight as a drum, sure that he would be caught. The next moment he exulted, reflecting that, so far, the police had not asked him a single question. He had not tried to evade them, they just hadn't contacted him. He was keeping all of his relationships on an even keel, everything normal. Go to work, play some bridge, show no signs of unusual behavior.

Betsy says they're investigating Jack, he reflected. That shows the intelligence of some of the cops. That'll never go anywhere. But the longer they drag that out, the better I like it. They'll tie up all their manpower. They won't have time to think about me. He slept a little less fitfully that night.

The next morning Art Fraser called him at his office. Art knew that Charles and Betsy had had a poor game the night before and Charles would not be feeling any pride in their performance.

"You guys didn't shine as usual last night," said Art.

"Below average," replied Charles. "I'm trying to forget it."

"Happens to everyone. We weren't great either. There were some fun hands, though."

"Usually are," came the sullen reply.

"Listen," said Art. "Are you real busy today?"

Warning bells went off in Charles' mind. Show no signs of unusual behavior. "We're always busy. Do you need some paint?" he joked.

Fraser laughed. "Not today. I wonder if you can drop over for a chat. We're talking to a number of bridge players about Bob Smithers' murder. I'd like to get your slant."

"I don't know what I can tell you that you don't already know," said Charles.

"We can just run over the facts," said Art. "Every little clue will help us. You know Jack Duffy pretty well."

"And?" said Charles.

"You know he had that argument with Bob the day of the murder. You were there for the whole thing."

"You mean for the argument?"

"Exactly. We believe that's an important part of the whole picture, and we're pulling together all the details of the incident. How about late this afternoon? Could you drop over to headquarters about four?"

"I guess I could. I may be a little late if something urgent crops up."

"That'll be no problem. You know how to get here?"

Charles assured Fraser that he knew where headquarters were and hung up the phone. His stomach began to churn. He decided to skip lunch. Concentration on work became difficult early in the afternoon, and impossible as the day wore on. He could think only of the upcoming talk with Fraser, and how he should handle himself. Panic struck. Should he leave town? Should he invent some false evidence that might incriminate Jack? His mind became numb and his thoughts were all blanks. There was no experience in his background that he could draw on. He muddled through the afternoon, accomplishing no work and finally arriving at police headquarters at four-thirty.

CHAPTER 30

EARLIER THAT DAY, FRASER HAD CALLED A MEETING of his investigating team. Wilson gave his report first. "Here's the latest, guys. They called in the Sonata like I asked, and Werkman left it there all day. They gave him a vehicle to drive. There are good people at that dealership. I had a couple of hours to go over the car with nobody bothering me. Guess what? There was no tire wrench in the car."

Nelson said, "Damn. That tells us something, but it probably won't help us with the D.A."

"Maybe it will. All the Hyundais come with a little pouch in the spare tire pocket. The pouch holds three items – a wrench, and two levers. The pouch had both levers, but the wrench was missing. The service guy swore that the car went out with a tire wrench. He says he personally inspected it, and he even showed Werkman how to use the small tire for a spare."

"It sounds like we're on the right track about Werkman."

Fraser asked, "Any luck with the hotel staff?"

"I'm going to see them at one. I got a couple of great mug shots." He showed Nelson and Fraser his black and white enlargements of Werkman, and notes on the suspect's physical characteristics.

"Good work," said Fraser. "I talked to Smithers' teammates, but I drew a blank. None of them saw anything helpful. We're down to our last chance for a witness. It'll have to be one of the hotel staff."

Nelson said, "I got a search warrant for Werkman's place from the D.A.'s office. He went along that far anyway."

"Werkman is coming down here about four. I told him we needed to talk about Duffy and the argument he had with Smithers the day of the murder. But I'm getting an idea," said Fraser.

"Again?" asked Nelson.

"Two ideas, actually. Do you still have that tire wrench the dealer gave you?" he asked Wilson.

"It's in my car."

"How about this. Werkman got rid of his tire wrench somewhere. We'll never find the damned thing unless he was very, very careless. Or maybe we get very, very lucky searching. I agree we should go through the motions, but a guy as smart as that could find a million places to hide the thing forever."

"Okay."

"So, take your tire wrench to a butcher shop."

"A butcher shop? What in hell for?"

"Get the butcher to show you some fresh blood from somewhere. Pig's blood. Sheep's blood. It doesn't matter. Dip the end of the tire wrench. No, wait. Take along a small artist's brush. Paint the end of the wrench, you know, a design consistent with the wound. Blood on one side of it. Don't make it too neat. If Werkman washed off his wrench before he threw it out, he'll know right away. If he didn't, when I spring the thing on him, he'll go gaga."

"I see where you're going. This might work. It just might work. It's certainly worth a try."

"I'll pick my time to unwrap this wrench at some point during our interview. I won't say a word, but I'll make sure Werkman sees it. If it is the same type of wrench, and it's covered with dried blood, it might scare the hell out of him."

"Another thing, even if he did clean the wrench he chucked out, he might have forgotten exactly how well he cleaned it. He was in a hurry maybe. He might have given it a quick, careless wipe, and then flung it out the window of his car or something. Or maybe he dug a hole and buried it in the woods."

"Right. If he rushed, that's in our favor. I don't have to say a word. You just bring the wrench up where he can see it clearly. You unwrap it. We'll get his reaction and go on from there."

"I'd like to be there," said Nelson. "This ought to be interesting."

"I'll tell you what. This might work even better. I'll discuss the Smithers murder until he's tired of it. I'll go over every minute detail I can think of. Then I'll switch to Volcker's death. I'll feed him a few details, and then ask him what he thinks. Then I'll call you in. Have the wrench all wrapped up in a white sheet or some white packing material. You put it on my desk and unwrap it. We say nothing for a while. Give him lots of rope."

"I like that."

"Don't get your hopes up too high. Maybe we'll strike out. But maybe not."

"I'm thinking about Volcker," said Nelson. "Does Werkman know what we know there?"

"What do you mean?" asked Wilson.

"The word was that Volcker had a heart attack. At least, that he died of natural causes. The three of us know that he was murdered. Does Werkman know that?"

Fraser replied, "No. Werkman may not know that. We've told a few people. I told Helen and she will have told Jack. We told Orono when we questioned him."

"Don't forget we told Appleton the day we visited the bridge club," said Nelson.

"That's true, but we asked him to keep quiet about it. Let's hope that he did. The rest of the crowd still assumes that Hermann died naturally. We might surprise Werkman when we tell him we know Hermann was murdered. We can hit him with Hermann's murder and with the so-called murder weapon."

"That might do it," said Nelson.

"You said two ideas," remarked Wilson.

"Okay. If you have any luck finding a witness down at the hotel, let me know as soon as possible. If we can hit Werkman with a witness report, the chances that he'll fold are much better."

"Even a suggestion of a witness might soften him up," said Nelson.

"I think you're right," said Fraser. "But a real witness would go a long way. Not to mention help with the D.A. So, Russ, if you come up with something let me or Bryan know right away. I'd like to work it into the grilling."

CHAPTER 31

FRASER KNEW HE HAD TO APPEAR RELAXED AND off-hand. This was the most important interview of his career so far. Somehow, he had to extract some sort of damning evidence or best of all, a confession, out of Werkman. And he had to respect Miranda requirements in the process. He was not quite sure how he could accomplish all that, but at least he had a plan. Werkman must be the murderer, so he'll be uptight about everything. I've got to be very cautious and non-committal. I can't offer anything or admit anything. Maybe he'll lie about Jack's activities and try to incriminate Jack. He'd like to divert suspicion away from himself. These are surely the first murders he's committed. As far as we know, he's not a hardened criminal. I've got to surprise him and make him think he's not on the suspect list. Then I need to pull something out quickly that'll unbalance him. If I do it right, he'll crack. Fraser's policeman's instinct told him that his approach was going to work.

"Coffee?" he asked, when Charles walked into his office.

"How long are we going to be?" asked Werkman. "I've got things to do."

No doubt you do, thought Fraser. "Couple of hours maybe. This is murder we're talking about." Fraser was pleased to see the gamut of emotions that Werkman's face reflected at this statement. He liked a suspect with a sensitive face that concealed nothing. Maybe I have one here, he thought.

"I'm taping this," he continued. "We get into so many interviews in these cases it's impossible to keep our evidence straight without tapes. You okay with that?"

Werkman nodded his head indicating that it was of no concern. Fraser was silent for a few moments, letting the news sink in, hoping that Werkman would start talking out of nerves.

Fraser continued, "We need to know about Jack Duffy the day of the murder. Jack owned the murder weapon, his fingerprints were on it, he had access to the deceased at the time of the murder, and he had a strong motive to kill Bob Smithers. When you piece that all together, things look pretty bad for Jack right now."

"Fingerprints?" asked Charles. "I don't know how you could... I mean I didn't know you had Jack's prints on the knife."

"It was his knife. There was never a doubt about that. He admitted it, as soon as he saw it. His wife gave it to him for a present." Werkman's face went from slightly white to pink back to white, and his lips quivered as if he were about to mouth different words. Say it, thought Fraser. He waited a while, but Werkman's lips produced nothing.

"Now, you were playing bridge with Jack during the Swiss when he had the big run-in with Bob Smithers. Is that right?"

"Oh, yes, I was there. I heard the whole thing. But there was nothing there that... I mean... it was just bridge talk. In fact, Jack was defending me. See, I hesitated before making my bid. But you know that you're allowed to think. That's all I was doing. The laws say your partner is supposed to bid his own cards, not take advantage of the hesitation. Jack made a perfectly normal bid after that. He's one of the most ethical players you'll find in the game. But Smithers was a real bastard. He would start a row at the drop of a hat. Everybody hated him. Out of the blue, he and Jack are at each other's throats. Jack is a great guy. Everybody likes him. He told Smithers I had a right to think. That's all. Like I say, he was defending me. Then things blew up. Smithers, my God, everybody had it in for him. Even I did. I mean... he got what he deserved."

That's three, thought Fraser, thinking of Werkman's interrupted sentences. The tape will tell us something. He carried on as though Werkman had said nothing.

"Pretty much everyone in the world of bridge disliked him," said Fraser. "Now tell me about Jack's moves the night of the murder."

"Bob was murdered just after the tournament ended, wasn't he?" asked Charles. Fraser just looked on calmly, waiting for an answer. "That's what the paper said, anyway. We all left the tournament hotel together, the four of us and two or three others. We just got in our cars and went home. A couple of people car-pooled from Buffalo to the club here."

"How about you? Did you drive by yourself?"

"Yeah. I don't live close to anybody."

"Okay. Finish the story of the tournament. So you met your team at the hotel at game time and went straight home from downtown Buffalo late that night. Is that right?" asked Fraser.

"Right," said Werkman. "I wouldn't say it was that late on Sunday, though. Maybe nine-thirty at night. You know yourself that the team games on Sundays always start early and end early. We were finished by eight o'clock, easy."

"I see. Who was the other person on your team? You said four. There were you, Helen and Jack."

"Hermann was Helen's partner. He plays a lot with her. They do okay."

"Did okay, anyway. Poor old Hermann." Fraser watched Charles very closely now.

Werkman surprised Fraser by looking directly into his eyes. "Yeah. Everybody liked him."

"You mentioned that there were some other people who car-pooled or at least drove from the hotel."

"Yeah. That's common. Couple of other regulars at Stewart's club. Stewart himself, in fact. I don't remember them all. I could find out though, if that's important."

"No, not right now. I'm getting the picture. Now that night, after the game, Bob Smithers was murdered. Did you see Jack leave the hotel parking lot?"

Charles paused at this question. He's got his composure back, thought Fraser. Too bad. "No. It was so damned cold out; I wasn't paying attention to the others. I just wanted to get home."

"So you just finished the tournament and you came right home without talking to the other players."

"Not very exciting, but that's the way it was."

"Now, Sunday night is the night Bob was stabbed," said Fraser.

"We all know that," said Werkman, in a weak voice.

He's losing it again, thought Fraser. "You played against him in the evening session?" continued Fraser.

"Yes, I did. That's when he and Jack had the big argument."

"And Bob provoked Jack," said Fraser, watching his mark closely for any sign that he might be cracking.

"He provoked anyone he talked to. The man could say 'hello' and make you want to take a swing at him."

Fraser didn't see much emotion in Werkman as he answered. I'd better turn the heat up a notch, he thought. "Did anything special happen between the players that night? I mean, how did Jack seem? Normal? Nervous? Did he act any way that might seem suspicious?"

"Not that I can remember. Jack is Jack. I've never seen him do anything suspicious in the six years I've known him. He fights with his wife at the bridge table. That's all. Never with me. We're good friends. I can tell you that he had nothing to do with the murder."

"How can you be so sure?" asked Fraser. "Look at the same evidence that I have. He had a motive. He owns the murder weapon. He had the perfect opportunity to kill the victim. It all adds up."

"You're missing something," said Charles. "Look at the motive. You're making a big thing out of Jack's run-in with Bob. That was no big deal. I've seen Jack go through that sort of thing many times. He gets mad and a few minutes later, he's forgotten about it. He and Helen do this all the time. Big fight and then two minutes later they're lovey-dovey."

"Are you sure you're not underestimating Jack's anger?"

"Positive. You have to remember how every bridge player around hated Bob Smithers. Nobody liked him. He made enemies wherever he went. The club. Tournaments. He had a knack. I'll bet everyone who knew him was glad when they heard he was dead."

"You were, I take it."

"Sure I was. He got what he deserved. Well, I mean... Nobody deserves to get murdered. But Bob... Let's say he came close."

"Okay. So you were together until eight-thirty. Then who was in the crowd at the time you left?"

"Oh hell. I don't remember all that. All the players in the game, I guess. The directors are always the last to leave."

"So you were one of the first to leave, and you don't know when Jack left. Or Bob Smithers?"

"No, not that I can... I mean yeah. I told you, Jack left when I did. Bob was there when I left. I guess. You know that."

My boy's getting flustered again, thought Fraser. "I know that?" asked Fraser. "Oh, because he was murdered that night. He had to be there when you left."

"Yes. I mean... Well, he won that night. I mean after the committee reversed a score in his last match."

"Did you witness the argument Smithers had with Lew Orono?"

"I was there. I wasn't close enough to see it all. I could hear some of it, though."

"Okay. Let's look at the parking situation. Can you show me a diagram of how you all parked? Here, I've got a piece of paper. Let's make a little sketch of the whole scene." Fraser had a diagram of the hotel area and put it on the table in front of him. Werkman was beginning to perspire and lick his lips. "Here is the hotel. This square. Here is Bingham Street. This is the cut-rate parking, where we found Bob's body. Here is where Jack Duffy parked his car, not too far from Bob Smithers' car. So Jack had a great position to watch Bob come out of the hotel and walk toward his car."

"Yeah, but Jack was gone... I mean, well, so what? I parked on the street," said Charles. The room seemed to be getting hotter.

"You were parked well away from Bob Smithers."

"Yeah. I parked on Charles Street. There are a few spots there, if you get there early enough. Nowhere near Bob." Charles suddenly seemed to become nervous and wary. Fraser thought, I'd better ease off a bit.

"How do you suppose Jack Duffy could get to him, get at him all by himself? It almost looks as if Helen Duffy was an accessory here. That's strange. I hadn't considered that before."

"I'm telling you, there's no way Jack or Helen would ever be involved in a murder. Helen is a kind person."

"I hear you. But there's too much against Jack now. I just have this feeling we've got the right man. Jack Duffy I mean. I need to reconstruct the events of that night, after the game. You're helping a lot. Now just tell me the sequence of events after the game. A few of you stuck around for the scores. Right?"

"Yes."

"That would be who? The directors, right? And anybody who wanted to find out their placing."

Charles nodded. "You know all of this as well as I do. A lot of people stick around after a Swiss."

"Jack Duffy, his wife and her partner, Hermann Volcker, you, Bob Smithers. Anyone else?"

"We were among the last to leave. In fact, Jack and Helen pulled out before I did. Smithers' team went to the bar and I... Nobody else was there then..."

"I see," said Fraser. He acted as though this was all a matter of course, and nothing surprising was being disclosed. "Did you go to the bar with Smithers and his team?"

"No, I don't like to drink at night. Anyway, I wouldn't have anything to do with that S.O.B. I left right after the game."

"You went directly home, right after the game?"

Werkman nodded assent.

"I guess Jack must have waited for Bob Smithers to come out of the bar and circled back, then done his thing. The murder, I mean."

"I could never believe that Jack would do that. I suppose he must have had the opportunity. But he's not that kind of guy."

"I can understand you protecting your friends. That's natural. But you're helping us a lot. I couldn't see before how the murder was done. It's obvious now that Jack Duffy, and you say his wife was there also, just circled back, stopped Smithers and nailed him. I think we're making a lot of progress."

"You're not listening. Ask anybody about the Duffys." Charles was perspiring now.

"I will. Definitely. I'm going to take another look at the parking lot, maybe get a detailed drawing of the whole thing. A good professional sketch. I'll get you to help me mark the position of the cars exactly on it. Then I can talk to Jack again. I bet he confesses on the spot."

"He'll never do that," said Charles. "Not unless you beat a confession out of him."

"Oh, no. We don't work that way. But if he's an honest man, not a criminal, I can't see him not confessing. It'll go easier on him if he just confesses. Maybe we'll charge him with manslaughter. That's much less serious than first-degree murder."

"You're all wrong," persisted Charles.

"Tell me why? Tell me."

Charles was looking uncomfortable. "He just couldn't have done it. He's not that type."

"Let me tell you something, Charles. I've been a cop for a lot of years, and one thing I have found is that people surprise you. You take murder. The most unexpected person you can think of is capable of murder. I'll bet even a nice guy like yourself could kill a person under certain circumstances. I mean really special circumstances. Am I right?"

"Yes, I guess. I-I m-mean no," stammered Charles.

"I bet you could," continued Fraser. "I mean if something really important or threatening cropped up. Say something that might destroy your reputation. People surprise you."

Charles just stared at the wall, now unable to meet Fraser's gaze.

"Bridge players are a funny lot. Some of them are brilliant people. Very good at planning, I suppose. Then there is Hermann's case, too. Tragic."

"Hmm?" said Charles, sitting up abruptly.

"Hermann Volcker?" said Fraser. "You know he was murdered on Wednesday?"

"He died of a heart attack," said Charles in the highest pitch he had used for the past hour.

"That's what the doc thought at first. When the coroner took a close look at the body, he found a crease in the skull. Did you know that?"

"No," whispered Charles, his face white.

"Yep. And his jaw was broken. Terrible way for an old guy to go. Makes you wonder about the kind of people around nowadays. Eighty-three years old, harmless."

"I wouldn't call him exactly harmless," blurted Charles.

"Why is that?"

"Well, I mean, he poked his nose into... I mean he could be a nosey old bugger."

"I know. I know. A lot of us have no time for old people. We have to get smarter. There is something else. The crease in Hermann's skull, the murder wound I'm talking about now, it matches exactly the shape of a tire wrench. Strange thing is we can tell the wrench comes specifically from a Hyundai product. The shape of them is just a little bit different. Lucky break for us, don't you think?" Fraser hesitated for several seconds to let that sink in.

"A Hyundai?" Charles was whispering again. "That's ugly," he continued after a pause, in a stronger voice now. "Who would want to kill Hermann?" He's going to bluff it out, thought Fraser. Charles' face reminded Art of a mouse destroyed in a trap — eyes protruding noticeably and snout prominent.

"Let me show you something." Fraser moved to the door of his office and pulled it open. "Hey Bryan," he shouted. "Bring that exhibit in. Be careful with it. Don't drop the damned thing or you'll blow our case before we get off the ground."

Nelson brought in a package wrapped up in white cloth and set it on Fraser's desk. "Don't touch this," said Fraser. "We haven't tested it for prints yet. Come on over and have a look." He unwrapped the package, exposing a tire wrench with the socket end covered in a reddish-brown stain of dried blood.

Charles walked over at Fraser's invitation and took a close look at the object. "How…?" he moaned, and collapsed back in his chair.

At that moment, they heard a pounding on the partially open office door and glimpsed an excited-looking Russ Wilson. "Hey, Art," said Wilson. "I just got back from the hotel."

"Have a good time?" asked Nelson.

"I talked to a waiter at the Mark. He was on duty Sunday night."

Werkman sat up sharply in his chair.

"Do you guys know Charles Werkman?" asked Fraser softly, hoping to quench some of Wilson's excitement. "Charles, this is Bryan Nelson and Russ Wilson. They're in our criminal branch, looking into homicides." Fraser turned back to Wilson. "What did your waiter have to say?"

Wilson took a good look at Werkman. "I showed people this mug shot," he said, waving an envelope. "One of the waiters said this guy was in the restaurant drinking coffee until about nine thirty. He was pretty sure of the exact time because the guy got up, dropped a five-spot on the table and left real quick. He didn't go to the cash to pay and didn't wait for any change."

Fraser took the envelope from Wilson, opened it, and took out the pictures of Werkman. He laid them in front of Charles. "So you left right after the game, did you?"

"What are you talking about?" said Charles.

Nelson spoke up. "We have a warrant to search your apartment, and we're going to do that right now."

Thinking of his bedroom, his printouts on the walls, even the pouch of the Nighthawk tucked away in his closet, Charles took his head in his hands and groaned. "Okay. Okay. I did it. I did them both. Just leave me alone."

Nelson looked across at Fraser and nodded congratulations as he pulled the Miranda card out of his pocket and began to read aloud from it.

CHAPTER 32

JACK DUFFY WALKED THROUGH HIS FRONT DOOR and for the first time in a while heard the beautiful sound of ice cracking against the walls of a metallic cocktail shaker. Something has changed, he thought. He hung up his coat in the hall closet and headed for the living room. Helen appeared with a conical glass in each hand, offering him one.

"Poor Charles," she said.

"I never suspected him for a minute. I should have remembered his black Chevy. Taking my knife. You were right about him being after the hand records the night we surprised him."

"Now that this is all over and you have lots of time on your hands, you can join the U.P.A."

"What in hell is U.P.A?" asked Jack.

"Ugly Partners Anonymous," she replied. "An organization for people with horrible bridge manners who can't help themselves."

By now, Jack was feeling more than a little sheepish about his behavior. "Never heard of it," he grunted. "Look. I'm sorry for the way I've been acting. I didn't mean to say those things. I was just dumb."

Helen said, "I know, dear. This organization is for people just like you. People who can't help themselves. They have a twelve-step program based on Alcoholics Anonymous. Same idea."

Jack laughed. "Okay. I agree I've got to do something about my behavior at the bridge table. I don't know how you put up with it. I'm ashamed of myself, as a matter of fact."

"I hear they're looking for a president. I think you should apply. You could be their inspirational leader."

"Honey, I'm crazy about you. I don't know why I say the things I do. They just come out when we play bridge, I don't know why."

"Tell you what. To get a start in your organization, I have some words you can use as your main teaching."

"Huh?"

"Love is patient. Love is kind. It is not rude. It is not easily angered."

While Helen was talking, Jack noticed that she was wearing red shoes, a dark green skirt, and his favorite, a sheer pale green silk blouse. He definitely detected dark green bra straps showing through the blouse. He set down his glass, got up from his chair and interrupted her to say, "I think we should go upstairs."

She laughed, picked an olive out of the clear liquid she was drinking, savored it, swallowed, and took his hand. She decided she probably wouldn't talk to Jack about divorce, not just yet, anyway. Maybe the leopard could change his spots, maybe not. But she was prepared to wait a little and see.

☠ ♥ ☠

Eight weeks later, Jim Kesten called Art Fraser into his office and informed him that he was to become captain in charge of the criminal investigation branch of district seven of the New York state police at the end of the month, when Kesten retired. Later that day Fraser invited Nelson and Wilson out for a couple of beers to celebrate. Fraser asked the waiter for three large drafts.

"One second, Art," said Wilson.

"What?"

"You payin'?"

"Of course. This is my treat."

"Okay. You serve rum martinis?" asked Wilson of the waiter.

"Among the best anywhere," said the waiter, who had never before heard of a rum martini.

"I'll have a double."

Fraser looked at Wilson quizzically and nodded assent to the waiter. Nelson burst out laughing. When they were into their second round of drinks, he said, "You know Russ, maybe you and I ought to sign up for some of Applecore's bridge lessons. I hear it's a great game."

"Nah, I'm sticking to golf. At least I don't have to learn a new language to play it."

"Hmm. I thought I heard Kathy was taking lessons," said Nelson.

"Yes, I think I saw her at the bridge club the other night," Fraser went along with the joke.

Wilson glared at the other two suspiciously. Finally they both broke down into helpless laughter.

"All right you guys, that's it. Waiter, another rum martini — and it's still his round!"